THE NEW SOUTH

SABRA WALDFOGEL

CONTENTS

Cover Design: www.bookflydesign.com

A978-1-953354-04-4 Ebook

978-1-953354-05-1 Print

Sabra Waldfogel, Publisher

www.sabrawaldfogel.com

Published in Minneapolis, Minnesota

CHAPTER 1

AMANDA GARDINER

WHEN I BRING the wash to Missus Kershaw's house, I come in the back door, like I always do, and Missus herself come into the kitchen. She look mad, and it bother me before she say a word to me.

Missus Kershaw always been sharp and peevish. If she have her monthlies and her back ache, if her husband raise his voice to her, if her dog relieve himself on her carpet, she get riled and take it out on me.

She open up the bundle of clean wash and look at it. Bend down and sniff it. Make a face. "This isn't clean," she say.

Of course it clean, and I know what it smell like because I fold everything careful before I bundle it up. It smell like soap and starch. I say, as polite as I can, "Missus Kershaw, begging your pardon, but it as clean as I can get it."

She poke the bundle like it a nasty, dead critter on her kitchen table. "That's not clean enough," she say. "Take it away and get it clean the next time."

1

We know when the missus of the house have her monthlies because we wash the bloody rags. We know when the missus have relations with her husband because we wash the soiled sheets. We know what her sweat smell like. That's an awfully private thing to know about a person you don't really know and don't like in the least.

White ladies, they act like they some kind of angel that don't sweat and don't use the chamber pot and don't make a mess doing their marital duty. It shame them that we know different. That's why they look at us like we something nasty. Because they the ones who are nasty, and they know it, and they hate themselves for it. That's why they hate us.

But all I say is, "Ma'am, it clean, and I need my wage for it."

She get bright-red spots on her cheeks. "Do you think I'll pay you for dirty laundry? You'll get your money when you bring it back clean."

"Ma'am, I surely need that money." I think about my husband, who can't work as hard as he could when he a young man, and my last two girls at home, too young to go out to work.

"You'll get it when you do this right."

"Ma'am."

"Are you being insolent with me?"

Insolent. Like I a bad child. It rankle me all of a sudden. I'm a grown woman, and she talk to me like I ain't old enough or wise enough to understand her. "No, ma'am."

"If you're insolent, I don't want you to work for me anymore. And I'll tell my friends that you're lazy and insolent into the bargain. They won't employ you, either."

I bite my tongue because I remember hearing them words, *lazy* and *insolent*, from my missus back in slavery. Wasn't true back then, and it ain't true now.

But my family got to eat. They need what I earn, every dime. Can't get by without it. I swallow my pride and my anger both, and I reach for the bundle. Tie it closed again. "Missus Kershaw, I take it back. I wash it again."

"That's better, Mandy."

My mama called me Mandy, but my friends call me Miss Amanda, and now that I free, I like to be called Mrs. Amanda Gardiner. "Mandy" sound to me like a child. Or a dog. I hate the sound of it.

I leave the house and heft the bundle to my head. It don't weigh any more than it did when I carried it into the house, but it feel heavier. My head ache with the burden.

I have a walk from the Kershaw house on Peachtree Street back to my own house on Fraser Street. I have too much time to think while I walk. My thoughts don't cheer me.

I was born in slavery in Bibb County, not far from Macon. I'm close to fifty, but I don't know for sure since no one trouble to write down when I was born. My mama do the wash in the house, and I help her since I could reach into the washtub. Massa own nearly sixty slaves, and he grow cotton. He a wealthy man. Because I spend my time in the house, I know Missus. She the one who call me lazy. Massa have his overseer or driver whup the field hands, but Missus slap anyone who vex her, and she do it all the time. Ain't as bad as a whip, but it hurt just the same.

I never forget the day that I learn that we all free.

General Sherman's army come to our place, and his men tell us. My mama and I, my husband and my children, we free ourselves on the spot. We join the crowd that follow the army, and we march with them to Atlanta.

I still do the wash for the Union army, but they pay me, and that make all the difference in the world.

Wasn't easy, the war years in Atlanta, but while we struggle along, we do it in freedom. After the war, things get better. We find a house to rent in Shermantown, on Houston Street, and so many of us women are washer-women that we work together in the courtyard behind the street. We talk about who we work for, how they treat us, how they pay us. Some missuses ain't bad, and others never got their minds out of slavery. We talk about that, too.

My husband, Zachariah, and I, we go to the church nearby, Bethel A. M. E., and we hear Reverend Peck talk about how Black people have to help themselves. It ain't just talk. He start a mutual aid society to pay for funerals and to help widows and orphans, and for a few years I help to run it. It please me no end to be vice president of the Daughters of Bethel. I go to the bank, the Freedman's Bank downtown, with the president and the treasurer, and we put all the mutual aid society money in an account there.

Lost every dime of it when the bank failed in 1874. Church kept on, and the mutual aid society started up again. This time we put our money in a bank that ain't likely to fold up, one run by white people. They don't like us much, Black women in their bank, but the only color our money got is green. That should be good enough for anyone.

A few years ago, Zachariah and I move from Sherman-town to Summerhill. Nicer house, better place. We live on Fraser Street, and our block is all Black folks. Can't tell you how many washerwomen live on that street. We work together in the yards behind the houses, and we talk among ourselves. It not too different from Shermantown.

I join a new church, Pleasant Grove Baptist, because it close by and because the minister used to be at Bethel. He believe that Black people have to help themselves, like Reverend Peck always say. He start a mutual aid society, and I get elected to it, just like at Bethel A. M. E. We ain't a big congregation and the good Lord know we ain't a rich one, but we good at coaxing a dime here and a dime there from the faithful. Everyone know that you need help for a funeral when death come. Death come too often for Black people who ain't got much. The congregation trust us, the Mutual Aid Society of Pleasant Grove Baptist, to take good care of their money for them.

When I get home, I go into the yard. My neighbor, Miss Ophelia, wave to me and come close enough to see that I'm downcast. "What happen?" she ask me.

"Didn't get paid."

"Why not?"

"Missus say I didn't get the wash clean."

"That's a dirty lie, and she know it! She just don't want to pay you."

Ophelia young enough to be my daughter, a little older than twenty, but she fiery. She was three year old when she got free, and she don't have the memory of slavery that I do. She live in Atlanta since she was ten, and she get mad when things ain't right. Don't keep it to herself. Don't always bite her tongue with white people. I say, "It ain't any better if they talk nice and apologize and wring their hands and tell you they have it next week. You still go home without your money."

"It ain't right and we all know it."

"Of course it ain't." I sigh and rub my head where the weight of the bundle aggravate it. I been carrying laundry on my head all my life, and suddenly my head ache from it something awful.

"We ain't slaves no more, no matter what some white missus think."

"I know that. But I got to make a living. Need that money. Can't say no."

She look at me, and suddenly she smile like she think of something that please her. "What if we do?" she ask. "Say no?"

"They find someone else who say yes," I say. "Someone more desperate even than you or me. That's what happen."

"Maybe not," she say.

I shake my head. "You a little crazy," I say, and she laugh.

CHAPTER 2

MATT'S RETURN

A DEPOT PORTER, a dignified, dark-skinned Black man who wore his uniform, modeled on pre-Civil War livery, approached him with the aplomb of a general. "Mr. Matthew Kaltenbach?" he asked. "Come with me. We find your father."

The Atlanta depot was not much different from the one he left in San Francisco four days before. It was similarly crowded and smelled of coal and smoke. The porter moved easily through the crowd and stopped before the man he sought. "Mr. Henry Kaltenbach?"

Matt's childhood memories of his father were so patchy and so distant that he didn't recognize the man who stood before him. He searched the face—the liquid eyes, the prominent nose, and the mobile mouth—trying to remember the man who had left for the Civil War when he was a baby and again for Atlanta when the war was over. He was jarred to see the family resemblance. It was eerie to resemble someone for whom he had so little feeling.

His father spoke first to the porter. "I see you've become acquainted with my son Matthew," he said. "Matt, this is Mr. William Dozier. A neighbor of mine, and a friend."

Matt was utterly at a loss to be introduced to a Black man who worked as a servant. Should he shake the man's hand or not? As he hesitated, Mr. Dozier helped him. He didn't extend his hand, but he nodded.

Matt's father said, "My son has come all the way from San Francisco for a visit."

Mr. Dozier inclined his head. "I hope you enjoy your time here, young Mr. Kaltenbach."

Startled by this courteous exchange, Matt replied, "So do I."

When they were alone, Henry Kaltenbach shook his son's hand, saying, "It's good to see you."

Matt was disappointed at the formality. He had hoped for greater warmth, but his father didn't know him, either. He could hardly hope for a prodigal's welcome.

His father said, "I've hired a hansom. Do you have a trunk?"

In the driver's seat of the hansom sat a Black man, not dressed in livery but wearing a well-fitting dark frock coat. He smiled in greeting. "Mr. Henry Kaltenbach, I don't usually drive anymore, but this is special. To see your boy come all the way from San Francisco!"

Matt recognized the driver. "You're Zeke's son," he said. "Tom." Zeke had been his father's slave, as had Zeke's two sons, Tom and Luke.

He smiled again, this time at Matt. "Mr. Thomas Hutchens now," he said.

His father said, "Mr. Hutchens runs a cartage company. Wagons and now hansoms, too."

"Yes, I do well in Atlanta," Mr. Hutchens added. "Hop in! It ain't far, but you never know, with so many wagons on the street these days."

Matt settled into the hansom and stared out the window. Atlanta was much smaller than San Francisco, but the streets near the depot bustled with traffic, both horse-drawn and on foot. He had read about Atlanta's rise from the ashes of the war. In the newspapers, Atlanta thought of itself as prosperous and progressive. But the streets downtown were still unpaved, hard-packed dirt like a town on the frontier.

"Where are we going?" Matt asked his father.

"My house is on Clarke Street," his father said. "It's in Summerhill, just a little south and east of here."

When they left downtown, they drove through a neighborhood full of small wooden houses. They stopped at a house as modest as the rest, even though it was newly built and well-maintained. His stepfather, hardly a magnate in San Francisco, had bought a three-story house that would dwarf this little cottage.

Matt read about the Rich brothers, the most prosperous dry goods merchants in Atlanta, who were Jews like his father. Now he wondered whether his father's business prospered or not.

The door opened, and a Black woman, her apron spotless over her dark dress, smiled as Mr. Hutchens brought in the trunk. She wore her gray hair braided neatly around her head, a housekeeper's crown. Matt wondered if all the Black people his father knew were so dignified.

Inside, his father once again made introductions.

"Matt, this is Mrs. Amanda Bailey, who is employed as my cook and housekeeper." As though he were warding off scandal, his father said, "She lives close by and comes in every day to keep me in order."

Uneasy again, not knowing whether it was right to call her "Mrs. Bailey," Matt nodded and smiled.

"Pleased to meet you, young Mr. Kaltenbach," she said.

So few Black people lived in San Francisco that courtesy toward them was never a question or a source of confusion. In San Francisco, white people exercised their racial antagonism in dealing with the Chinese.

Matt's experience with people of color, like his relationship with his father, was in the past. He tried to stay in touch with the friends of his childhood from Cass County. He wrote to his friend Ben until it was clear that distance and diverged experience now separated them. If he met Ben in Atlanta today, he would have no idea what to say to him, or how to say it. He doubted he could recognize Ben if they passed on the street.

"Mrs. Bailey will take good care of you," his father said.

Matt nodded again and hoped that was polite enough.

Mrs. Bailey said, "I make a special dinner tonight for you, young Mr. Kaltenbach. Do you keep the kosher laws?"

He shouldn't be surprised that she asked. Their servants in San Francisco, German and Irish and Chinese, had all learned about the dietary peculiarities of their Jewish employers. "I'm not religious," he said. "But I don't care for ham or bacon."

She nodded. "Like your daddy."

~

HE AND HIS FATHER ATE THE EVENING MEAL IN THE diminutive dining room. The whole house was small. It was mean to think so, Matt knew, but he did. The parlor was cramped. The three bedrooms upstairs were close. He didn't venture into the kitchen, but he'd bet that it was tiny, too.

He thought not only of the house in San Francisco but also the house in Cass County, which had felt so spacious. Was that because he had been so much smaller himself?

Mrs. Bailey cooked a meal that reminded him of his childhood: chicken fried in a batter, beaten biscuits, and greens. The taste of the biscuits brought him back to Cass County, where he had eaten in the kitchen with their cook, Minnie, and his mother's maid, Rachel, whom he called "Aunt," as slaves were called, before he knew the truth. Rachel was his mother's half sister, and the slave epithet coincided with the real relationship. Rachel's daughter Eliza, about two years younger than himself, was always present in the kitchen, as she was now present in his memory. She resembled her mother, but she had the complexion that ensued when a Black child had a white father. In this case, his own father.

She was the half sister he couldn't admit to.

Now his father asked Matt politely about his family in San Francisco. His "people," as the Southerners said. "How is your mother?"

Matt knew that his mother and father didn't write to each other. "She does well."

"Has she found a new cause to crusade?"

Matt's mother took a stand against slavery during the war, and after it, started a school for the children of former slaves. It earned her the notice—and the fury—of the Ku Klux Klan. Those memories were still too vivid. Matt said lightly, "Yes, and she's always pulling the Temple Sisterhood along to get them to agree with her."

His father laughed. "Good for her," he said. "And your stepfather? Does he flourish?"

Now that was hard to answer. Lewis Hart had provided the reason for his parents' divorce, which had been hastily accomplished in 1868, after they left Cass County. But Hart had been a kinder father to Matt than Henry Kaltenbach had. It was awkward and disloyal to talk about his affectionate stepfather with his absent father. He swallowed hard and spoke as politely as he could. "Yes, he does. His business does well, and life in San Francisco suits him."

"And you? Does it suit you?"

"It has," he said. "But I remember Georgia from my childhood, and I wanted to see it again." It was too hard to say, *to see you again.*

"You attended college in California, did you not?"

"Yes, the University of California at Berkeley."

"What did you study there?"

"The general course. Latin and Greek, history, philosophy, mathematics, and science."

"What did you like most?"

"I couldn't decide," he said, the first thing he had said that wasn't a pleasantry. "I liked all of it."

"What are you inclined to do?"

"Mr. Hart offered to help me find a position in San Francisco," Matt said. "But I insisted on coming to Atlanta. I don't know. I thought I would make some inquiries."

"Atlanta prospers," his father said, smiling. "I'm sure you'll find an opportunity."

Without your help, evidently. "I hope so," he said, not wanting to sound as rude as he felt.

AFTER DINNER, MRS. BAILEY WASHED THE DISHES AND LEFT, and when she was gone, his father rose from his chair in the parlor. "You'll have to excuse me. I have an engagement this evening. Mrs. Bailey will have readied your room upstairs for whenever you want to turn in."

Matt asked the question that had been bothering him all evening. "My aunt Rachel and her daughter Eliza. How are they?"

"Quite well," his father said, resting his hand on the back of his chair as though he were unhappy to be detained. "Rachel is in business, and she makes a handy profit, and Eliza just graduated from Atlanta University."

"Do they know that I'll be in Atlanta?"

His father nodded. "I'll tell them. You'll excuse me, Matt?"

After his father left, Matt thought, *Is that where he's going now?* In San Francisco, his father's enduring connection with Rachel was too far away to cause any scandal. It would mean something else in Atlanta.

Both his mother and his stepfather had tried to dissuade him from returning to Georgia. They had talked around the real problem, telling him that Atlanta was a small town, a backwater, a place where prejudice got in the way of a decent life. It was his stepfather who finally lost his composure and said it outright. "Why do you want to run after the man who abandoned you?"

"He didn't abandon me," Matt said, startled at his step-father's vehemence.

"He let you go and he never cared to ask after you. What do you call that?"

"He's still my father."

"There's nothing for you in Atlanta. Nothing but disappointment."

"Shouldn't I find that out for myself?"

"He'll cause you pain. As he caused your mother pain."

Matt said, "I don't think so." He made his arrangements and packed his trunk, certain that he was right.

THE HOUSE ON CLARKE STREET, UNLIKE THE ONE HE HAD left in San Francisco, was not yet piped for gas. Before she left, Mrs. Bailey filled the candlesticks in the parlor and put out a chamberstick and a box of matches on the hallway table at the base of the stairs. As darkness fell, Matt appreciated her thoughtfulness. He would not have known to light a candle, let alone where to find a match for one.

He sat for a while in the summer dusk. He was alone in the house, and it was silent, save for the small creaks and groans of any wooden house. Outside, the street was bereft of human sound. The people on this block were either quiet by nature or early to bed. He heard the rasp of crickets and the low, haunting calls of birds. If San Francisco had wild creatures, they were submerged in the noise of a population ten times that of Atlanta's.

Matt sighed. He closed the downstairs windows—he had lived in a big city, and he couldn't lose the habit in a smaller one—and lit the candle in the chamberstick to make his way upstairs.

Even in the low light, he could appreciate Mrs. Bailey's handiwork. She unpacked his trunk and laid all his clothes in the press, carefully refolded. He opened the dresser drawer to find his socks, ties and handkerchiefs carefully rolled. She plumped the pillows on the bed, smoothed the counterpane, and laid out a nightshirt. She left him a slop jar on the dressing table. He cast the candlelight into the corner of the room. She also provided him with a chamber pot.

He sighed again. No indoor plumbing on this street, either. He thought of his childhood home in Cass County, where all the household's water was drawn from the well, and a pump in the kitchen had been a great convenience.

He undressed, carefully draping his clothes over the dressing table's chair. He would spare Mrs. Bailey a little effort tomorrow. He pulled on his nightshirt and got into bed. The sheets were crisp with starch and smelled of lavender. He wondered if Mrs. Bailey washed them.

Matt never prayed at bedtime—he had been raised by lax and secular Jews—but when he was a little boy in Cass County, he listened to his half sister say her prayers. He wondered if he would feel any better if he addressed a few words to God. All that came to mind were a few words from the Yom Kippur service. *For all the sins we have committed...pardon us and forgive us.* That seemed a bit much for a God who expected to hear "Now I lay me down to sleep."

He closed his eyes and sank into the pillow. Under the

crisp pillowcase, the pillow was very soft, cradling his head as sweetly as a mother's touch. He fell asleep.

~

MATT DREAMED. IN THE DREAM, HE SMELLED THE PERFUME of magnolia, with it, the smell of smoke. It was an ugly odor, a house burning. The sky was bright red, and flames leaped from a roof. The smoke billowed and sent the stench of charred wood and tarpaper his way.

He heard men shouting. Horses neighing. Men on horseback, their faces hidden by white hoods, surrounding a crowd.

Women screamed. Black women. He heard their cry: "Help us! Lord, help us! They're killing us!"

The sound of gunfire, and the smell of cordite.

Where was he? He wasn't in the crowd, but he wasn't safe. The men in hoods, the men with rifles, would find him.

They would shoot him.

He woke and bolted upright, gasping for breath. It wasn't just a nightmare. It was a memory that disturbed his sleep after his mother and stepfather took him away from Cass County. It persisted for months after they settled in San Francisco. It really happened, even though the dream conflated two horrors into one.

The Ku Klux Klan set his mother's school on fire one night in 1868, and several months later, they came back to try to murder her. Sitting up, in a sweat of terror, he remembered himself and Eliza, cowering in a back room of the plantation house, with their arms wrapped around each other.

"Will they kill us?" he whispered to his half sister.

She whispered back, "I don't know."

Now, thirteen years later, he wrapped his arms around himself in the quiet dark of an Atlanta night. In the balmy air of late spring in Georgia, with the smell of magnolia blossom drifting through the open window of the bedroom, he remembered Cass County and the childhood he thought was long over, and he felt a chill too deep for comfort.

CHAPTER 3

LONG TIME COMING

ELIZA COLDBROOK HESITATED on the front steps of the house on Fraser Street. She had just graduated from Atlanta University, and after going to school every year since she was seven, she didn't know what to do with herself. Her friends had each answered a calling. One was bound for Augusta, where she would teach in a Black grammar school. Another was packing her trunk for her missionary work in Africa. The least ambitious among them had said yes to her sweetheart's proposal and was planning her wedding to a young man who was a minister, also an Atlanta University graduate, who would expect her to join him in his work. Atlanta University, the only school in Georgia to bestow college degrees on young women, liked to inspire them to dedicate themselves to uplifting the less fortunate.

This morning, Eliza managed to write a letter to a former classmate who now lived in Savannah and to finish her chores. Despite their relative comfort, unusual for a Black family, her mother insisted that a Black woman know how to take care of herself. Her mother ran a successful business that was the envy of many a man in Black Atlanta and was self-sufficient at home. She refused a maid to help her dress and arrange her hair, and she still worked alongside the cook to get dinner. She had been known to lend a hand to their maid with the dusting.

The Coldbrook family didn't really need servants, but they were part of her mother's effort to use her good fortune to quash any resentment from her less-fortunate neighbors. It was also a way to help that didn't seem like charity. Many of their servants were girls who had gone on to study at Atlanta University.

Eliza grew up in a home that never knew a lack of food or money, whether for necessities like new clothes or expenses like school fees. Every day, she went to school in a clean, starched dress with fresh ribbons in her hair, and when she wasn't helping the maid or the cook in an effort to stay unpretentious, she was reading. Her mother spared no expense for books.

But a Black child, no matter how pampered at home, couldn't be sheltered from the realities of life in Black Atlanta. The Coldbrooks lived next door to families on a knife edge of poverty, sickness, and want. Eliza knew how lucky she was. She saw the result of misfortune every day.

Because of her mother's down-to-earth manner, as well as her largesse, she was well-liked in Summerhill, and Eliza was greeted with genuine friendliness by everyone on her block and in their church. Today she ran down the steps and through the yard to wave at their nearest neighbor, Ophelia Taylor, who made her living as a washerwoman. She was up to her elbows in suds when Eliza greeted her.

They were unlikely friends. Ophelia was only a few years older than Eliza, but she was married to a man thirteen years her senior who brought her two stepchildren from a previous marriage broken by death. Ophelia couldn't read or write, and despite Eliza's offers to teach her, she had yet to agree to learn. "Something always need taking care of," she would say. Even though her husband was employed as a drayman, a good and steady job, they needed the money she made by washing. Her hands were roughened by lye soap, and her fingers were permanently wrinkled from being immersed in soapy water.

Ophelia was full of sauce. She was bolder to speak her mind than Eliza dared to be. When Eliza tried to explain that her mother wanted her to act like a lady, Ophelia would laugh—she had a deep, musical laugh, bigger than she was—and say, "I'm a Black woman. Can't afford to be a lady."

Today Ophelia raised a dripping arm from the tub in greeting. "Are you going to the church meeting tonight, Miss Eliza?"

"Is the Mutual Aid Society meeting tonight?"

"No, something else. But you and your mama should be there. Any woman who attend Pleasant Grove Baptist should be there."

"What's it about?"

"Be there tonight, you find out."

"Is it about women voting?"

Ophelia laughed, an explosive splutter. "Voting! That ain't a bad idea, either. No, it ain't about voting. And don't keep asking me busybody questions to find out. Got to get back to work."

Eliza sighed.

Ophelia said, "What? It bother you that you don't have to make a living? You should be glad of it and get married, like your mama want you to. Ain't Mr. Ben Mannheim sweet on you? He ask you."

"There's more to life than getting married."

Ophelia shook her head. "You mighty lucky to be able to say that."

Eliza didn't reply. Her mother set her a complicated example. She'd never married, but she had two children besides Eliza, both of whom resembled their father. Their white father. At eight, Eliza's baby sister, Ada, was so fair of skin that it had already started to cause her trouble. Eliza and her brother, Charles, looked like her mother, even if they were a few shades lighter in color. Ada was the spit of their Jewish father, in color as well as in feature.

It was a situation that caused unease among Black people, but no one liked to talk about it much. Too many people traced their ancestry to their masters for the subject to be easy. So they tried not to stare at Ada Coldbrook in church, and they bit their tongues instead of saying anything pointed about Black women and white men they weren't married to.

It was further complicated by the fact that her father, Henry Kaltenbach, loved her mother, doted on all three of his children, and ran a dry goods business that catered to Black customers and employed young Black men and women as clerks. Henry Kaltenbach lived in Summerhill —the block was white, but the neighborhood was mixed —and he was as familiar a figure in the Black community as his wife, a former slave who was not his legal wife, his lifelong companion, her mother, Rachel Coldbrook.

Eliza stared at a spot behind Ophelia's head. "I know I'm lucky. The question is, what should I do about it?"

Ophelia snorted. "Something useful. That take your mind off worrying about yourself all the time."

"You're right," Eliza said.

"You come to the meeting tonight?"

"I believe I will."

ELIZA DECIDED THAT SHE WOULD GO DOWNTOWN TO MAKE sure her mother knew about the meeting. She changed her dress. Looking fashionable was no protection against the rudeness of white Atlanta, but it gave her a sense of dignity. She knew she was a lady, even if white people wouldn't admit to it.

Her mother, who learned to read, write, and figure at an early age, had a talent for business. While still a slave, she made Henry Kaltenbach a fortune in cotton run through the blockade during the war, and he paid her a handsome commission on it. That money was the seed for her comfort today, and it funded the business she began a few years after the war. It was a most unusual business for any woman, and even more so for a Black woman. Rachel Coldbrook was a general contractor. She started by building houses for Black families in Shermantown, the neighborhood where they had first settled in Atlanta, and now she built houses for her neighbors in Summerhill. She hoped to try her hand at a commercial building. But the bidding process for any commercial building meant one fight after another that she couldn't win.

Her mother still worked from her first office on

Wheat Street, the main street of Shermantown. The original building, a brick office building badly damaged by General Sherman's army, was rebuilt just after the war and refurbished since. Eliza took pleasure in the neatly tuckpointed façade and the gold lettering on the window.

Rachel sat at her desk, a blueprint before her. With her, conferring over the specifications, was her foreman and chief builder, Luke Hutchens. They had been Henry Kaltenbach's slaves together. Luke always had a talent for carpentering. When he came to Atlanta, his first job was at Peck's Lumber Mill. Peck, a white man, took full advantage of the craze for rebuilding that seized Atlanta as soon as the war ended. He recognized Luke's talent and made him a carpenter, then a foreman. When Rachel decided to build her own house, she hired Luke Hutchens. And when one of her neighbors asked her to build a house, too, Rachel went into business with Luke.

Luke looked up from the blueprint. "Miss Eliza! Congratulations on your graduation. It's a wonderful thing to have a college education. A special thing."

"It is, thank you," Eliza said.

"What you plan to do now? You teach for a while?"

"I don't know yet," she said, smiling.

He chuckled. "I see that young Mr. Ben Mannheim interested in you."

"I don't know about that, either."

"Luke, leave her be. She hasn't been graduated for more than ten minutes," her mother said.

Luke said, "We all watch her grow up. That's why we fuss over her and hope for her."

Her mother sighed.

Eliza asked, "What are you building?"

"Another house in Summerhill," her mother replied. "It's for the Badger family." The Badgers were a family of dentists, fiercely proud of their professional status in the Black community. "For the son, Robert. Nothing fancy. But solid. He wants a lot of room for children."

"I hope he can afford to send all of them to Atlanta University," Eliza said, a little tartly.

"Well, that isn't our lookout, is it? Just enough rooms for them to sleep in, after they arrive."

"Any hope for a commercial project?"

Her mother reflected. "I hear that the Temple, the Hebrew Benevolent Association, wants to do a little expansion," she said.

"I thought they just put up the building," Eliza said.

"Evidently they're bursting at the seams already."

"Won't they employ the firm that did the original construction?"

Her mother looked pensive. "They might, and they might not."

"Why would they even consider us?"

"Mordecai Mannheim," her mother said.

Her mother, like Eliza herself, had a Jewish father who was her master. He died a few years before, but he had been a pillar of the Jewish community, and he never hid his relationship with his Black daughter. He loved her, in a difficult, prickly way. He said with pride, "She has a good, hard head for business. She got it from me."

They were descended from Jews, but they were not Jews. Eliza said, "They don't care. They won't even let you bid." Eliza was surprised how bitter she sounded.

"Someday," her mother said, and she sighed. "Someday I'll bid on a commercial project and I'll get it."

Her mother declined to walk home with Eliza for midday dinner, saying, "I can't, sugar. I got too much to do right here." Eliza never did tell her about the meeting at Pleasant Grove Church, but she knew that the neighbors would buttonhole her and let her know.

Her father's shop was just down the street from her mother's office. The clerk behind the counter was a young woman, her hair neatly smoothed into a bun, her dress crisp and fashionable. She looked as smart as any student at Atlanta University. She smiled pleasantly at Eliza and asked, "Miss? May I help you?"

"You must be new," Eliza said, smiling in return.

She was taken aback. "I am, but how would you know?"

"Mr. Kaltenbach is my father. All his clerks come to know me."

She was light-skinned enough to show a blush. "Excuse me."

Eliza was about to introduce herself when the familiar voice called from the back, "Eliza? Is that you, *Liebchen?*"

The clerk looked askance. She was brand-new if she hadn't learned any German yet. Eliza said, "That's the way Germans say 'sugar.'"

Her father emerged from the back, smiling broadly. "What brings you to Shermantown?"

"I had a message for Mama."

"Do you need anything? Ribbons? Trim?"

"No, and even if I did, you shouldn't be giving it away. You have a business to run."

"You sound just like your mother," he said with affection.

"She believes in making a profit, and you should, too."

The clerk watched this exchange in astonishment. Eliza said to her, "You must not be from Atlanta."

She was further surprised. "I'm not," she said. "I grew up in Macon. How would you know that?"

"Because everyone Black in Atlanta knows about the connections between the Kaltenbach and Coldbrook families. Even if they don't like it, they know of it."

The clerk's face showed that she had a master's ancestry in her family somewhere. She closed her mouth in a firm line to stay tactful.

AFTER SHE LEFT HER FATHER'S SHOP, ELIZA HEADED FOR Peachtree Street. She wished, as always, that she could take a horsecar home. But the practice of making Black people sit in the back infuriated her mother so much that she forbade the horsecars for all her children, and she herself walked to and from work in all kinds of weather. Eliza was tired of stepping into the gutter whenever a white person wanted to pass her. She was tired of the looks and the catcalls from white men. If it were up to her, she would dispense with worrying about anyone's opinion and buy a carriage and a team to pull it.

A block from downtown, she saw a familiar face, that of Ben Mannheim, the young man everyone was nagging her about. Ben was her playmate in Cass County when they were children. Six years ago, he came to Atlanta to enroll in Atlanta University. Back then, she teased him for having cotton fluff in his hair. It was unfair of her. His father, Charles Mannheim, a former Mannheim slave but no relation to the family, farmed a hundred acres and sat on the county's board of education as the advocate for the county's Black schools. His older sister, Josey, attended Howard University and was now the principal of a Black school in Washington. All the Mannheims had high aspirations.

Today Ben wore his new suit, made with cloth from her father's shop and carefully tailored by a friend of her father's. He had meticulously parted his hair and secured it with pomade. He looked like a gentleman, as she looked like a lady.

"Don't you look fine today," she teased.

"I am seeking employment," he teased back, poking fun at the high-toned way that ministers and teachers spoke.

"Have you had any success?"

He said, "The *Atlanta Constitution* was willing to hire me as a messenger boy. And Rich's would take me on as a porter." He wasn't bitter; it wasn't worth the effort. But he sounded tired.

"Perhaps you would have better luck with a Black man of business."

"If I could find one."

She sighed. "You could work for my father."

"I know."

"You could work for my mother."

"I'd rather not be beholden to your mother."

"Think about it."

"It's easier for you. You can get married. That would decide it for you."

She snorted. "Is that how you're proposing to me?"

"Are we that far along?" he asked. "I didn't think we were."

"An understanding to have an understanding," she reminded him.

"When I propose to you, I'll do it right," he said. "But a man who wants to marry needs employment first."

"Maybe a woman needs employment, too."

"As a washerwoman? A maid? A cook?"

Eliza thought of all the women in Summerhill who worked because the family needed their wages: the washerwomen, domestic servants, nursemaids, and cooks. That kind of work was beneath her, as being a porter or a messenger boy was beneath Ben.

"There has to be something better." She meant for both of them.

Now he sighed. "When you find it, tell me."

THAT EVENING, AS ELIZA AND HER MOTHER WALKED DOWN the street to the church, her mother asked, "What is this meeting about?"

"Didn't Ophelia tell you?"

"I didn't have time to ask."

Pleasant Grove Baptist, just two years old, met in a wooden building that was the house of someone prosperous just after the war. The first floor had been opened up—the congregation had no shortage of carpenters and plasterers—and pews installed. Tonight it wasn't full. About twenty women sat together in the first few rows. Most of them had the swollen hands of washerwomen.

Amanda Gardiner sat amid them, and so did Ophelia Taylor.

The Reverend Jones faced them and raised his arms, as if in benediction. They quieted. He said, "We have serious business here tonight, you washerwomen. Mrs. Gardiner has asked me to welcome you as you gather together. I know firsthand about the travails of a washerwoman. My wife works at the washtub, and so does my daughter. But this meeting is for you. Mrs. Gardiner, I believe you have something to say?"

Amanda Gardiner rose from her pew, glancing backward as she did so. Mrs. Gardiner took the central spot that belonged to the reverend on Sunday morning. As she stood before them, her eyes rested on one face after another. Eliza felt that gaze, and she saw it settle on her mother's face, too.

The church was hot and still, even with the windows open. "Sisters," she began. Her voice was low but resonant, and she betrayed no unease at standing before them. "I bet you all wonder why you been asked to come here."

Laughter. Someone said, "Miss Ophelia keep it a secret."

"Secret no longer." She looked at them, her eyes resting on them, her friends and neighbors, one after another. "Most of you earn your living by washing." She held up her hands and showed them her swollen joints, her wrinkled fingers, and the backs of her hands, scarred by iron burns. "Work hard, all of us, don't we?"

"Yes, we do," the crowd agreed.

"We talk among ourselves, don't we, many a time. Talk about this missus and that missus. How they treat us. How they pay us. Now none of that a secret, not on Fraser

Street or Rawson Street or Martin's Alley, where we all do the wash together."

"That's right."

Mrs. Gardiner's voice resounded. "But tonight we gather together and we do something new. We don't just grumble about our work and our wages. We bear witness to them, in our church, before God and each other." She paused and again swept her gaze over her audience. They were very quiet. "Mrs. Taylor, you tell me before this meeting that you have something to say."

Someone in the back row said, "Miss Ophelia always have something to say!" The women erupted in good-natured laughter.

Ophelia rose from the pew and turned to nod at the women behind her. She was laughing, too. "That I do."

Mrs. Gardiner said, "Would you tell them what you tell me a few days ago?"

Ophelia nodded. "I go to see a new missus, hope that she give me work. She look at me, and I can tell she don't like me much, just from the look of my face. She say, 'How is a colored girl called Ophelia? Who named you that?'

"I say, 'My mama name me Ophelia, and people call me that.'

"And she say, 'Ophelia, that too fancy a name for a colored girl. You should be called something plain, like Annie or Polly. I call you Polly.'

"And I tell her, 'No, ma'am. My name Ophelia. Ophelia Taylor.'

"She say, 'Are you sassing me?'

"I say, 'No, ma'am, just stating a fact.'

"And then she get mad. She say, 'You impudent nigger. I won't stand for sass from you. You won't work for me.'

"And I say, 'I wouldn't work for you. My name ain't Annie or Polly. Ophelia. Ophelia Taylor.' And I walk away, and I don't get the work."

Several women laughed, and one of them said, "Miss Ophelia ain't afraid to speak her mind."

Another woman said, "I can't afford to speak my mind, even though I would dearly love to."

"Mrs. Lee, will you tell us? Will you witness?" Mrs. Gardiner asked.

Mrs. Lee stood and took a deep breath. It was hard for her to raise her voice like this. "I bite my tongue all the time. When missus call me by a pet's name, when she complain that the wash ain't clean enough, when she late with the wages. My husband used to work regular at the planing mill and now he sick. He don't work half the time. We need what I bring in. So I press my lips together, even though I think just what Miss Ophelia do, and I shoulder that burden along with the load of wash and carry it home."

"Ain't right!" someone called out, and another woman echoed her: "No, it ain't!"

As Mrs. Lee sat down, another woman rose swiftly to her feet. "My husband pass on last year. You all know that because we had his service in this church. My eldest already at work—she a maid for a family on Whitehall Street—and after my husband gone, my oldest boy go to work, too." She stood very still. The words were a burden for her. "My youngest, my little girl, twelve year old, she go to the grammar school at Atlanta University. We scrimp and we go without to pay her school fees. But now I don't see how we manage. I wake up in the middle of the night and I cry, thinking about her losing her chance to go to school. She my hope for the future, and I don't know how I forgive myself if she leave school to work as a washerwoman like I do." She wiped away a tear.

Eliza found that her own eyes were full. She tried to blink her tears away. Her mother squeezed her hand.

"Ain't right!" more than one voice called out.

Another woman stood. She was Mrs. Gardiner's age. She was dark and worn-looking, like a weathered tree. "I ain't afraid of hard work. Never have been. But I need to get paid." She looked around her. "How many of you follow General Sherman's army to Atlanta?" She nodded as the hands rose in the air. "I work for the army. I still work as a washerwoman. But I get paid. She held out her palm and slapped it. "Money in my hand every week. That money the difference between freedom and slavery. Slavery over. We ain't slaves no more. We free. We get paid."

Another woman jumped up. "Don't get paid enough! My missus complain to me that the wash cost her too much. And every other week, she don't have my pay. Whine to me that she short. I need that money every week." She slapped her palm, too. "Money in my hand, and more than a dollar a week!"

Now they were all on their feet, shouting, "Ain't right!"

Ophelia's voice rose above the rest. "We got to do something!"

Someone else caught her fervor. "We stop work! That show them!"

The woman who bit her tongue managed to speak out. "You crazy? We don't work, we don't eat! We starve to death!"

And then there was a din, too loud to tell who said

what. Mrs. Gardiner didn't stop them. But after a while, she nodded to Reverend Jones.

He called out, "Sisters, sisters! Quiet yourselves! Mrs. Gardiner wants to speak!"

They quieted. "We all riled up," she said, and they responded, "Yes, we are!" She called back, "We got to do something!" and they responded, "Yes, we do!" She said, "But we ain't ready yet. How do we get ready?" Her gaze swept over the group. "What do we do to get ready?"

They waited for her to answer.

"We spread the word. We let our sisters in Sherman-town and Jenningstown witness, too. We ask them what they want to do. We test the waters. Then we get together in Bethel A. M. E. We get together at Friendship Baptist."

They grumbled. Mrs. Gardiner said, "What do they say? That it take more than a day to build a city? It take more than a moment to get us together. Got some work to do first." She turned to Reverend Jones. "Reverend, would you talk to the ministers and spread the word among them?"

He wasn't the least bit surprised to get an order from her. Eliza thought, *They talked about this before we met.* "Yes, Mrs. Gardiner. I'd be glad to talk to Reverend Carter at Bethel A. M. E. and Reverend Quarles at Friendship Baptist. And at some of the other churches in Summerhill, too."

She faced the group again. "Sisters, can you do the same? Take the word of this meeting, and what we talk about, to your friends, your neighbors, and your kin, not just in Summerhill but in Shermantown and Jenningstown? Get them ready? Then we gather again,

33

test the waters once more, and figure out what we do and how to do it."

One woman waved her hand in the air. "My sister live on Green's Ferry Avenue, and they all washerwomen there. I see her every week."

Mrs. Gardiner smiled. "Spread the news!"

Someone began to sing, the old song from slavery days with new meaning now. "Roll, Jordan, Roll." Yes, we cross the river. Yes, we hope to go to Heaven. And now yes, we want to get every washerwoman in Atlanta riled up and ready to do something.

As they rose to leave, Mrs. Gardiner positioned herself at the church door, the minister's spot, and as they left, she murmured words of encouragement to each. When it was the Coldbrooks' turn, she smiled. "Miss Rachel, are you with us?"

"It depends on where you're going, Miss Amanda."

"Cross the Jordan with us?"

Eliza's mother laughed. "I have to talk to that woman about keeping her daughter in Atlanta University."

"That, too."

Her mother said, "You didn't think of this just yesterday. You've been thinking about it for a long time, haven't you?"

Mrs. Gardiner smiled. "Yes, it been a long time coming." She clasped Eliza's hand between her own. "What about you, Miss Eliza? Are you with us?"

Eliza couldn't speak. She didn't trust her voice.

CHAPTER 4

NOT WELCOME

MATT ATE his breakfast alone in the dining room, as he had every day since his arrival in Atlanta. He ate his dinners alone, too. He felt so lonely that he asked Mrs. Bailey if he could eat in the kitchen with her. She refused. "It isn't seemly," she said.

This morning, as she proffered the coffee pot, he asked her, "Where does my father go at night?"

She maintained a tight-lipped silence.

He asked, "Does he go to Miss Mannheim?"

He had always known his aunt Rachel as Miss Mannheim. He was surprised when Mrs. Bailey corrected him. "That's not her name anymore."

"What does she call herself now?"

"Mrs. Coldbrook."

So she had changed her name and let the world believe that she had been married.

Now there was another tight-lipped silence. On the Cass County place, slaves would reply to a question they didn't want to answer with "Can't say." That meant they knew, but they wouldn't tell. Mrs. Bailey's silence was no different.

The Coldbrook house was just around the corner, on Fraser Street, but it would be as unseemly for him to call on Mrs. Coldbrook as it would be to eat dinner with Mrs. Bailey.

Mrs. Bailey let slip that Mrs. Coldbrook had a place of business on Wheat Street. Matt decided that a business call was different from a social one. After his solitary breakfast, he left the house to find a horsecar bound for downtown.

He had spent too much time in the damp, cool fog of San Francisco and had forgotten the wet heat of an Atlanta summer. He cursed his wool suit. He felt as though he were wearing a wool blanket. As soon as he sat down on the horsecar, he loosened his tie. He took off his hat and fanned himself with it.

The horsecar was open to the air, which made staring out the window easy. He was still adjusting to the sight of so many Black people on the street. In all his memories of Georgia, he had been surrounded by Black people, but San Francisco was bereft of Black faces. California's strangers were from China, and they were concentrated in Chinatown. His mother, who cared about the down-trodden, had raised her voice in the Temple Sisterhood to prod them to help Chinese immigrants. She told Matt that anyone who had been despised should have a fellow feeling for others who suffered the same way.

The horsecar stopped and a Black man got on. He gave the driver his dime and looked around the car. He wore the clothes of a working man, a coarse shirt and nankeen trousers. Even though the car was empty save for Matt, the newest passenger walked past him, not raising his eyes, and sat in the farthest seat in the back.

Curious, Matt asked the driver, "Why did that man sit in back? There are plenty of seats in front."

The driver said, "They can ride the horsecars if they sit in the colored section."

Matt drew in his breath and said nothing.

He got off the horsecar at Wheat Street and walked eastward. The farther he went, the more Black people he saw, and the worse the repair of the streets and the sidewalks. No neighborhood in Atlanta smelled sweet, since anything that lay in the gutter rotted in the heat, but Shermantown seemed more rank than Summerhill or downtown. He hurried past his father's shop.

The sidewalks were narrow and crowded. The children were in school and the men at work, but the street was full of women. Many of them carried huge bundles on their heads. He moved aside to give a woman so burdened room to pass. Under the bundle her face registered surprise.

"What are you carrying, ma'am?"

Further surprised, she replied, "Wash, young sir."

"On your head like that?"

She said, "Been washing all my life. I'm used to it."

A few blocks farther east, he was the only white man on the street, and the Black people he passed looked askance from the corners of their eyes. He wanted to ask for directions to Mrs. Coldbrook's place of business, but it was clear no one was glad he was here. No one would challenge him or tell him to go somewhere else. But there were plenty of subtle ways to make a white person feel unwelcome in a Black neighborhood, and he felt them all.

He saw the bright gold lettering on the window, artfully done: "Coldbrook Construction Company." So his aunt Rachel was a builder, an odd business for a woman. He pushed the door open. Unlike a dry goods shop, it had no bell to jangle to announce his arrival.

A woman sat at a desk, writing. She had a good vantage point to see whoever came in. She wore a dark, well-tailored dress with a white collar and cuffs, the feminine version of a black suit. Even before she lifted her head, Matt recognized her.

The years had taken some of the roundness from her face, and her expression had lost the sweetness he remembered. She looked as though she spent a great deal of time in practical worry. A businesslike face. She asked, "Sir, can I help you?"

She hadn't recognized him. Full of sorrow, full of shame, he took a deep breath. "Mrs. Coldbrook," he said, knowing that "Aunt Rachel" was unseemly, too. "It's Matthew Kaltenbach. Matt."

She rose. She didn't extend her hand. "It's been a long time," she said. "You're much changed."

"Thirteen years," he said.

"You grew up."

He struggled to keep the pleading tone from his voice. "Did my father mention that I was in Atlanta?"

"Yes," she said. "He told me that you were here for a visit."

He wasn't ready to tell her that he was considering more than a visit; he hadn't told his father, either. "How is Eliza?" he asked, not knowing what else to ask.

She thawed, just a little. "She does very well. She just graduated from Atlanta University."

"You must be proud of her."

She inclined her head, as though nodding was more than she could manage. "Your father told me you just graduated, too."

"Yes, from the University of California at Berkeley." He breathed a little easier and waited for her to make a further inquiry.

"All of Henry's children seem to be scholars," she said.

He seized this bit of warmth. "I hear that Eliza has a brother and sister."

"Called Charles and Ada."

He didn't know how to reply, and the silence made him so uneasy that he blurted out, "Mrs. Coldbrook, might I call on you? And Eliza, and the others?"

She gave him a long, appraising gaze, as though he had brought her a contract she didn't want to sign. If she was remembering his childhood, it gave her no pleasure, and it produced no connection between them. She said, "We're at home on Sunday afternoons."

"Will my father be there?"

Her face remained impassive. "He usually is."

On Sunday afternoon, Matt dressed carefully. He plastered his hair with pomade, a doubly useless gesture, since the heat encouraged the curl. He smoothed the recalcitrant locks, knowing that the nerves weren't about his appearance.

They were about Eliza.

Would she recognize him? Would she remember

anything of their shared past? He stared at himself in the mirror. Did she have a nightmare like his own?

As a rougher man would say, *That's a damn fool thing to think.*

He left the empty house to walk around the block to the Coldbrook house.

He hesitated on the sidewalk as he had hesitated on Wheat Street. The house was new and fresh with white paint. It was the compact city version of the four-up-and-down where they had all lived in Cass County before the war. It even had two modest pillars in front. They looked useful, holding up the second story and not announcing that the householder had pretensions to be a planter in a plantation house.

He swallowed hard, walked up the steps, and knocked on the door.

The young woman who opened it wore a fresh white dress that made her skin look darker, even though she was not dark in complexion. She wore her hair in a neat bun, and it had been as fiercely tamed with pomade as his own. She looked like her mother, but he knew to look for the resemblance. If he had passed her on the street, he would not have recognized her, either.

"Miss Coldbrook," he said.

Her voice was cool. "Mr. Kaltenbach." She opened the door all the way. "We've been expecting you. Come in."

He had been a fool to contemplate it, but he thought for a moment of a different reunion, one in which she exclaimed over him, clasped his hand, and fell on his neck, crying out, "Matt! It is so good to see you again!"

They were half brother and half sister, and the years apart had made them strangers.

He asked, "Is my father with you?"

She looked surprised. "Yes, as always."

Matt began to stammer. "This may not be a good time," he managed to say.

"As good as any."

"Excuse me. I won't trouble you. I won't come in." Without waiting for her reply, he turned away and fled.

HENRY KALTENBACH DID NOT ATTEND A SYNAGOGUE. MATT asked Mrs. Bailey if she knew someone who might guide him to one.

She said, "Oh, you mean the Temple up on Garnett and Forsyth."

"How do you know about the synagogue?"

"Have a friend who work for a Jewish family. She know all about the holidays and the Temple. I can ask her when they have their service."

They didn't meet on the Jewish Sabbath; they held their services on Sunday. The temples in San Francisco were no different. It was part of their far-reaching reform of Judaism, which meant making it more like a Protestant church. There was a practical reason, too, and Matt was sure that the Jews of Atlanta felt it as much as the Jews in California. Saturday was the best day for retail business. On Sunday, blue laws demanded that shops stay closed.

On Sunday morning, as Mrs. Bailey went off to her church, Matt again put on his good suit and took himself to the new synagogue building. The architects had been inspired by the synagogues of Moorish Spain; the Gothic building had been topped with an onion-shaped dome.

Inside, he felt shy and slipped into a pew at the back to wait. He watched as the Jews of Atlanta entered, the men in black suits like his own, the women in brightly colored dresses in the newest fashion. The elders, German immigrants, had heavy accents, while the younger generation was Southern in their speech. Some of the families had pretty daughters, but no one cast a glance in his direction or greeted him.

In accordance with their name, they kept to a Reform service. Men and women sat together, and in the choir, they sang together. The congregation prayed in English, and the rabbi gave a sermon in English. It was familiar enough to take the edge from his unease about not belonging there.

But afterward, when they gathered to bless the wine and take a little refreshment in the reception room downstairs, they clustered together, all of them friends and all of them familiar with each other. Matt hung back. No one approached him, welcomed him, or asked who he was and what brought him to the Temple and to Atlanta. Was it fitting to be bold? To introduce himself to these strangers? He thought not. He should go.

But as he turned to leave, a young man, also by himself, said to him, "You must be new." He had a New Yorker's accent.

"I am," Matt said.

He was skinny and lively, with a pleasant, blue-eyed gaze. He stuck out his hand; his coat sleeve was too short for him, and it showed a knobby wrist. "Artie Cohen," he said. "I'm new, too. Just got here from up north."

"Matt Kaltenbach. San Francisco."

Artie gestured to the crowd, so thick among themselves. "You think they'd been Southerners for a hundred years instead of Germans who got off the boat a few years ago." His speech was clipped and swift. Southerners must think he was impatient.

"If they fought in the war, they're Southerners through and through."

Artie said, "I thought that was over and done."

"Not here," Matt said.

"How do you know? You're from California." It wasn't a challenge, just a friendly inquiry.

"I grew up there. I was born in Georgia."

"And you don't have any *mishpokhe* here?"

"My family left after the war. They were on the Union side, God help them." Why had he told a stranger that?

Artie said, "What's your business? Where do you work?"

"I just got here. I'm looking for a position."

"They aren't hospitable here," Artie said, looking around the room. "But they hire their own. I work for Mr. Rich. Pillar of the Jewish community."

"The dry goods man?"

"Yes, that's the one. Would you like me to put in a word for you?"

Matt thought of his father's shop on Wheat Street. He couldn't imagine he'd get a warm reception from Mr. Rich. "Thanks, but I'd rather not work in dry goods."

"There's sure to be something for you. There's plenty to go around in Atlanta. I can do a little nosing for you elsewhere, if you like."

Matt felt a rush of gratitude at this enthusiastic stranger's kindness. "Thanks."

Artie grinned. "We outsiders have to stick together, too."

~

Resourceful Artie finagled him an introduction to Cohen and Sons, telling him that they were cotton buyers. "No relation to me," he said, grinning. "Moses Cohen is the father, and James and Edward are the sons."

"Were they here before the war?"

"I thought you'd be the one to know."

"I think they were. I think they used to be planters. Cotton growers. Slave owners."

Artie said, "You're as bad as the local men. Always talking about the Lost Cause. War's over."

Matt didn't reply.

When he left the next day to call on the Cohens, Mrs. Bailey said, "You wear out that suit."

"When I get a position, I can order a new one."

"A position? Thought you were just visiting."

"Maybe not."

"Do your daddy know?"

"Don't tell him."

She brushed something from his shoulder. "Who you call on?"

"Cohen and Sons."

"Cohen? From the Temple?"

"I'm sure they go there. But I don't know them."

She sighed. "I wish you luck."

The Cohens did business in a five-story brick building on Whitehall Street. Its façade shouted, *See how we rose from the ashes of the war!* Inside, marble gleamed on the floor. Behind a mahogany desk sat a light-skinned man in a resplendent blue uniform. With great dignity, he asked, "Who are you here to see, sir?"

"Mr. Moses Cohen."

"Second floor, sir."

The Cohens, whether they were fit or infirm, were spared the climb up four flights of stairs.

When he was led back to Moses Cohen's office, he was suddenly in the study in the plantation house in Cass County. The chairs in the anteroom were red leather, and the walls were paneled in a dark wood. The air smelled of tobacco. Was it his imagination, or did he smell the faintest whiff of whiskey, too?

Moses Cohen was a stout man with grizzled dark hair. His eyes, which had a weary look, were still keen. He was dressed as a man of business, not as a planter. He settled Matt into a big leather chair and asked how long he had been in Atlanta and how he found it. Matt offered pleasantries. Moses Cohen asked, "Where do you hail from, young man? I hear the South in your voice."

"I spent my earliest years in Georgia," Matt said.

"Where?"

Inspired, Matt said, "In Cass County. My grandfather had a place there."

"Who was he, your grandfather? Perhaps I know him."

"Mordecai Mannheim."

Moses Cohen chuckled. "Mordecai! That old scoundrel. I knew him well. He turned his hand to selling cotton after the war. He lost everything when Sherman came through."

As Matt well knew. He kept his voice polite but

couldn't resist the dig. "Sir, did you have a place before the war?"

"We still have it. In Troup County. Good cotton land. We lost all our people, of course. Had to start over. Now we crop shares with our colored workers. We make as much as we did before the war."

"But in Atlanta, sir, you broker cotton? Buy and sell?"

"Yes, we do." He gave Matt a penetrating look. "Kaltenbach. Are you any kin to Henry Kaltenbach?"

"Yes, I am. He's my father."

Moses Cohen's gaze became keener. "Mannheim. Your mother was the Mannheim, then. Adelaide Mannheim."

"Yes, sir." He began to feel deeply uneasy. Nothing was history in the South. He waited to hear what Moses Cohen remembered.

"It was quite a scandal," he said. "She wouldn't marry a Pereira from Charleston, and her family managed to scrape up Mr. Kaltenbach. And after he came back from the war, they didn't suit anymore, and she ran off to California with the local Bureau man."

"Mr. Lewis Hart," Matt said. "He's my stepfather."

Moses Cohen chuckled. "There was a divorce, too. Another scandal."

Matt knew that in a moment Cohen would get to the scandal that was still fresh: that Henry Kaltenbach treated a Black woman as his wife and doted on his Black children. And he did. He licked his lips, as old Black men did when they told a good story. He said, "Henry Kaltenbach seems to be a little too much tangled up with colored people, by my lights. Sells to them, lives among them, has some very cordial relations with them. Intimate relations, some say."

Matt, despite his own hurt at his father's behavior, was furious on his father's behalf. He was surprised he could talk without choking. Or raising his voice. "Sir, I left Georgia when I was a boy. I haven't seen my father for thirteen years. These things are all very far away."

"It was a *shande* then, and it's a *shande* now." He used the Yiddish word that refined German Jews found vulgar. It meant both scandal and shame. "We Jews, we need to be above reproach. Any man I employ needs to be above reproach. I can't hire a young man with a cloud over his head."

Matt was so angry that he didn't bite his tongue. "Sir, if I may ask, how many slaves did you own before the war?"

"Not that it's any business of yours, but I had thirty hands on my place," he said.

He rose. "I was raised by people who hated slavery," he said. "Let those without sin cast the first stone."

He stumbled from the Cohen office, so angry that he had to grip the fine marble railing to get down the stairs. In the splendid lobby, the Black man at the desk asked, "Young sir, are you all right?"

Matt shook his head and walked away, speechless.

~

SEVERAL DAYS LATER, HIS FATHER RETURNED FROM THE SHOP and lingered long enough in the parlor to hand Matt an envelope. "This came to the shop, but it was addressed to you," he said.

Matt was too impatient to find the letter opener. He

47

tore the heavy rag paper of the envelope. In the best copperplate was written:

Dear Mr. Kaltenbach:

Mr. Cohen regrets that he has no opportunity for you. He recommends you to his lawyer, Mr. Howell, who may be in need of a clerk.

Respectfully,

James Cohen

"Is it good news?" his father asked.

"I hope so. It's about someone who may have a position."

"I wish you luck," his father said, before he left for the Coldbrook house.

Matt held the paper in his hand and wondered why Moses Cohen felt compelled to do anything for him.

The next morning, Matt put on his suit again and made his way to Mr. Howell's office on Whitehall Street. Whitehall, the center of downtown, was thick with carriages. Black-coated men crowded the sidewalks. Matt wondered what it would be like to become one of them, a man who had business every day on Whitehall Street.

In the street, careful to avoid any white people, walked a Black man in rough clothes, with a shovel resting on his shoulder.

The law offices were less ostentatious than Mr. Cohen's den of marble and mahogany. In the front room, with its worn wing chairs and plain white walls, he explained his business to a sandy-haired man who said he'd convey Matt's message to Mr. Howell.

In a few minutes he returned and said, "Mr. Howell regrets that he's too busy this morning to speak to you. I'm his head clerk. You can speak to me."

Under the lawyer's diction Matt heard the echo of an accent from northern Georgia. A planter's snobbery awoke in Matt. This man was a lawyer's clerk now, but before the war, he had been a hill country man, likely from a farm that struggled to grow enough corn to feed his family.

The clerk, whose name was Mr. Skaggs, asked where Matt hailed from. Matt explained.

"Cass County?" Mr. Skaggs said. "Bartow, now. I have kin in Walker County."

Walker County was on the border with Tennessee. Hill country, indeed. Mr. Skaggs said, "I came to Atlanta after the war. I was interested in the law, and Mr. Howell was kind enough to take me on."

Matt waited politely.

Mr. Skaggs said, "Are you interested in the law?"

"I just finished a course in college," Matt said. "I'd like to find out."

"College?" Mr. Skaggs bristled a little. "Where?"

"In California."

"Well, you don't need college to do well as a lawyer's clerk. You need a good hand and an eye for detail. Do you have that?"

"I hope so."

Mr. Skaggs had pale-blue eyes, like so many of the hill country people. He regarded Matt with a pale-blue gaze. "Kaltenbach," he said. "I seem to recall that name. Isn't there a dry goods merchant by that name? He has a shop on Wheat Street."

"Yes, he does," Matt said.

"Sells to coloreds, as I recall. Employs them, too."

Matt was silent. The door opened, and a Black man,

dressed in a black jacket and pants, a workman's version of the businessman's suit, slipped into the office. Under his arm he carried a large envelope.

Mr. Skaggs said, "Jimmy, what have you got for us today?"

"Messages, sir." *Suh.* He handed Mr. Skaggs the envelope. Mr. Skaggs fumbled in his pocket. He laid a dime on the counter. The man took it. "Thank you, suh," he said as he left.

Mr. Skaggs said, "It's all right for them to make a living. But they need to know their place."

Matt was silent.

"Is this Mr. Kaltenbach any kin to you?"

Matt thought, *There's nothing for me here, either.* He wouldn't wait for the rebuff. He said, "He's my father," and when Mr. Skaggs didn't reply, Matt rose. "I won't take any more of your time, sir. Thank you, and thank Mr. Howell for me."

Mr. Skaggs looked a little surprised, but he remained cordial. "You're welcome," he said, extending his hand.

Even though Matt had sworn not to return to the Temple, he attended the service on Sunday to find Artie Cohen. At the Kiddush, they blessed the wine that was served in tiny glasses. Artie asked him how his search for a position was going.

Matt turned the glass in his hand. "I need more than this to tell you about it," he said.

Artie laughed. "Ain't it a good thing that the saloons are open on the Lord's Day?"

Artie took Matt to Railroad Street, which ran parallel to the train tracks. The saloon was surprisingly well-appointed, the walls freshly painted, the wooden trim glowing, and the bar a shining marble. Behind the bar stood a Black man, broad-shouldered and tall, with a ready smile. "Young sirs, what can I get you?" He sounded cordial without being the least bit servile.

Matt said, "What do you have to drown a man's sorrows?"

"Sorrows?" the barkeeper asked, smiling. His teeth were very white. "Fine young man like you, with your whole life before you? You lose your sweetheart?"

Matt said, "Thank goodness, no. I don't have a sweetheart to lose. I can't find a position."

"You keep looking, you will," the barkeep said.

"He's right," Artie said.

Matt was suddenly so upset that he didn't care if the barkeep, a man with acute hearing, overheard him. He said, "The Jews won't have me because my father is a *shande*. And the goyim won't have me either because he likes Black people too much."

"They won't have you because of your daddy?" the barkeep asked.

"Mr. Henry Kaltenbach. Evidently he's notorious all over Atlanta."

The man shook his head. "Don't know of him," he said.

Even if it wasn't true, Matt felt better.

The barkeep said, "You know, when I first came to Atlanta, I had high hopes. Wanted to better myself. I looked and looked for a position. Couldn't find a thing better than a laborer. A porter. A messenger boy. A grown man. Too old to be a boy." He smiled to soften his words, knowing he was taking a chance with a white stranger. "Found a spot working in a saloon. Saved my money and had enough to start a saloon of my own. Did well enough to buy this place." He gestured, a sweeping motion that took in the entire saloon. "Made my own way."

Matt said, "Perhaps I should work for you."

The man laughed. "Wouldn't be seemly," he said. "Now, what can I get the two of you?"

Matt drank a glass of whiskey, then another. He had never drunk more than a little wine at the Passover Seder. After an hour, he was dizzy. He said the first thing that came into his head. "Artie, does your father love you?"

Artie held his liquor better than Matt. "I guess so. When I left New York, he shook my hand and told me he'd miss me. He gave me twenty dollars for the trip. My mother was the one who cried."

"I want my father to love me." Matt was appalled to realize he was this drunk.

"I thought he doted on you."

"That's my stepfather. My father here in Atlanta."

"Doesn't he?"

"I don't know."

"What do you want him to do?"

The room seemed to be spinning. "I don't know that, either."

Artie shifted in his chair. "I think you've had enough." He asked the barkeep, "What do you think?"

The barkeep spoke to Artie. "Young sir, I think your friend needs to go home."

"I think so, too. Can we get a hansom around here?"

CHAPTER 5

GET IN UNION

ELIZA WAVED TO OPHELIA, who wasn't in her usual tattered washday dress and dingy apron. She had doffed her Sunday best. "No washing today," she said, her eyes gleaming.

"I thought it wasn't time to quit working yet."

"It ain't. But it's time to spread the word. Want to come with me?" Ophelia held out her arm. The stripes on her dress glowed red in the sunshine.

Eliza laughed. "I can't refuse if you put it like that." She took Ophelia's arm and they ambled down the street like friends on a promenade. The air was already hot, promising more heat later in the day, but Eliza didn't mind the way it warmed her. She was an Atlantan, used to it.

Ophelia led her down the alley. Some alleys were wide enough to build houses in, but the one behind Fraser Street was for utility, to give access to the backyards where the washerwomen worked.

Ophelia sauntered down the alley, waving.

"Why don't we stop?" Eliza asked.

"Nearest neighbors already know. Today I go farther afield." Ophelia stopped and waved to a woman bent over her washtub. "Miss Mary!" she called. "How you doing?"

Miss Mary, a slight woman in a worn gray dress, didn't look up. Behind her, a girl of about ten looked after three younger ones. The littlest, not old enough to walk yet, began to cry. The girl picked up the baby and rocked him, her eyes on Ophelia.

"I'm busy," Miss Mary said.

"We all busy. Won't take but a moment. Do you hear about that meeting we have a few days ago at Pleasant Grove Baptist?"

Miss Mary wiped her forehead with a soapy arm. "No, don't hear a thing. Thought was for Bible study. Can't read, so I didn't pay it no mind."

"Wasn't Bible study. We washerwomen on Fraser and Rawson, we meet. We talk about how it ain't right that we treated so poor and paid so little."

Miss Mary rocked back on her heels. "That ain't news to anyone."

"No, but we all testify to it. Before the minister and each other. Mean something more than just grumbling among ourselves."

Miss Mary didn't move. "What good is that? Whether you moan and complain in the backyard or in the church?"

"We think about doing something about it."

Miss Mary sighed. Eliza had never heard a woman sigh with such melancholy. "Like what?"

"Don't know yet. But we decide to gather again, more of us, at Bethel A. M. E. on Wheat Street to talk it over."

Miss Mary turned her head toward Eliza. "You ain't a washerwoman."

"No, I'm not."

"What do you think? You think this a good idea?"

Eliza took in a quick breath. "Yes."

"You going to this meeting?"

"I am."

"What do your mama think about it?"

Eliza said, "She says she's pondering it."

Miss Mary considered this.

Ophelia bent down and touched Miss Mary's soapy arm. "You ponder it, too," she said. "About coming to the meeting."

Miss Mary gestured toward the washtub. "Busy," she said, as she had begun.

"I know. That why we have the meeting in the evening."

The little girl, who had been soothing her brother, spoke up. "We should go, Mama."

"You want to go?"

The little girl said, "I don't want to be a washerwoman when I grow up." Eliza felt an intent gaze on her, big round brown eyes. "I want to go to school."

Miss Mary didn't reply.

Ophelia tapped Miss Mary on the shoulder. "Ponder it," she repeated, casting a glance at the little girl.

As they walked on, Eliza said, "Didn't think anyone would say no."

Ophelia grinned. "Some say no and some say maybe. I come back again before the meeting. See what I can do." They made their way a little farther down the alley. In the yard, a woman straightened herself, wiping her hands on her apron. Her greeting was cheerful. "Miss Ophelia, why ain't you working? Why you come to see me today?"

"Do I need a reason?"

"To keep me from my work, you do." But she was smiling. She was tall and broad-shouldered, with the weather-beaten skin of someone who had spent her youth in the cotton field.

"I got good news for you."

The woman laughed. "Do Jesus come again? I miss that, if it happen."

"Day ain't over yet," Ophelia replied, with good humor. "No, it about the meeting at Pleasant Grove Church, since I don't see you there. Do you hear about that?"

"Yes, I do. I hear that you intend to have another meeting."

"Bethel A. M. E. on Wheat Street."

She put her hand on her back, just where it would ache from bending over the washtub. "You have a healing? Ease my sore back?"

"You make more money and don't work so hard, that ease your back. And pay for liniment, too."

She rubbed the sore spot. But she was smiling again. It transformed her face; she looked ten years younger. "Miss Ophelia, I believe you could talk a bird out of a tree. Yes, I'll be there."

"Tell your neighbors! Tell your friends! Tell your kin!"

As they returned to the alley—Ophelia sauntered as though she had all the time in the world—Eliza said, "You like doing this."

Ophelia's smile dazzled. "Yes, Miss Eliza, I surely do." She held out her arm. "Help me snare a few more."

Down the alley, Ophelia stopped to talk to a woman

Eliza knew slightly from church, Mrs. Ida Watkins. She was stout, and everything about her was swollen. She moved with difficulty on rheumatic knees. "How you doing, Miss Ida?" Ophelia asked, and Eliza braced herself for a raft of complaint.

Instead she asked, "Miss Ophelia, I hear you run up and down the alley to tell my neighbors about the washer-women meeting together."

Ophelia nodded. Eliza was a little weary of her friend's enthusiasm. She felt sweaty under her corset, and she began to think with longing of the glass of iced water she could have at home.

A man walked down the alley. His pace was slow, as though he might be lost. He was refined-looking and slender inside his frock coat, and he carried a black leather bag. Seeing them, he stopped. His hair was close-cropped, and his skin was the warmest shade of sepia brown. "Excuse me," he said. His accent was Northern. "Where can I find the Oliver house? They've asked me to call."

"Miss Minerva?" Mrs. Watkins asked. "She live on the other side of the alley. The house front on Terry Street. You in the alley behind Martin."

"I've just moved to Atlanta, and I'm still finding my way around."

"You're a Yankee!" Ophelia said.

His smile was swift and warm. "Philadelphia born and bred. My name is Franklin Chesney."

Ophelia asked, "What you got in that bag?"

He lifted it. "I'm a doctor. Everything I need to call on a patient."

"How do a man of color get to be a doctor?" Mrs. Watkins asked.

"I just finished my medical degree at Howard University in Washington."

"University! Miss Eliza here, she just graduate from Atlanta University."

He glanced at Eliza. His eyes were a deep brown, and they were as warm as his smile. "Congratulations. A college degree is an achievement."

She said, "And a medical degree, even more so. Are you planning to set up your practice in Atlanta?"

"I hope so," he said. He smelled of wintergreen, a pleasantly medicinal smell. He laughed. "If I can find Mrs. Oliver to attend to her."

Mrs. Watkins said, "Doctor, do you have a moment? My ankles hurt me something terrible."

Eliza thought, *He'll be here for half an hour, if she'll let him.*

"Yes, but for just a moment. Mrs. Oliver is expecting me. Can you show me?"

She lifted her hem. He bent to look and said, "May I touch your ankle?" His finger left a depression in her skin. "You're retaining water."

"I know. I have the dropsy. Run in the family."

He straightened. "Come to see me. My office is on Wheat Street. Just down the block from the dry goods shop. Kaltenbach's, I believe it's called."

Mrs. Watkins's face fell. "Don't have the money for it, Dr. Chesney. Dearly wish I did."

He said, "I hope to make a living, but I came to Atlanta because the need is so great. Dropsy is a serious condition. Let me help you."

"Never met a doctor who work for free," she said.

He sighed. "I must go. Which way to the Olivers'?"

~

WHEN ELIZA RETURNED HOME THAT AFTERNOON, HER mother was home as well, sitting in the parlor, the newspaper in her lap instead of the sewing that occupied most women. "Eliza? Where have you been?"

"Ophelia wanted to tell the women on the street about another meeting."

"The washerwomen again?"

"Yes, at Bethel A. M. E. this time. I thought you'd heard."

"I hadn't. I have my own business to run. Were you planning on going?"

"Yes," Eliza said. "Weren't you?"

Her mother sighed. She had the troubled, distant look that meant she was thinking of Cass County. "I'm a little worried to see you get involved in this."

"To tag along with Ophelia? To go to a meeting? That's not much."

"Not yet. But if the washerwomen decide to strike, it's a different matter."

Her mother's worry upset Eliza. She pushed the past away. "Mama, we're in Atlanta. I'm going to a meeting in church. I'm with Ophelia, talking to our neighbors. It's all right."

"Be careful. Don't let Ophelia pull you along. She's worked up about this, and she's very persuasive."

"Don't you think I can decide this for myself? Can't I decide to do this because I want to?"

"Oh, Eliza," her mother said, and her tone was no longer censure but sadness. "I don't want to see you hurt, and believe me, the world can hurt a Black woman a lot worse than it can a white woman."

The memory of that night in Cass County swept over Eliza. "Mama, when are we going to stop thinking about that? Remembering it?"

"Do you still have that nightmare?"

"I haven't. Not for a long time."

A shadow of pain passed over her mother's face. She had owned a farm in Cass County and she was prideful enough to put glass windows in the house she built for her Black tenants. The Klan burned that farm to the ground. "We're in Atlanta now. But we're still Black, all of us. Don't forget that."

Eliza felt a chill. "I can't. And I won't."

❧

THE WASHERWOMEN OF SUMMERHILL, ELIZA IN THEIR MIDST, left for the next meeting at Bethel A. M. E. in small groups, families and friends walking together. In Summerhill, a crowd of Black women wasn't unusual, but as soon as they passed Foster Street, where McDonough became Peachtree, they were conspicuous. They were Black; they were women; they were numerous. And they were a stone's throw away from the white folks' mansions west of Peachtree.

Eliza walked with Ophelia Taylor, who thrummed with excitement. "Look at how many of us there are. Fifty, maybe more! And I talk to most of them myself!"

Amanda Gardiner, who led the band, turned to say,

"Keep your voice down, Miss Ophelia. Don't want to call attention to ourselves."

Ophelia stuck out her tongue when Amanda turned back. Eliza thought, *Even if we stood silent and stock still, we'd call attention to ourselves.*

A policeman eyed them as they turned onto Wheat Street. He wore a bright-blue coat—no one would mistake it for Union blue—with very shiny brass buttons. He was stocky, with a ruddy face, and he tapped his baton on his palm. Eliza felt a clutch of unease. The policemen of Atlanta reminded her too much of the rural patrollers of her childhood. And hard on the heels of those memories were the ones she tried to shut away, her memories of the Klan.

The policeman barred Amanda Gardiner's way, his baton still resting on his palm. "Where are you going?" he demanded, letting them hear the rudeness of "you."

Mrs. Gardiner stopped on the sidewalk, and those behind her halted, too. She dropped her voice. She was careful to look somewhere behind his head. "Sir, we going to church."

He stared at the crowd of women behind her. "Church? On a Tuesday night?"

"Sir, every day is a good day to listen to the word of the Lord."

The policeman let his eyes rove over Amanda. He shifted his gaze to Ophelia, then to Eliza. Eliza began to tremble, as much with fear as with anger. Ophelia clutched her arm tightly, trying to steady them both. He turned his attention back to Mrs. Gardiner. "Don't you cause any trouble."

Mrs. Gardiner stretched her lips in a servile smile. "Oh no, sir. We certainly won't."

He tapped his baton on his palm once more and said, "Get on with you." He remained in the middle of the sidewalk. It was clear that he wanted them to walk in the street.

Amanda Gardiner squared her shoulders. She stepped delicately into the street, as though she were a lady and ladies always walked in the gutter.

Eliza thought, *Twenty years out of slavery, and she has to act like this!*

Ophelia tugged on Eliza's arm and pulled her into the street to follow Mrs. Gardiner. And as the policeman watched, all fifty of the Black women of Summerhill, cluster by cluster, stepped carefully into the gutter and proceeded down the street with dignity.

When they were safely past—when they could return to the sidewalk, a block or two from the church—Eliza muttered to Ophelia, "It makes me furious to watch her act the slave."

Ophelia bent close. She whispered, "She act, all right."

BETHEL A. M. E., BIGGER THAN PLEASANT GROVE AND built as a church, had room for several hundred people. All the pews were full. In this protected space, reserved for Black people, no one was quiet. The noise rose from the crowd like the hum of a giant beehive. Eliza hesitated at the door. "Look at all these people," she murmured to Ophelia.

Ophelia's eyes were bright. "We spread the word in

Shermantown, too." Ophelia pulled on her arm. "I want to sit up front. Come with me."

Not entirely willing to be so visible, Eliza let Ophelia pull her down the church aisle. Heads turned as they walked. She whispered, "Why are they staring?"

"You dressed too fine for a washerwoman."

Eliza had put on a plain white dress that she had often worn to class at Atlanta University. These women had hurried from their washtubs, and they wore the dresses they worked in.

The first pew was crowded, but no one minded that Ophelia wanted to squeeze in. Eliza found herself crushed between Ophelia and a substantial woman who smelled of sweat and lye soap.

Unlike Pleasant Grove, which was too plain for a pulpit, Bethel had a proper dais and lectern for the minister. Reverend Carter, who presided at Bethel A. M. E., stood there now. Two people flanked him: Reverend Jones from Pleasant Grove and Amanda Gardiner. Reverend Carter raised his arms and called, "Ladies! Ladies! I call you to order!"

They fell silent. They turned their faces to him, eager to hear what he had to say.

"We come here today for a special purpose. My good friend from Pleasant Grove Baptist Church, the Reverend Charles Oliver Jones, told me that the washerwomen of his congregation came together to testify that they are weary of working too hard and being paid too little. He told me that his flock would spread the word of their meeting to their sisters in Shermantown. I see many of my own congregants among you. They sowed that word among you, and I see what they've reaped. You've come together in a multitude!"

They called out, "Yes, we have!"

Reverend Carter waited as they responded. "We have a guest who wants to speak to you. Like yourselves, she is a washerwoman, and she knows in her back and her hands and her bones what it's like to earn a living at the washtub."

Eliza thought of the cheerful woman that she and Ophelia had talked to, whose back ached. Was she in this crowd tonight?

The reverend said, "Mrs. Amanda Gardiner, will you come forward? Will you speak?"

Mrs. Gardiner smiled, her face alight with joy. "I surely will."

He stepped away from the lectern. "I yield this meeting to you."

Mrs. Gardiner stepped forward and rested her hands on the lectern as though she spoke at a lectern every week. She let her eyes roam over the crowd. Eliza remembered how she had seemed to meet every eye at Pleasant Grove. She wondered if Mrs. Gardiner could manage that with an audience of several hundred.

"We all wash for a living." As in the first meeting, she held up her hands and showed them the evidence of her labor. "It's hard work, ain't it?"

"Yes, it is," the crowd agreed.

She reprised her first speech. "Don't we know it. Tell each other about it. Talk about this missus and that missus. How they treat us. How they pay us. We all hear about that in Summerhill, where we have our first meeting." She took in the crowd. "And it ain't no different on Wheat Street or Houston Street here in Shermantown."

"That's right."

"No matter how hard we work," Mrs. Gardiner said, "we don't get paid enough. And sometimes we don't get paid at all."

"Ain't that the truth!" someone called, and someone else responded, "That ain't right!"

"No, it ain't. We want better than that. Need our money. Families need our money. Can't go without. Can't live on a pittance." She rested her gaze on them, seeming to meet everyone's eyes. Eliza had seen preachers who could do that. Mrs. Gardiner was their equal.

Mrs. Gardiner paused. "We deserve better. We deserve more."

"More!" they chorused. "Deserve more!" They clapped their hands, not in applause, but in rhythm. For Eliza, it stirred a memory of the rhythm of a ring shout, a long time ago, back in Cass County.

Mrs. Gardiner raised her arms, as Reverend Carter had done, and they obeyed her. They quieted, eager to hear what she had to say next. "You all fired up, I can see it. Ain't enough to hope for better or for more. Ain't enough to pray for it." She took a deep breath, as though preparing herself for something arduous. "It's time to ask for it."

They stayed silent.

"That's why I come here today, when all of you gathered here, thanks to our sisters who talk to all of you. I come here to find out if you ready to ask for better and for more. If you ready to work for it, too."

They were still silent. And in the silence, Ophelia rose.

She turned to the audience. In a voice that could travel the length of a cotton field, or a city block, she yelled, "We stop work!"

They erupted into a furious response, nothing like their previous rhythm of before. Eliza could make out a few words in their angry din. "Stop work?" "How we eat?" "We starve to death!" "That's crazy!"

Mrs. Gardiner, whose voice could also travel a distance, called out, "Hush! Sisters, hush!"

They were so worked up that it took them a while to hush.

"To stop work, that's a frightening thing. No money coming in, and you don't know how long it take. I see why you scared even to think about it."

"That's right!" They were back in chorus. Back in agreement.

"We don't stop work on a whim. We don't stop work in a flash of anger. We plan for it. Agree on what we want. Agree on when we stop. Agree to do it together. Imagine, all the washerwomen of Atlanta, on strike together! Ain't no one can get a pair of clean drawers in the sweatiest month of summer!"

Laughter, at first a ripple, then a wave, and clapping, this time like applause.

She waited for them to quiet. "And we figure on how to take care of those who suffer if they stop work. How to help them. Feed them. Keep a roof over their heads. Make it easy for them to stay with us, no matter how long it take to get what we want." Her eyes traveled over the crowd again, and Eliza had the oddest feeling that Mrs. Gardiner met her eyes alone. That this message was for her, although everyone heard it. She said, "We get the better treatment we deserve. We get more money. But we get more. We get dignity. We get respect."

"Oh yes!" The rhythm of hands clapping resumed, like an army's drumbeat. Anyone who had followed General Sherman knew that sound.

Mrs. Gardiner called, "Sisters, are you with me!"

"We with you!"

"We all together?"

"Yes! We together!"

"Then we come together again to make that plan. Are you ready for that?"

"Yes, we are!"

Mrs. Gardiner said, "You ready to witness to that?"

"Yes, we are!"

Ophelia's eyes were shining. She said to Eliza, "Got more work to do!"

Eliza thought, *Was my mother right?* She glanced around the church. At the back, in a press of washerwomen, stood her mother, in her good businesslike black dress.

She was here. Despite all her reservations, despite all her fears, she was here. She saw Eliza and nodded. She worked her way through the crowd, all the way to the front of the church, to hold out her hand to Eliza.

"Miss Rachel!" Mrs. Gardiner greeted her mother. "It's good to see you. You with us? Or you still pondering?"

"I'll talk to you later, Miss Amanda." Her mother held out her arm to Eliza. "Come on home."

CHAPTER 6

THE BEACON

When Matt returned to temple the following week, Artie didn't seek him out after the service. He saw Artie from afar in the reception hall where the Kiddush was held, and he could plainly see how uneasy Artie looked. He'd clearly made a fool of himself, embarrassing Artie with his confidences in the saloon last week. He snaked his way through the crowd to greet Artie as he took a sip of the Kiddush schnapps. "How are you?" Matt asked.

Artie swallowed the rest of the schnapps and set down the glass. "All right," he said, his face impassive.

Matt waited for Artie to ask after him, too. But he did not. Instead, Artie turned away.

Matt watched Artie leave. Artie was his only friend in Atlanta, and the thought of losing the friendship, however slight, made Matt feel wretched. He rested his hand on the refreshment table to steady himself. *So that's done*, he thought. As he walked back to his father's empty house, he admitted to himself that his stepfather had been right.

So had his mother. There was nothing for him in Atlanta but sorrow.

By Monday morning, Matt had decided to return to San Francisco. He'd buy the ticket today. At the breakfast table, when Mrs. Bailey came out to pour him another cup of coffee, he asked her, "Can you help me pack up my trunk?"

She carefully filled his cup. Holding the coffeepot, looking at him, she asked, "You going back home?"

"I think I've given Atlanta a fair chance."

"When you thinking of leaving?"

"As soon as I can. Tomorrow, maybe."

"You might want to wait a little."

"Why?"

"Because your daddy want to have dinner with you tonight. He tell me just as I leave yesterday."

"My father wants my company?"

"I reckon so."

"Why? Why now?"

"That he didn't say. You'll have to ask him for yourself."

Matt spent the day in restless anticipation. Instead of packing his trunk or visiting the depot, he fidgeted his way through the house, unable to settle comfortably in his room or in the parlor. When Mrs. Bailey served him lunch, he left most of it on his plate. She shook her head as she cleared the table.

He waited in the parlor for his father's arrival, the *Atlanta Constitution* unread on his lap. At the sound of the door opening, he had to force himself not to jump up. What would he do? Throw out his arms and cry, "Papa, Papa"? When his father walked into the parlor, he rose, as he would for any gentleman.

"No, sit," his father said. He was smiling. "Take your ease. I'm going to pour myself a little brandy. Just a taste. Would you care for some?"

He thought of getting drunk in the saloon and shook his head.

"Coffee, perhaps? I'll ask Mrs. Bailey."

His throat was dry and tight, and his voice came out thin. "Yes, thank you."

As they sipped their drinks, Matt waited for his father to ask after him, but he did not. Finally Matt made the inquiry that every Jewish man of business could answer. "How is the shop?"

"It goes well. Business is steady, which is something to be grateful for. I have a new clerk, a young lady. She's very good with the customers." He took a sip of brandy. "You should stop by. We have some lovely silks for cravats."

Matt searched for another topic of conversation, but his mind had gone blank. They sat in painful silence.

Finally his father asked, "How goes your search for a position?"

He should tell his father that he had given it up, but it was too hard to admit it. "I'm still looking."

"The Israelites haven't snapped you up? I'm surprised."

Matt had to restrain himself from saying what he wished he could say: *Your reputation has preceded me wherever I go.* Instead, he said, "Unfortunately not."

His father drank the rest of his brandy. His eyes brightened, and his cheeks grew pink. Evidently Matt had inherited his low tolerance for alcohol from his father. He wished that it were a bond between them. But it was not.

His father said, "I'm sorry for the way I've been neglecting you."

Matt tensed. *Was it true, or was the brandy talking?* He didn't reply.

"The shop takes a great deal of my attention. And the little ones need me. Charlie and Ada. It would be wrong to make them feel that I've abandoned them."

Matt, sober as a stone, felt his chest constrict with anger. *I was a baby when you left for the first time,* he thought. *I was five when you left again. And when I was eight, you let me go without a word of regret.* Instead he said, "How old are they? Charlie and Ada?"

His father smiled. "Charlie is eleven and Ada is eight. They're clever, both of them. Precocious. Great readers. Ada wants to learn German. She asks me to speak to her in German."

Matt nodded. He was trying to imagine a little girl of color who spoke German.

"I worry about Ada," his father said. "She's very fair of complexion. Fair enough to have difficulty when she walks down the street with her mother and to have a different sort of difficulty when she comes into the shop." He sighed. "I don't know how we'll manage to make her at ease in the world, Rachel and I."

Matt said, "How is Mrs. Coldbrook?"

"Your aunt Rachel? Have you seen her?"

"I stopped at her office. She was…very polite, but she was cool. Eliza is the same. I think they want to keep me at arm's length."

His father regarded him, and for the first time, seemed

to see him. He reached across the gap that separated the wing chair and the settee and put his hand lightly on Matt's arm. "It's hard for them, too," he said. "It's a relationship they're uneasy with."

Matt drew in a breath. His father's light touch seemed to burn into his skin. "So am I. I remember...I remember Cass County. I loved Aunt Rachel, and I loved Eliza when we were both children. I haven't forgotten that. I can't."

His father patted Matt's arm. In a rueful voice, he said, "I've made quite a tangle for you, haven't I?"

It was the kindest thing he had said since Matt came to Atlanta. "We seem to be all tangled up together."

"Give it a little time to untangle. And let me help you a little."

Warmth surged through him. "How?"

"I'll talk to Rachel about inviting you to her house. You should meet all of them, including the little ones."

My half brother and half sister. "I'd welcome that," he said, the tightness in his chest easing.

THE TRUNK REMAINED UNPACKED AND THE TRAIN TICKETS unbought. A few days later, Matt took the horsecar down McDonough Boulevard. He walked down the sidewalk with fresh eyes, mingling with the black-suited white men, politely allowing the few ladies on the sidewalk to pass, and smiling at a Black woman who balanced a load of wash on her head. He looked at the storefronts anew. This block of Wheat Street, the border between white and Black Atlanta, housed businesses that wanted to pay low rents: a grocery, a cotton brokerage, a struggling lawyer.

He didn't belong here, on this street of threadbare employers. He didn't know what he was looking for, but he turned toward downtown, toward the firms that might have an opening for a young man who wanted to make his way in Atlanta.

He was just about to cross Peachtree Street to walk downtown to Whitehall, where the lawyers and brokers kept their offices, when he saw the nondescript one-story building of pitted brown brick. The plate glass window was unmarked, giving no hint of the business inside. But the placard in the window caught his eye. Printed on it, in letters as bold as a headline, were the words: "Help Wanted. Inquire Within."

He hesitated. He decided that his reception could hardly be worse than it had been at Cohen's or the lawyer's office. Suddenly he wanted to know if anyone in Atlanta might welcome him. He pushed open the door. No bell to jangle—not a shop, then—and the hinges groaned, as though no one had bothered to oil them for a long time.

The office was cluttered with paper. Newsprint. Facing the door was a large, flat desk piled with foolscap, and behind the desk sat a man who had not changed his appearance since the Civil War. He wore a frock coat and an old-fashioned cravat, and he sported the muttonchop whiskers and long hair of the 1860s. He looked up. Despite the gray threading through the brown of his hair, his expression was youthful and untroubled. He looked as though he thought of pleasant things during the day and slept well at night. At the sight of Matt, he laid down his pen, shook out his hand to ease his wrist, and asked, "Young man, how may I help you?"

He was a Yankee. A New Yorker, if Matt heard right.

"I saw your placard, and I've come to ask about it."

He smiled. "Ah, the position!" he said. "Please, take a seat, and I'll tell you about our business."

Matt settled himself in the chair, which had a hard, wooden seat. They must not have many visitors. He wondered again what their business was.

The man extended his hand. "I'm Thomas Endicott."

Matt shook his hand and introduced himself. Matt braced himself for the question about his father, but Mr. Endicott showed no flicker of recognition, and better still, no opprobrium. He gestured around the room. "This is the office of the Atlanta *Beacon*. Have you heard of us?"

Matt shook his head.

Endicott sighed. "I suppose that you take the *Constitution*."

"A newspaper," Matt said slowly. "You publish a newspaper."

"Yes, we do, young Mr. Kaltenbach. And we take quite a different point of view from the *Constitution*. That's why I've had so much difficulty filling the position for an editorial assistant."

Matt waited to hear what the *Beacon* stood for.

Endicott said, "The *Beacon* speaks for the dignity of labor. We speak to the equality of people of color. And we speak to the rights of women." He looked at Matt as though he expected a violent reaction.

Matt wanted to laugh. They were progressive in a way that his mother would delight in. "You must be very lonely in Atlanta."

"It's true, our views aren't the most common ones

here." His gaze was suddenly very keen. "You can see why it's been difficult to hire someone."

Matt leaned back in the uncomfortable chair. He was so pleased that he wanted to laugh. "I have no argument with your views. With the *Beacon*'s views. I grew up in San Francisco."

"So you're not a Southerner."

Matt leaned forward. "I was born in Georgia. Cass County, now called Bartow County, north of Atlanta."

Mr. Endicott's brow furrowed. "Was your father a planter?"

Matt took a deep breath. "Yes, he was, but my mother was an abolitionist. She started a school for freed slaves during the war. After the war the Klan forced her out. That's why we left."

"And you? Do you follow in your mother's footsteps?"

"Yes." Matt took another deep breath. "Do you know of Mr. Henry Kaltenbach?"

"No, I haven't had the pleasure of his acquaintance."

"He's my father. A planter no longer. He owns a dry goods shop on Wheat Street, and he sells to people of color. He employs them, too."

Mr. Endicott took this in. "Wheat Street, did you say? I should visit his shop. I should give him my custom." Endicott hesitated. "But I thought your family left Georgia."

Matt thought, *Let's see how liberal-minded you are, Mr. Endicott.* "My parents divorced after the war. My mother married the man who had been the Freedmen's Bureau agent in Cass County."

Mr. Endicott grinned. "Had the courage of her convictions, didn't she?" Then he sobered. "A divorce is a sad thing, even if it gives people a renewed chance at happiness."

Matt was sweating in his black wool suit. He thought, *I want to work here, if they'll have me.* "Sir, you take a very liberal view."

"Oh, I do. As does my wife. And our few but dedicated friends here in Atlanta. I'm delighted to meet you, Mr. Matthew Kaltenbach." He grinned again. "I'd be equally delighted to take you on as an editorial assistant. How clear is your handwriting?"

Is that all! Matt thought. "I write a good hand, sir."

"Editorial assistants are like clerks. They copy manuscripts. Our reporters and correspondents give us a scrawl, and we make it into fair copy for the printer. Would that suit you?"

"Yes, it would."

"And other duties, too. You'd work with our printer. And perhaps find an advertiser or two, as we all struggle to do. And if you don't mind, bring me some coffee in the mornings."

"I won't mind."

Mr. Endicott beamed. "Can you start tomorrow morning? Be here at nine?"

"Yes, sir." Matt thought, *I'll come clean about this, too.* "I'm an Israelite, sir. Does that matter to you?"

"Israelite? Our reporter, Miss Birnbaum, is an Israelite. You'll have something in common when you meet. She's a New Yorker, so she has something in common with my wife and me as well." He held out his hand. "Five dollars a week, the same as Miss Birnbaum."

Matt shook Mr. Endicott's hand. "Thank you, sir. Nine o'clock tomorrow morning."

"I look forward to our association, Mr. Kaltenbach."

Matt was about to rise from the chair—he suddenly realized how much his backside hurt—when the door opened and a young woman entered the office.

Mr. Endicott's smile was sunny. "Nina! I've found a young man to work as my editorial assistant!"

She laughed. She turned to Matt. "You must not be from Atlanta."

She wasn't tall, but she had a presence. She wore a plain dark-blue dress, the color he would always associate with the Union army. Her waist had a natural shape. Matt realized that she wasn't wearing a corset. He was surprised but not shocked. His mother, who was too stylish to dispense with lacing, had friends who espoused dress reform.

"I was born in Cass County, Georgia, but I've lived in California since I was eight," he said.

"California! I envy you. I've never been there."

"But you're a New Yorker. I envy you. I've never been to New York."

Mr. Endicott looked pleased that they were getting along. He made formal introductions. Nina held out her hand in a businesslike way, and they shook like business associates. Her fingers were stained black with ink. He looked from her hand to her face. Her eyes were fiercely intelligent in her oval face. It took him a moment to see that she was handsome, too. Her hair had escaped its pins, and she pushed it behind her ear with a carelessness that told him she didn't think much of her looks.

Mr. Endicott said, "Mr. Kaltenbach shares our liberal views."

"Do you believe in rights for women?" she quizzed him.

He didn't miss a beat. "My mother would have my hide if I didn't."

She looked at Mr. Endicott and grinned. "He's one of us, all right."

"Tomorrow, young man?" Mr. Endicott asked.

Matt grinned. "Nine o'clock."

CHAPTER 7

THE WASHING SOCIETY

ELIZA WAS surprised when Mrs. Gardiner invited her to meet in the parlor. She hadn't been inside the house before, but she knew what the small, one-story houses of Summerhill were like. The parlor and dining room crowded the front of the house and the bedrooms crowded behind, with a tiny kitchen sandwiched between the two. Eliza and Ophelia squeezed onto the settee, which was not new but was in good condition, and Mrs. Gardiner sat in the wing chair that her husband appropriated when he was home. Another woman, whom Eliza hadn't met, took the ladies' chair. She was slight, with bowed shoulders and work-worn hands that she rested on her knees. Her breath came in little gasps. Eliza wondered if she was ill.

Mrs. Gardiner had closed all her windows and drawn her curtains against the midday heat. The shadows in the room gave it a conspiratorial air.

Mrs. Gardiner introduced the stranger. "This is Mrs.

Susan Bell, who live on Green's Ferry Avenue in Jenningstown. She have a sister in Summerhill, and she go to the meeting at Bethel. Now she join us."

Mrs. Bell said, "Pleased to meet all of you." She wheezed a bit as she spoke.

Eliza asked, "Ma'am, are you all right?"

"I'm fine, young miss. I have the asthma. It bother me whenever I feel worked up, for good or for bad. It come over me at church, too. Ain't nothing to worry about."

Mrs. Gardiner said, "Well, we have quite a time at the meeting at Bethel. I hear that three hundred washer-women join us. Three hundred! That's a big number."

Ophelia grinned and Eliza nodded.

"Now we have to figure what to do with all them people who get worked up at Bethel."

"Spread the word," Ophelia said.

"Yes, Miss Ophelia, and I know how good you are at doing that. But what do we tell them? Not just to come to another meeting. Need something to give them. Something more."

"Stop work," Ophelia said.

"To get what?" Mrs. Gardiner's gaze was too majestic for the tiny parlor.

"Better wages, Miss Amanda, like you and I and every woman on Fraser Street been talking about for a long time."

"Can't just say better wages. What do that mean? Have to fix on something in particular."

"On Green's Ferry, we all talk about how much we hate getting paid a dollar a load. We talk about getting paid by what the load weigh." Mrs. Bell looked from one of them to the other. Her gaze was penetrating, too. "A dollar for a dozen pound of wash, that's what we hope for."

"What we ask for," Ophelia said, her tone fierce. She looked at Mrs. Gardiner. "A dollar a dozen!"

"Have a sound to it," Mrs. Gardiner said, her tone mild.

Eliza thought, *She doesn't want Ophelia to run off with this. She wants to be in charge herself.*

Mrs. Bell laughed. "It do have a good sound to it, Mrs. Gardiner. Easy to say. Easy to remember."

Mrs. Gardiner asked, "Miss Eliza, what do you think?"

Eliza sat up straighter. She had been called on; she was a good student. "Good words. But words aren't enough. If we want the washerwomen to call a strike, and to stay with it, they need more than words."

Mrs. Gardiner smiled and nodded. "Ain't enough to quit work. Need to get organized. Get in union. We start a society, like the Mutual Aid Society but for washerwomen. So we can pull together. Stay together. Take care of each other."

Ophelia said, "The Washing Society."

"I like it," Mrs. Bell said.

Eliza asked, "What do they get if they join?"

"Besides knowing that we all together?" Mrs. Gardiner's eyes gleamed. "Yes, Miss Eliza, I know you think that ain't enough. But what do the Mutual Aid Society do? It collect money and put it into a fund to help people out when they need it. To bury someone who pass away and to care for the widow and the orphan left behind. You all hear, as well as I do, what frighten us washerwomen most about a strike. No money coming in.

We got to figure that out before we ask anyone to quit working."

"You'll need more than a dime here and a dime there," Eliza said, thinking of the neighbors who scraped together a weekly contribution for the Mutual Aid Society.

"I know."

"Where would that money come from?"

"Have to figure that, Miss Eliza."

It took Eliza ten seconds to figure it herself. Amanda Gardiner was as sly as Br'er Rabbit. "You have a notion, don't you, Mrs. Gardiner?" That was the old expression from slavery days. A notion was more than an idea. It was a plan.

Mrs. Gardiner beamed like a teacher with a clever student. "Yes, Miss Eliza. I do."

A FEW DAYS LATER, OPHELIA ASKED ELIZA TO JOIN HER again, but she had a suggestion. "Dress for it. Old washday dress."

"No," Eliza said. "I go as myself, Miss Coldbrook who went to Atlanta University. I'll lend my name to this, but I don't pretend to be something I'm not."

"Pretty white dress get dirty."

"We'll wash it."

Ophelia laughed. "If everything go right, nothing get washed for a while!"

"Don't get ahead of yourself."

They went out together, the washerwoman in her

grayed cotton and the graduate in her clean, white lawn, to see what Fraser Street thought of "a dollar a dozen."

Ophelia, who liked a challenge, started with Miss Mary, who looked as tired and burdened as she had the last time they talked to her.

Ophelia waved and bounced into Miss Mary's yard. "You hear about the meeting at Bethel A. M. E.?"

Miss Mary rubbed her back as she straightened. "Yes, I hear. I hear plenty. Got everyone all riled up to quit work and act foolish. That's what I hear."

"Three hundred washerwomen come to meet at Bethel."

"They could meet at Mount Gilead for all I care. Don't matter to me."

As before, Miss Mary's daughter held the baby and listened to the conversation, her eyes wide with attention.

"You want to get paid better?" Ophelia asked.

"What I want and what I get, that ain't the same thing," Miss Mary replied.

"What do you get now?"

"A dollar a load. A dollar a week."

"Is it enough?"

The girl didn't speak, but she mouthed "no" at Ophelia. Ophelia asked Miss Mary, "What if you get a dollar a dozen pound instead?"

Miss Mary snorted. "My missus would do the wash herself before she pay me that much."

"Think about it. How much do a load weigh? Near fifty pound? Say four dozen pound. That's four dollar a week, Miss Mary."

"I can figure that well, Miss Ophelia. I know."

"A dollar a dozen," Ophelia said. "Think about it." She glanced at the girl, whose expression was wistful. "Think of what you could do for your babies, all of them, with a dollar a dozen."

Miss Mary returned to her tub. "Get on with you, Ophelia Taylor."

Ophelia grinned. As she left, pulling Eliza by the hand, she called to Miss Mary, "Ponder it!"

In the alley, out of Miss Mary's earshot, Eliza asked, "Why do you try so hard with her?"

"Can't you see?" Ophelia said. "She ponder it, and that girl of hers ponder it with her. And when she tell her neighbors, all up and down the alley, they get all worked up. And then it start to go around." She laughed. "A dollar a dozen!"

It did go around—so swiftly that the next day, when they ventured into Martin's Alley, the first woman they visited grinned at Ophelia. "You the gal who start that talk about a dollar a dozen? A dollar for a dozen pound of wash?"

"I surely am."

"Dear Lord, if I could get a dollar a dozen, and my daughter, who wash too, could get a dollar a dozen, we earn almost as much as my man who get a dollar a day." She pressed her hands to her back where it ached and stretched backward to ease the muscles that cramped from bending forward. "What we could do with eight more dollar a week!"

"Your neighbors already know?" Ophelia asked.

"We all talk about it. We abuzz!"

"Go tell it on Rawson Street. On Clarke Street. On Fulton Street. On Richardson Street. Spread the word!"

Eliza accompanied Ophelia around Summerhill, watching as she smiled and cajoled and joked her sister washerwomen into thinking about the benefit of "a dollar a dozen." Eliza herself didn't say much. When a woman glanced at her, wanting to know, "Do you agree, Miss Eliza?" she smiled and nodded. She continued to wear her white dress. They became well-known on the streets of Summerhill, the voluble washerwoman and the college graduate who shadowed her.

The excitement over "a dollar a dozen" didn't affect the rhythms of the week at the Coldbrook house, where Henry Kaltenbach always presided at dinner. He knew about the agitation since his customers in Shermantown were abuzz with it, too. He teased Eliza at the dinner table. "So you take after your old father, don't you? Fomenting revolution in Summerhill?"

"Hardly a revolution. Just a matter of fairness, I'd think. You're generous in what you pay your clerks. You understand that."

Her mother said, "Henry, it ain't exactly dinner table conversation." She only lost her good grammar when she was upset—or when she wanted to make a point.

"You're right." He turned to Ada. "How are you coming along with the *Grimm's Fairy Tales*?" He had read her the tales in English translation when she was very small; he meant the German version he recently gave her.

Ada blushed with pleasure. "Better. I can understand nearly all the words. I like the pictures, too."

Eliza thought that teaching Ada to speak and read German was a conceit, but it wasn't her business to object to it.

After dinner, they retired to the parlor, her mother

and father sharing the newspaper—they complained about the *Constitution*, even as they read it from cover to cover—while her brother and sister played checkers. Charlie was an aggressive player, taking Ada's pieces with undisguised glee.

At the knock on the door, Eliza said, "I'll get it." She opened the door to Ben Mannheim, her childhood friend and now the subject of gossip as her suitor and potential fiancé. She wasn't any more convinced of him than she'd been at the beginning of the summer. He hadn't called for several weeks. "Come in, come in. We've missed you."

He stepped inside. "I was hoping I'd have good news about a position."

"We're glad to see you, whether you've found a position or not."

He sighed. In the suit he wore to seek work, he looked stiff and starched and miserably hot. She thought of Dr. Chesney, who smelled of wintergreen in the summer heat.

Her mother called, "Ben! Come in and sit down. Do you want anything? We have coffee left over from dinner."

"No, I'm all right." He glanced from her mother to her father. "I came to ask if I could spirit Eliza away. Just for a little promenade."

Her mother smiled. "Even though it's hot as Hades outside."

"Mama, if we didn't go out in the heat in Atlanta, we'd never leave the house," Eliza replied.

Outside, Eliza said, "It is too hot to walk, Ben. Would you mind standing in the shade in the backyard?"

"All right. I wanted to talk to you alone. That will do."

She led him into the yard. "What do you have to say

that's so private?" She didn't think he'd come to propose marriage to her. He'd ask her mother and father first.

He glanced at her and glanced away. "I hear you're going around with Mrs. Ophelia Taylor to talk to the washerwomen."

"I have been. What of it?"

"Do you think that's seemly? To walk the streets talking to laundresses?"

She laughed. "Ben, I'm hardly doing anything improper. I talk to my neighbors about something that concerns them. Don't you think they should get paid fairly for the hard work they do?"

A Black man could hardly fault Black women for insisting on decent treatment. "Of course I want them to get better pay. I just don't like seeing you out in the street helping them do it."

Ben's interference rankled her. "Did you forget? I'm a Black woman, too, Ben Mannheim!"

He gave her a pointed look. "You're an Atlanta University graduate. You're a lady."

She thought of Ophelia's words: *I can't afford to be a lady.* "Am I?"

He reached for her hand, presuming on the fact that they were all but promised to one another. "It bothers me."

She thought of Dr. Chesney's smile. She drew her hand back. "Let it."

A FEW DAYS LATER, ELIZA SAT ON THE FRONT PORCH, taking in the cool air of early morning and watching as

Fraser Street woke. The draymen, the maids, the porters, and the cooks were already gone for the day, and the washerwomen were just setting up their tubs. Mrs. Gardiner waved as she approached the house. "Miss Eliza, would you come downtown with me?"

"What is it, Mrs. Gardiner? Is it about the Washing Society?"

She smiled to hear Eliza use the name. "In a way. I plan to call on your mama."

"You can talk to her at home anytime, you know."

"I go to her office to talk some business. Come with me. You can help."

Eliza remembered Mrs. Gardiner's slyness at the meeting of the inner circle of the Society's organizers. She scrambled up from the rocking chair.

At her mother's office, her mother greeted Mrs. Gardiner and invited her to sit. "Eliza, will you excuse us?"

Mrs. Gardiner said, "No, I ask her to come with me. Let her stay. What we talk about ain't a secret."

Thoroughly intrigued, Eliza sat.

Mrs. Gardiner said, "Mrs. Coldbrook, we all know the sticking point about stopping work. Money. We talk about women who can't afford to lose their wages. A lot of people excited about the idea of better pay, but not everyone sure enough to stop work. I have a notion, and I come here to talk to you about it. I been the president of the Mutual Aid Society at Bethel and now at Pleasant Grove. We raise money, dime by dime, for the time when tragedy come. People used to the idea of an association to help those who need it."

Her mother nodded politely. In slavery days, Eliza

knew, her mother had called this kind of circumlocution "going roundabout."

"We have a difficulty, though. The people we ask to give us money are the people who have the least to give. And even if they give us a dime here and a nickel there, that ain't enough. Not to replace the wages they lose. Not to keep their families fed. Not to keep a roof over their heads. Because who know how long we stop work."

Another polite silence. Eliza had seen her mother use silence to her advantage many times. People hated silence and talked to fill it.

Mrs. Gardiner's eyes rested on Eliza's mother. Her gaze was as powerful a weapon as her mother's silence. "Mrs. Coldbrook, I come to you, appeal to you, because you have the means to help us."

Her mother put her hand on Mrs. Gardiner's arm. "It's all right, Miss Amanda. It's just me. You don't have to preach to me."

Mrs. Gardiner chuckled. "Still got to talk you into it."

"Miss Amanda, I've always been generous with my money when it's for a good reason."

"Do you think this a good reason?"

She let the question hang in the air so Amanda Gardiner felt the weight of her pause. "Yes, I do."

Now Amanda Gardiner paused. She broke the silence to say, "Will you help?"

"Money never hurts. But you'll need more than money if you stop work for more than a week or two. How long will this go on? We don't know. But if we want to see it through, we'll have to look ahead."

"I think about that," Mrs. Gardiner said. "Food and shelter, like I already say."

Her mother said, "I'm glad to give you some money to start. But there are others you can ask. And there are people who can give something besides money."

"Yes," Mrs. Gardiner said. "If you a grocer, you have food to give. And if you rent a place, like Mrs. Toussaint do, maybe you don't collect the rent for a month."

Mrs. Toussaint, who owned many properties in Shermantown and Summerhill, was her mother's oldest friend in Atlanta, but Mrs. Toussaint had made her fortune before the war. In 1860, she was called Madame Toussaint, and she owned a bawdy house. Now she was so respectable that Bethel A. M. E. was glad to welcome her.

"If it comes to that," her mother said, her voice low.

Mrs. Gardiner said, "You know it might."

"You try my patience."

"I mean to." Mrs. Gardiner smiled. "How much can you spare for us, Miss Rachel?" She let that question hang in the air, too. Every moment of silence was a greater appeal.

Her mother was very still. She was doing sums in her head, Eliza knew. Finally she spoke. "I can spare a thousand dollars."

Eliza gasped. *A thousand dollars! A washerwoman earned less than a hundred dollars in a year.*

When Mrs. Gardiner didn't reply, her mother said, "Would that be enough help to begin, Mrs. Gardiner? Enough to tell anyone who signs on with you that we have a fund for anyone who loses her wages?"

Mrs. Gardiner let herself smile. "It would. It ain't the end, but it's a good beginning."

Her mother laughed. "You'll be back, Miss Amanda. I know you will."

"Maybe. Maybe not. We don't know how long we stop work. No one do."

"Would you like me to talk to the bank? Or to give you the check?"

"Give me the check. I open the account for the Mutual Aid Society. They see me before at the bank, they know I make deposits for the church." Her eyes gleamed. "We fox them. Open the account and call this something that don't tip our hand. Even if we know that we the Washing Society." She rose. "Thank you, Mrs. Coldbrook. God bless you." And she was gone.

Eliza said, "I thought you didn't want us involved with the Washing Society."

"To give money you have? That's easy. That's safe." She gave Eliza a penetrating look. "It's entirely different from exposing yourself to peril in the street."

THE WASHERWOMEN OF SUMMERHILL AND SHERMANTOWN streamed into Jenningstown for the meeting at Friendship Baptist Church. Jenningstown had been the site of the first refugee camp after the war. Eliza heard stories of the wretchedness there in the earliest years. People lived under pieces of torn canvas discarded by the Union army. They dug themselves shelters in the hollows carved by Union bombardment. The business of Jenningstown was always industry, and since the war, the mills returned: rolling mills and planing mills and sawmills. The Black men of Jenningstown worked in the mills at the worst jobs, and they were the last hired and first fired. The women who did the wash desperately needed that money, that dollar a load, to feed their families. Susan Bell, whose friends and neighbors had inspired the slogan of "a dollar a dozen," lived among the washerwomen on Green's Ferry Avenue in Jenningstown.

From its earliest days in 1867, Friendship Baptist Church encouraged uplift through education. The church was now home to two colleges, the Atlanta Baptist Seminary for young men, and since April of this year, the Female Seminary for young women. Eliza hadn't met the students at the Female Seminary, but she could imagine them, their shoulders straight despite the burden of expectation they carried, their faces serious, their hearts full of a fragile feeling of hope. She wondered if they would attend this meeting, and if they would wear white dresses like her own. She wondered if they were like herself, caught between being a lady and a Black woman.

The church was full, Black women of every condition together, and a few white women as well. And men, husbands and fathers and brothers who felt their wives' and daughters' and sisters' labor ache in their own bones. The room smelled of sweat and soap and starch, the smell of labor at the washtub.

Mrs. Gardiner stood on the pulpit with the minister of Friendship Baptist. The Reverend Frank Quarles had been the pastor here since the church began, just after the war. Now he looked tired; he had been ill, and his congregation worried about him. Nonetheless, he surveyed the crowd with a joyful smile on his face, clearly glad to see so many souls in the pews.

Ophelia ran down the aisle to join Mrs. Gardiner. Behind her, hampered by wheezing, was Susan Bell. They joined Mrs. Gardiner and Reverend Quarles on the pulpit.

Before the reverend could speak, a chant rose from the crowd. It was as loud as the cry at a ring shout.

"A dollar a dozen!" They took it up, clapping and chanting it together. "A dollar a dozen!"

Ophelia whistled. "What do we want?"

"A dollar a dozen!" they responded.

"What do we ask for?"

"A dollar a dozen!"

"What do we get?"

"A dollar a dozen!"

Mrs. Gardiner and Reverend Quarles exchanged a glance. They waited. They were both used to high emotion in church. The reverend finally raised his arms, indicating that he wanted to speak, and they quieted.

He said, "Sisters, my heart is glad to see so many of you here today. Mrs. Gardiner, Mrs. Taylor, and your friend and neighbor and fellow congregant, Mrs. Bell, have been spreading the word about better working conditions and better pay for washerwomen. And I know now how well they have succeeded!"

A swell of laughter rose from the crowd. Eliza saw no one she knew. Not her mother, and not a single young lady in a white dress. If the Female Seminary was represented here, it had come in the same washday dress as the rest.

The reverend raised his arms again. "Sisters, I turn this meeting over to Mrs. Amanda Gardiner."

Mrs. Gardiner stepped forward and the crowd began to clap, not in applause but in unison. They called out, "Miss Amanda! Miss Amanda!"

She beamed. She didn't wait for them to stop. Over the

clapping, she called, "Thank you! All of you! Now you hush a bit and we get down to business!"

"A dollar a dozen!"

"Yes, I hear you and we all hear you and I believe the Lord hear you, since you loud enough." She took on a serious mien. "Now, we have something to ask for. We all know what that is. What we do tonight is figure how we work together to ask for it and how we stay steadfast until we get it. Because no one hand it to us. No one give it to us. We have to struggle for it. Keep our hand on the plow and hold on until we get a dollar a dozen."

Ophelia couldn't wait. She sang out, "We stop work!"

And instead of any objection, a new cry rose from the crowd. "Stop work!"

Mrs. Gardiner didn't try to hush them. She let them chant and clap, and finally she spoke in a voice as loud and resonant as a field holler. "Are you ready?"

That silenced them.

"I know that you worry. Stop work, lose your wages. Lose your wages, can't feed your children, can't pay your rent. We need a society like the Mutual Aid Society but for us washerwomen. A Washing Society."

They were quiet.

"What do I tell you last time we meet? That we take care of each other. Hold together. Keep everyone fed and housed, no matter what happen. That's what the Washing Society do. We sisters, and sisters help each other in their moment of need."

"Is there money?"

"Yes."

"Who give it?" someone called out.

"Can't say. Just that it come from someone generous."

"Is it enough?" asked a worried woman in the front row.

Amanda Gardiner said, "Enough to start. And I just begin to ask. You all know how I can persuade someone to find a dime, or a dollar, once I ask."

Laughter rippled through the crowd from those who knew Amanda Gardiner to be fierce in collecting for the Mutual Aid Society.

She said, "Now we know what we want. A dollar a dozen. We know who we are. We the Washing Society. Are we ready? Are we all in union to stop work until we get what we want and what we deserve?"

"Yes." It flowed through the crowd.

"Can't hear you yet. Have to talk louder."

"Yes!" The response swelled.

"What do you say?"

"Yes!"

"That's better. Now we have a show of hands. Those who want to go on strike, raise your hand."

They didn't raise their hands. They rose from their chairs. Eliza saw that anyone who was slow to stand—unless she was old or infirm—was pulled to her feet by someone else. Without a word, all of them stood.

Mrs. Gardiner surveyed the crowd. She paused. When she spoke, did she have a catch in her voice? "Are we in union?"

"Yes," they called back. "We in union!"

"Are you ready to stop work tomorrow morning?"

"Yes, we are!"

The song rose from the crowd. Eliza knew the traditional version, about getting in union with Jesus, but they put the tune to a new use. They sang about getting in union to go on strike and staying in union to triumph. Eliza stood in the midst of the crowd, pressed in so tight she could barely move her hands to clap, and she sang, too. She felt tears start in her eyes. *Get in union and stay in union.* White dress or no, she belonged here.

CHAPTER 8

OPHELIA TAYLOR

I ALWAYS BEEN good at talking. My mama caution me against it. "It don't help a Black woman to say whatever come into her head," she tell me. But I don't. I say what I feel, after I think about it. That ain't the same thing.

After that first meeting at Pleasant Grove Baptist Church, I start to feel different. Everyone see it. My friends tell me that I always been lively, and now I send off a spark. They feel brighter when they talk to me. And my husband, Jack, he see it too. He say, "You lit up, Ophelia." He like it because he get the benefit of it in the marriage bed. Now, that, I keep to myself. Wouldn't even tell Eliza, and she smart enough to hear a secret like that, even if her mama the most high-rumped Black woman in Atlanta with enough money to try to make Miss Eliza into a lady.

When I first go to those meetings, I never dream what happen next, that I get swept up like I do. Never dream that Amanda Gardiner would take to me. She ain't high-rumped, but she a person of consequence, especially at the church. I always think that she see me as a little flighty because laughter come easy to me. So I feel surprised when she take me along to bring the word to the washerwomen.

And I never dream that a few words I say matter so much. "A dollar a dozen" wasn't my idea, but them words come from me. They catch like a fire and tear through Summerhill. They jump over Foster Street into Shermantown, and they cut a swath down Marietta Street into Jenningstown. Now I ain't the only one lit up. All over Atlanta, washerwomen afire with the words I say. "A dollar a dozen."

After that meeting at Friendship, when we start the Washing Society and decide to go on strike, I look at Mrs. Gardiner, and I feel a hot wave of worry.

"What do we do now?" I ask Miss Amanda.

Her eyes gleam. She got a glow, too. "We got work to do. Now we get every washerwoman in Atlanta in union with us." She give me a good hard look, like my mama used to. "You go out and do what you so good at."

I'd be glad to do that all day long, but first I have to go on strike myself. I have a missus who's young and pretty, and she carrying her first baby. But she don't have my money half the time. Don't know if her husband don't do well or if he a skinflint who begrudge her housekeeping money. Those woes ain't my worry, as long as I get my pay. But when I don't get paid, I have a lot of worry of my own.

I bring her the clean wash, the last load—dear Lord, that thought give me joy!—and I leave it on the kitchen table. She fumble around in her pocket, and I know she ain't got nothing for me. That give me resolve. Even if I can sass like nobody's business, I still feel a tremor defying a white woman who can pay me.

I take a deep breath to brace myself. "I won't take another load from you, ma'am. No washing." And I say it aloud and I hear it. "I stop work. I go on strike."

She get flustered. Set her hand on her belly like the baby kick her or she have a cramp. "You won't work? Well, I'll find someone else."

Then it dawn on me what it mean to be in union. "No, ma'am, you won't. We all on strike, all we washerwomen, all over Atlanta."

"Why would you possibly do something like that? You're treated right!"

"No, ma'am. Ain't paid enough. That why we stop work."

"My stars. I pay you a dollar a week."

The words come to me. My words, the words that travel all over Atlanta. "Ma'am, we all ask for a dollar a dozen pound of wash."

She get bright-red spots on her cheeks. Her voice rise. Didn't think she could talk so loud. "That's highway robbery!"

"No, ma'am. It's only fair."

"I won't pay it!"

"No washing, then, ma'am."

She crumple up. Get a pleading tone in her voice. "What am I going to do? With a new baby on the way? Babies make for a mountain of dirty laundry. No washing!"

God forgive me, but I feel a surge of joy at that. "It ain't my worry, ma'am." And I walk out. No load of wash in my arms or on my head. I take a deep breath and relish how light I feel. Now I just know what the old song mean, *When I lay my burden down.*

I hurry with a light step back to Summerhill. Still a lot of work to do. Got a lot of washerwomen to get in union and to keep in union.

CHAPTER 9

NINA

MATT LEFT the *Beacon* office in a daze. He didn't wait for
the horsecar. He needed to walk to clear his head, never
mind the heat. He took off his coat and loosened his tie,
not caring that white Atlantans stared at him as though
he'd done something indecent.

Employed at last, and by a man who delighted in his
mother's abolitionist history. Who expressed no horror at
hearing about his parents' divorce. Who didn't mind his
father's racial sympathies. Who welcomed him as a Jew.

Five dollars a week, and Miss Nina Birnbaum for a
colleague.

Mrs. Bailey noticed his mood as soon as he walked in
the door. "You hear something good today?"

"I have a position."

"That's good. Who take you on?"

"The *Atlanta Beacon*." Her face registered no recognition. "The newspaper."

"Didn't think Atlanta had a newspaper besides the
Constitution."

"Well, we do. I'll bring you a copy, Mrs. Bailey." He realized that he didn't know if she could read or not. "They advocate equal rights for Black people and for women."

Mrs. Bailey shook her head. "Must not sell many papers that way."

"I'll change that. I've been hired to assist the editor, but I'll sell advertising, too." He grinned. "Do you think my father might advertise there?"

"It ain't my business to say. When he come here for dinner again, you ask him."

"I will." He was still grinning.

"You look like the Chessy cat," Mrs. Bailey said. "You want something to eat? You have an appetite?"

He felt ravenous. "I'm so hungry, I'd eat a roast pig."

Mrs. Bailey cocked her head a little, like a thoughtful bird. "You a bit addled, I think. Well, best wishes, even if I never hear of this newspaper in all the days I live in Atlanta."

MATT WAS SO EARLY THE NEXT MORNING THAT THE *Beacon*'s door was still locked. He fidgeted as he waited on the sidewalk until he saw the stocky figure of Mr. Endicott approach. Endicott beamed to see him. "Mr. Kaltenbach! Good morning, young man. Let's get you settled, and then I'll send you out for coffee."

"Will Miss Birnbaum be in the office today?"

"She may. She's off to ferret out a story. She's tenacious and not easily insulted. Good qualities in a reporter." He unlocked the door, and the smell of paper and newsprint wafted from the office. The air was hot and still. "You don't mind fresh air, do you?"

"Of course not."

"Help me open the windows to bring a breeze in."

The breeze was warm, and it brought the smell of the street with it: manure and mud. Matt didn't mind.

Endicott had cleared a desk for him and provided the tools of his new trade: an inkwell, a plethora of pens, and a ream of paper. "Your realm, Mr. Kaltenbach."

Matt rested his hand on the scarred wood of the desk-top. "I am so glad to be here, sir."

"Good, good. Now for the essential thing that oils our business. Coffee! There's a restaurant around the corner." He rummaged in his pocket and found a coin. He laid the quarter in Matt's palm. "Get some for yourself, too. They'll put it in a jar. Have them cover it!"

Matt clasped the quarter in his hand as though it were a Hanukkah present. He found the restaurant easily. "Restaurant" was a misnomer; the place had a counter with a half dozen stools all occupied by white men bent over their plates. The place smelled of coffee and bacon grease.

Behind the counter, a slender Black man fried eggs and potatoes in a cast-iron pan. At the sight of Matt, he said, "How can I help you, sir?" He had a fine-boned face and wore an apron that someone had ironed just this morning.

"I'm from the *Beacon*," he said. "I'm here for coffee for Mr. Endicott."

The man broke into a smile. "You the new man at the *Beacon*?"

"Do you know the paper?"

"Sir, read the *Beacon* every week and tell my friends they should take it, too." He deftly filled a jar with coffee. "Cream?"

"Yes."

He fastened the lid, handed Matt the jar, and easily made change for the quarter. All his movements were graceful. He smiled and said, "Hope to see you tomorrow, sir."

Matt's heart surged with pleasure at the thought.

At the office, Mr. Endicott thanked him. "There's a cup if you want some."

"No, thank you." He glanced at the paper and suddenly had a horror of spilling something on it.

"Well, let us commence." Mr. Endicott took a manuscript from the top of a pile on his desk. "If you would, make a clean copy."

Matt took the manuscript and scanned it. "I'll do my best."

"I'm sorry it's such a scrawl. But I have great faith in you, Mr. Kaltenbach, in your ability to decipher it and to create order from chaos."

Matt sat at the desk. He regarded the pens and chose one. He dipped it into the inkwell and began. Mr. Endicott had exaggerated the difficulty of reading the handwriting; he had no trouble making it out. It was an essay on the unfairness of the low wages paid for Black contract labor in Bibb County and sympathy for the men who refused to work for so little. Matt followed the situation with interest as he made the copy. By the time he was finished, he was irate, as the writer wanted him to be.

He stopped and, without thinking about it, shook out

his hand to ease the cramp in his wrist. "Do you have anything else for me?"

"Are you done already? Let me examine the fruit of your labor."

Matt gave him the pages, handling them by the edges. Endicott scanned them and said, "You write a very clear hand. This can go straight to the printer." He smiled. "What did you think of the sentiment?"

"The laborers of color in Bibb County seem to be wronged, sir."

"Yes, exactly!" He beamed. "I do have another manuscript for you. Don't overtax yourself, Mr. Kaltenbach. We need that writing hand of yours in tip-top shape."

MISS BIRNBAUM MADE HER APPEARANCE CLOSE TO THE noon hour, flushed with the heat and dressed again in dark blue. Matt, the son of a fashionable woman, saw that it was a different dress from yesterday's. Nina Birnbaum was attractive despite her frock, which no one could call fashionable.

"Nina!" Mr. Endicott said. "My dear, what have you unearthed for next week's edition?"

Matt wondered at the familiarity.

"Just the usual injustices," she said. "Nothing newsworthy. It should be an outrage instead of a commonplace that the Atlanta police arrest Black men *for walking down the street and minding their own business.*"

"We have several pieces from our correspondents in

rural Georgia," Mr. Endicott said. "They're full of outrage, and I can write an opinion piece myself."

"That may have to do." She addressed Matt. "So we didn't frighten you away."

Matt rose. "Of course not."

She looked at his hands, which were ink-stained. "I can see that Mr. Endicott has put you right to work."

"Earning my keep."

"Oh, you will." She laughed, a low, pleasant sound. She reached to take off her hat.

Mr. Endicott said, "No, leave your hat on. I'm just about to leave for dinner." He took in Matt as well. "Please join us, Mr. Kaltenbach. My wife will be glad to meet you."

"Sir, I wouldn't want to put you to any trouble."

"It wouldn't be any trouble, I assure you. My wife and our cook are used to guests."

Nina glanced at Matt. "Mr. Endicott, can it wait? I'd like to stand Mr. Kaltenbach a meal. We haven't had a chance to get acquainted yet."

Matt was astonished at this dual impudence, to an elder and an employer, but Mr. Endicott laughed. "You're right. I'll let you two get acquainted. Enjoy yourselves!"

Nina led him down Wheat Street and halted before a modest wooden building a few blocks shy of Kaltenbach's Dry Goods. She opened the door, releasing the good smell of gumbo. Inside, the place was modest, with wooden tables that had seen better days and wooden chairs to match. All the customers were Black, dressed in the clothes and caps of workmen and laughing and joking over their food. It reminded Matt of the kitchen on the Kaltenbach place in Cass County. As a little boy, he ate his meals there with his father's former slaves. A smiling woman in a spotless apron approached them. She was tall and slender, very dark of skin, with high cheekbones and an aquiline nose she had inherited from a European ancestor. "Miss Nina," she said. "Who you bring along?"

Nina made the introductions. Mrs. Harper asked, "Kaltenbach? Any connection with Mr. Henry Kaltenbach who own the dry goods shop down the street?"

Oh no. Not this again. "He's my father."

"He a good man."

Matt nodded, relieved to hear a compliment.

Nina said, "Mr. Matthew Kaltenbach just started at the *Beacon.*"

Mrs. Harper chuckled. "I put them old newspapers you give me to good use."

"Did you give them to someone who can read them?"

"I wrap fish in them. Keep them fresh!" She laughed outright.

Nina rolled her eyes. "You're fooling me. I know you can read, Mrs. Harper."

"Got some fine gumbo today, Miss Nina. Would that suit you?"

"Yes. Mr. Kaltenbach?"

"Do you have fried chicken?"

"Best chicken in Atlanta. I bring you some gumbo, too."

I'm buffeted by forceful women today, Matt thought, and suddenly he missed his mother, who exerted her own force.

As they waited for their gumbo, Matt asked Nina, "How did you come to work at the *Beacon?*"

"My mother was always close to the Endicotts. After

she died, Mr. Endicott offered to take me in and offered me a position with his newspaper."

"Your loss. Was it recent?"

"Yes. A few months ago."

So she was an orphan. "Miss Birnbaum, you have my condolences."

"Thank you." She gestured at her bodice. "I had no leisure to mourn. I came to Atlanta right after the funeral."

"Mr. Endicott seems kind-hearted as well as liberal in his opinions."

"He is," Nina said, pushing a stray lock of hair off her face. "Blasted pins, they won't stay put." She shoved a pin into place and winced. The pain wasn't about the hairpins. "He's still an abolitionist at heart, after all these years."

"It must be hard for him."

"He's never reneged on it, not a bit of it. He was raised in Syracuse, New York, that hotbed of antislavery, and joined the Union army the day after Fort Sumter. He marched through Georgia with Sherman and burned Atlanta to the ground. Were you here for that?"

"No, I was in the countryside."

She continued, "After the war, he stopped in New York long enough to captivate Mrs. Endicott and then came back here to finish the job he started in 1864. He's been here ever since, fighting the good fight for true progress in the unenlightened South."

She had the cadence of an orator and a storyteller. Matt wondered how she came by it. "Does the paper flourish?"

Their gumbo arrived, and before Nina picked up her

spoon, she said, "Laura Endicott was born a Tappan. You've heard of them? The great lions of prewar abolition? They had a great fortune, too, and enough came with her to make the Endicotts comfortable for the rest of their lives. It's thanks to her that the paper can flourish." She tasted her gumbo, and her face registered her pleasure in it. "They're the dearest people, the Endicotts, and I owe them an eternal debt of gratitude, but they haven't got a grain of business sense. Even I can see that. Which is close to a miracle, considering how I was brought up."

He took the bait. "How were you brought up?"

She put down her spoon. "How progressive are you?"

"Try me."

She sighed. "My mother was Friederike Birnbaum. That should tell you a lot."

"You'll forgive me, but I haven't heard of her."

"You're the only person I've met who hasn't."

He thought, *Whatever her mother's reputation, it's proceeded Nina everywhere.* "Enlighten me."

A deep sigh. "She was notorious. She traveled the country before the war, speaking against slavery, and they hated her so much in the South that some gentleman planter told her, 'If you weren't a lady, I'd tar and feather you and run you out of town.' After the war, she took up women's suffrage, no more popular a cause. When I was a baby, she brought me to her lectures in a basket. I grew up on the train, traveling from lecture to lecture. I thought that everyone lived hand-to-mouth like that, until we alit in New York for a few years."

"Where was your father?"

"He was gone by the time I was born," she said, and sadness shadowed her face. "I never knew him. One of the few things I do know is that he gave me my middle name. It's Ariadne."

"Nina Ariadne Birnbaum," he said, testing it, tasting it.

"So you can see why I have no patience with chaperones. Or corsets. Or with anyone who thinks it's wrong for a woman to make a living. Are you shocked yet?"

"No." He leaned forward and whispered, "I can tell about the corset."

She blushed. He didn't think she was capable of it. "You've met a dress reformer before?"

"Yes. Usually they dress very oddly. I'm glad you don't."

"Flattery will get you nowhere with me," she said, but she was smiling.

"Then I won't flatter you." Now that was outright flirtation.

"No, I mean it. I'm too busy for it. I came to Atlanta to write for the *Beacon*. I couldn't do that in New York. The only papers that would employ me didn't have any money to pay me. I look forward to a time when the *Herald* or the *Times* will take a piece from me."

"That's quite an ambition."

She leaned forward, her eyes alight. "Don't you have an ambition?"

"I don't know yet."

"I want to find a story. A real story, not a police blotter report. I haven't yet found it in Atlanta. I don't know how I will."

He was quiet.

She said, "I've overwhelmed you. I'm guilty of that, I know it."

Forceful women. They had raised him, and he was used to them. "At least you're able to see it," he said, feeling comfortable enough to tease. "That's the first thing if you want to do differently."

That quieted her. When she spoke, her voice was pitched low. "I see why Mr. Endicott brought you on. You're very much like him. Liberal in your thinking and kind in your heart."

Under her strident exterior, she was a fatherless child, something he understood all too well. She grieved for a mother who had given her a lonely, difficult childhood, despite the highest of principles and the best of intentions. He understood that, too. A powerful intelligence fueled Nina Birnbaum's fierce ambition. It was like a beacon. She could shine it into the hidden places as well as the dark ones.

LATER THAT WEEK, HIS FATHER STOPPED BY THE HOUSE TO tell Matt, "I've talked to Rachel, and she wants to invite you to dinner on Sunday. You'll be able to see Eliza, and you'll meet the little ones, Charlie and Ada."

Matt nodded. He felt a painful twinge. What would they think of him, his young half brother and half sister? Did they know who he was?

On Sunday, he pulled out his business suit, which Mrs. Bailey had brushed, but he couldn't find a clean shirt. That was odd. Where was the clean laundry? He found all his shirts sweat-soaked and crumpled on the bottom of his clothes press. Perhaps his father kept a spare shirt in the house. It felt wrong to rifle through his father's clothes. He found an unworn shirt, clean but a little musty and wrinkled from being folded for so long. It fit him.

That felt peculiar, too. He dabbed his cheeks with the eau de cologne his father used, the one in the little blue-and-gold bottle from Germany, hoping to overpower the smell of the shirt.

He gave himself one last look in his father's dressing table mirror, not for vanity's sake but for courage, and he squared his shoulders and marched down the stairs and out the front door.

This time, he didn't hesitate on the steps of the Cold-brook house. He rapped on the door, and when Eliza answered, he followed her inside. His father sat in the parlor, at his ease in his shirt sleeves. The younger children, who shared the settee, gazed at Matt with undisguised interest.

His father rose. "Children, this is Matthew, whom I've told you about. Matt, these are my youngest, Charlie and Ada." No mention of the relationship.

They stood up, side by side, and chorused, "Glad to meet you."

So these were his rivals for his father's affection. He should feel wrong being envious of these children. He couldn't help himself.

He sat. Too uncomfortable to start a conversation, Matt glanced around the room, which appeared as though a family spent time in it. The pillows on the settee were indented with use. The bookshelves were full, and more books lay on the tables on either side of the settee. Two Chinese vases graced the whatnot. Matt thought of his mother's parlor; she, too, had a weakness for Asian porcelain.

They were sisters, after all, and they had grown up in the same house, even if one of them had been young miss and the other her slave. *Stop it*, he told himself. *Let it go.*

The smell of dinner, a delicious aroma of roast beef and savory greens, seeped from the kitchen. Beneath it was the smell of beeswax, a sign that someone took care to polish the furniture, and the fragrance of cut roses. He hadn't seen rosebushes in the front yard. Did the Coldbrooks grow roses in their back garden?

Rachel emerged from the kitchen. Despite the warmth in the room—the kitchen must be hotter—she looked fresh, as though she had just rinsed her face in cold water. He was assailed by the memory of Aunt Rachel in her servant's dress and apron, smiling as he sat down at the kitchen table. He blinked the memory away and returned, with some pain, to the present. He rose for her, too. "Mrs. Coldbrook," he murmured, extending his hand, and she took it.

At the table—his father at the head, Rachel at the foot —they didn't pause to say grace. Matt remembered that his aunt Rachel had never been pious.

His nose hadn't deceived him. The meal was a roast of beef, an expensive cut of meat, with new potatoes and greens. These were the greens of his childhood, cooked in chicken grease instead of bacon fat out of respect for what their slave cook Minnie had called "the kosher laws."

Rachel said, "Your father tells me that you've been looking for a position for several weeks now. How is your search going?"

Matt hadn't yet told his father about the *Beacon*, so Rachel had no reason to know. "I've found one."

"What is it? Who are you working for?"

"The *Atlanta Beacon*. The newspaper."

"Is it new? I hadn't heard of it."

"Not new, but not as well-known as the *Constitution*," he said. "They take a liberal view on things. Equality for people of color, and rights for women."

She tucked in her chin. He remembered that gesture from childhood, too. It was the way that she tamped down the feelings she shouldn't express. "Well, it's good that their hearts are in the right place."

With sudden vehemence, he said, "I wish their advertisers were in the right place. They deserve a bigger audience."

"Bring me a copy," she said. She shot his father an odd look. "Didn't you know?"

"No, but I'm glad to hear," his father said, smiling.

Eliza asked Matt, "What are your duties?"

"I assist the editor. Mostly I make fair copies of articles for the printer. The other day, I helped to paste up the proof for this week's issue." He glanced around the table and tried to inject a drop of humor. "Just like at the *Constitution* but in miniature."

Charlie asked, "Will you be an editor someday, like Mr. Grady at the *Constitution*?"

His father smiled. "Charlie is already looking ahead in life. Only eleven, and he's already anticipating his time at Atlanta University."

Matt struggled to keep back the uncharitable thought that he couldn't voice: *In this house, even the little ones are ambitious.* He hadn't minded so much when Nina Birnbaum prodded him, but it galled him to be shown up by an eleven-year-old boy. His unacknowledged half brother.

"When I get old enough, I'm going to Atlanta University, too," said Ada.

"Yes, you will," her mother said, "but in the meantime, don't talk with your mouth full, and please take your elbows off the table."

His father said, "Eliza's found something useful to do this summer, too. Eliza, tell him about the Washing Society."

"What's the Washing Society?" Matt asked.

"You haven't heard about the strike?"

Strike? How could he have missed something as important as a strike? "I had no idea."

"You'll hear soon enough, when your laundress joins us," Eliza said tartly.

The dirty shirts. "When did this begin?" Matt asked.

"Last week. We started with five hundred washer-women on strike. Now we have a thousand."

"What are they asking for?"

"Better treatment and better wages," Eliza said. "A washerwoman is paid only a dollar for a load of wash."

Matt thought of the women who strode down Wheat Street, balancing huge bundles of laundry on their heads. "That's so little!"

"That's why they're asking a dollar for a dozen pounds of wash."

"I never thought that laundresses would go on strike," he said.

Eliza's voice was very sharp. "Well, they have. Their understanding of their own interest is as good as any white person's. And their resolve is stronger."

"Eliza!" Her mother's voice was a warning.

Eliza rose. "Don't you start with me, too." The color on her cheeks was heightened, a flush of anger under the brown skin. "Since I graduated from college, everyone—

everyone!—has been pestering me about what I'm going to do. And now that I've found something to do, you all pester me about that, too. Maybe I should go off to Africa to be a missionary. Or get married, like everyone wants me to. If anyone else tells me to hurry up and marry Ben Mannheim, I'll spit!" She threw her napkin on the table and stomped from the dining room.

His father put his napkin on the table and began to rise, but Rachel said, "No, don't. Don't go after her. Don't indulge her."

Ada asked, "Isn't it rude to run away from the table?"

"Yes, it is," her mother informed her. "Polite people fold up their napkins and ask to be excused."

After the meal, his father and the little ones returned to the parlor and tried to rope Matt into a game of Old Maid. He refused. He put his head into the kitchen, where his aunt stood at the stove, waiting for water to boil so she could wash the dishes. "Mrs. Coldbrook, I wanted to thank you for such a delicious meal."

"Can't say as much for the company." The irritation in her voice was absolutely familiar. Aunt Rachel had always had a sharp tongue.

"I hope it wasn't anything I said."

"It wasn't."

Encouraged, he took a leap. "Ben Mannheim? Are he and Eliza engaged?"

She turned away from the stove. "If it were up to him, they would be. But it ain't. He pay attention to her, that's all." Rachel lost her diction when she was upset, he remembered.

"Is he in Atlanta?"

"Yes, he just graduated from Atlanta University, in

116

Eliza's class. Thought you knew. Thought the two of you wrote to each other."

"We haven't written for years."

"Now that I didn't know."

"Where does he live in Atlanta?"

"Near the university. Why? You intend to call on him?"

"I might."

She didn't turn back to the stove, even though the water had come to a boil. "Why buy yourself grief?"

Eliza put her head into the kitchen. "I'm sorry," she said to her mother. "Do you need help?"

Rachel sighed. Clearly these two never stayed angry long. "No. Why don't you sit in the parlor?"

When Eliza shook her head, Matt seized the opportunity. "Might I have a word with you, Miss Coldbrook?" He let it sound odd. They were half brother and half sister, but they were "Miss" and "Mr." to one another.

Rachel said, "Why don't you go into the garden?"

"It's hot," Eliza said.

Rachel said, "It's always hot. Stand in the shade."

He followed Eliza into the backyard, where the roses grew. "The garden is beautiful."

Eliza didn't reply, and her silence was chilly in the summer heat.

Matt said, "I didn't mean to say a word against the washerwomen who are on strike. I was surprised. I hadn't known. I certainly didn't mean to anger you."

She remained silent.

"Might we try to be cordial to one another? Might we try to be friends?"

She was sharp again. "We haven't seen each other since we were children. We don't know each other."

Now he struggled to reply. "We were close once."

"That was a very long time ago."

"We've both changed a great deal. Perhaps we could start afresh. As we are now."

She shook her head. "We're too far apart." He knew what she meant. Their differences were a chasm between them. She turned and walked back to the house.

Matt stood in the hot, fragrant shade. He listened to the quiet chirps of the little birds that lived in the magnolia bushes. He watched as the bees sought the nectar in the roses.

He couldn't dismiss Eliza as he had dismissed Artie. He wasn't done with Eliza, and she wasn't done with him.

As the warm breeze caressed his cheek, he thought about the strike. About the dignity of working people and the equality of women and people of color. He thought of the *Beacon*.

Now he had a gift for Nina. The washerwomen's strike might be the story that her ambitious soul craved so much. And he had something for his unwilling half sister, too: the chance to tell that story to the *Beacon*, and to the world.

THE NEXT MORNING, HE RUMMAGED FOR ANOTHER OF HIS father's shirts. At the breakfast table, he asked Mrs. Bailey, "Was there a problem with the laundry this week?"

"Washerwoman don't come."

"I heard the washerwomen were on strike."

He recognized her expression, even though he hadn't seen it for fifteen years. *I know what you talk about, but I can't tell you.* "Can't say," she said. He remembered that evasion too. She set his plate before him. "Ain't nothing to worry about."

At the *Beacon*'s office, Mr. Endicott left as soon as he arrived. "I'm calling on someone who might advertise," he said, and that morning Matt was alone in the office, the only sound the scratching of his pen.

He was still alone when Nina arrived shortly before midday. She looked hot and discouraged. He teased, "Nothing newsworthy? Only the police blotter?"

"That's not amusing," she said, pulling off her hat and raking her loose curl away from her face.

"I heard something this Sunday that might interest you."

"Don't try to flirt with me," she said, still annoyed.

Of course he was trying to, but he delivered his news with a straight face. "Have you heard that the washer-women of Atlanta are on strike?"

She was instantly animated. "On strike?"

"Yes, they've stopped work, and they're asking for better pay."

"Where did you hear that?"

"I know someone who's a member of the Washing Society."

"Society? They have a union?"

"I don't know if it's a union. All I know is that they call themselves the Washing Society."

She reached for the notebook she kept in her pocket. "Who do you know there? Can you give me a name?"

"I can do better than that. I can introduce you."

"You know her?"

"Yes, I do. She's my half sister."

"Your half sister is a Black washerwoman?"

"She's a woman of color, but she's not a washer-woman. She's an Atlanta University graduate."

"And your half sister." Nonplussed Nina was surprised. "How do you come to have a sister who's a woman of color?"

"That's the rudest thing you could ever ask a South-erner. And don't tell me you don't have time to be polite."

"I don't. What's her name?"

"Eliza Coldbrook."

She stared at him until understanding came to her. "Coldbrook. Kaltenbach. It's there for anyone to see, if they know to look."

"It's a long story."

"There's nothing I like better than a story."

"I know. But this isn't about the strike. It's not for the *Beacon*. It's private."

She pulled her hand from her pocket and left the note-book there. "I promise not to use any of it as a reporter. I promise to listen to you as a friend, too."

He searched her face. "Do you consider me a friend?"

She blushed.

His family's shame hadn't bothered her, but the thought of his friendship did. He smiled at her and held out his arm. "Will you let me stand you lunch at Mrs. Harper's?"

CHAPTER 10

WILL YOU TESTIFY?

ONCE THE STRIKE BEGAN, Ophelia Taylor went out daily to talk to her neighbors about the Washing Society, and she took Eliza along. Now Eliza opened the door to Ophelia, who glanced at Eliza's white dress. "Really should put on something that won't show the dirt."

Eliza hesitated in the hot, humid air. She thought of the effort of standing in the backyards of Summerhill, so many without shade. "Let me get my hat."

As they walked down the street, Ophelia asked, "Who visit you on Sunday? That white man?"

"You mean my father?"

"No, I know your daddy. I mean that young man. Who is he?"

"Ophelia, that ain't the least bit your business."

Ophelia grinned. "Oh, you riled, you lose your education. You know me. I see something I wonder about, I ask."

"He's my father's son."

Very little silenced Ophelia, but this did. "Oh, Eliza,"

she said, knowing exactly what Eliza meant. "Sorry I ask you."

~

ELIZA AND OPHELIA TRAVERSED FRASER STREET, RAWSON Street, and Martin Street. When they were done, Eliza was wringing wet with sweat and desperately thirsty. At home, before she could run to her room to wash her face, there was a knock on the door, and she opened it to an unfamiliar white woman in a drab blue dress. "Excuse me?" Eliza asked.

The stranger stepped forward. "My name is Nina Birnbaum. I work with Mr. Kaltenbach at the *Beacon*. He gave me your name, and I hope I haven't taken a liberty in calling on you. I'm a reporter."

Eliza didn't open the door any farther. "You're a reporter?"

Miss Birnbaum held out her hand. "The washerwomen's strike is news, and not in the way the *Constitution* reports it. I'd like to get your side of the story. I'd like to talk to some of the washerwomen who are on strike. I hoped to start with you."

"Matt told you about me?"

"Yes, he did."

"Why didn't he come with you?"

"He thought it would be better if he didn't."

Eliza thought of how rude she'd been to him, and she felt ashamed. "Give me a moment to wash my face," she said. "I've been canvassing all morning, and I'm—"

"Glowing, as ladies do?" Nina Birnbaum asked, with a flicker of humor.

That this white stranger would call her a lady surprised her. She answered with sarcasm, as her mother would. "Sweating like a field hand, as you must be, in that dark twill dress of yours."

As Eliza washed her face, she found herself making the judgment of an Atlanta University graduate. Miss Birnbaum was handsome, despite the dowdy dress and the disheveled hair. But to not wear a corset! It was one thing to go around uncorseted if you were a stout washerwoman who had to exert herself all day. It was quite another if you were a lady, as Miss Birnbaum had teased her about being.

Was a white reporter a lady? Eliza wasn't sure. She wiped her face and smoothed her hair. She'd find out.

In the parlor, Nina Birnbaum had taken a seat on the settee and was absorbed in scribbling in a notebook. She looked up when Eliza sat and stashed the notebook in her pocket.

The maid had brought a pitcher of water. Eliza poured some for them both and handed her visitor a glass. "Tell me about your newspaper." She knew the *Constitution*'s point of view. Black people only appeared in the *Constitution* as criminals or figures of fun.

"I could give you a speech, but I thought it would be better to show you. I brought last week's issue." She held it out. "Please, look at it."

The paper was a little damp from Miss Birnbaum's sweaty journey through the streets of Atlanta. Eliza unfolded it, careful with the newsprint. The masthead read, "Dedicated To The Dignity Of Labor, The Equality Of People Of Color, And The Rights Of Women." She scanned the front page to find an article about the unfairness of labor contracts for Black men in the countryside and an essay about the struggle to pass a women's suffrage amendment. She looked up. "The *Beacon*'s views are quite advanced. Do many people in Atlanta read your newspaper?"

"There should be more," Miss Birnbaum said, and her eyes were alight with a familiar fire. It was just like Ophelia's.

"Why call on me? I'm not very important to the strike."

"Matt told me differently."

Eliza felt a spark of irritation at Matt's interference. "Mrs. Gardiner is the one who organized the Washing Society. You should talk to her."

"I'd like to. Will she talk to me?"

"I can make the introduction. I can't promise she'll say yes."

Nina Birnbaum put down her notebook. "Reporters are used to rebuffs. May I ask you a question?"

"You can ask. I don't know if I'll answer."

"Forgive me for the assumption, but I can surmise you're not a washerwoman."

"I'm not. I just graduated from Atlanta University."

"Why did you get involved with the Washing Society?"

She was just like Ophelia. She didn't watch her tongue and didn't care if she needled someone. Was that what reporters did? "Miss Birnbaum, I won't surmise anything about you, but why do you work as a reporter for the *Beacon*?"

Nina Birnbaum's tone was fierce. "To do something useful in the world. And maybe something important."

Startled, Eliza asked, "When did you know you wanted to do that?"

"I've always known it." She paused. Ophelia did that, too, drawing out a silence to poke someone into an answer. "Do you?"

Eliza stifled the impulse to respond as she would to Ophelia: *That ain't the least bit your business!* Instead she said, "Let me mention you to Mrs. Gardiner. We'll see how she feels about talking to the *Beacon.*"

That evening, Eliza fell in with the women who streamed to the meeting at Pleasant Grove Church. Many carried pots of food. Without prompting, the washer-women of Atlanta had devised their own form of mutual aid. Those who had enough brought food. Those who didn't were invited to come to eat.

When the figure in the blue dress waved and hurried toward her, Eliza waved back. Nina was even more disheveled than before, but she was smiling.

"You found us," Eliza said.

"It wasn't difficult. I followed the crowd."

Outside the church, women greeted each other as though they hadn't seen each other for days, even though they were neighbors and they'd come to the meeting last night. Eliza moved slowly through the throng, interrupted over and over by friendly greetings.

A woman who bounced a baby on her hip looked at Miss Birnbaum curiously and asked, "Eliza, who you got with you?"

"Miss Birnbaum. She's a reporter."

"From the *Constitution*? Don't think they care about us."

"I'm from the *Beacon*," Nina said. "We write about working people. Black people. We're interested in the strike."

"*Beacon*? Never hear of it," the woman said, as the baby reached for her nose, and she gently clasped the little hand in her own. She smiled at the baby, not at Nina, and said politely, "I can't read. Maybe somebody get that paper and read it to me."

As they moved on, Nina said, "So these people can't read."

"Some of them can. The younger women and the children who go to school."

"How do they get their news?"

Eliza said, "Someone reads the newspaper. Then they spread the news by telling their neighbors and their friends. In slavery days, we called it the human telegraph. It's swifter than any newspaper."

"Is that how they learned about the strike?"

Eliza nodded.

A woman who carried a pan full of cornbread called out, "Miss Eliza? Who you got with you?"

Eliza halted and made the introduction.

"Newspaper?" she asked. "Like the *Constitution*? When my nephew get arrested—and he don't do anything to get arrested for—the *Constitution* publish his name and shame our whole family."

Miss Birnbaum broke in. "We're not at all like that. We don't shame anyone. We try to treat people with dignity."

"Do you?" she asked, hugging her cornbread close, going on her way.

Miss Birnbaum glanced at Eliza, who said, "I thought reporters were used to rebuffs."

"I didn't say that we liked them." She dropped her voice. "These are people who don't trust a reporter."

"They don't trust white people," Eliza said, her voice a little too sharp.

Inside the church, the smell of greens with bacon and black-eyed peas was strong. "They set up dinner in back. It's plain food. Probably not what you're used to." Eliza thought, *Not what I'm used to, either*.

"I'm not the least bit particular," Miss Birnbaum said. "I'll eat what's put before me."

Eliza wondered what she made of a roomful of Black women in washday dresses that smelled of the sweat of heavy labor as they waited in line to serve themselves black-eyed peas. They were neither patient nor quiet. They stared at Miss Birnbaum and talked aloud. Eliza caught the word *reporter*.

When Miss Birnbaum served herself, Mrs. Hilliard, who was seventy years old, asked her, "Are you a washer-woman?" Mrs. Hilliard, born and raised in slavery, reverted to a servile tone with a white woman.

"No, ma'am, I'm not. I'm a reporter. And not for the *Constitution*. For a newspaper called the *Beacon*."

Mrs. Hilliard's eyes were too cloudy with cataracts for reading, even if she could read. "Reporter? Slip of a girl like you?"

Miss Birnbaum restrained herself and nodded politely.

"Well, that's all right, as long as you're a good Christian child."

At that, Miss Birnbaum laughed. "I guess I can be for tonight."

As they headed for a place to sit, Eliza asked, "What was that about?"

"I'm an Israelite. Like Matt."

"Just so you know, those greens have bacon in them."

She smiled. "I didn't say I was a religious Israelite."

They had just picked up their spoons when Mrs. Gardiner called, "Eliza! What's all the excitement? Who you bring to our meeting?"

"Someone who can tell Atlanta about the strike. Someone who wants to tell it from our point of view. She's a reporter. Miss Birnbaum, from the *Beacon*."

Miss Birnbaum rose and held out her hand, but Mrs. Gardiner didn't take it.

Mrs. Gardiner said, "A reporter? I ain't sure about a reporter, after I hear what the *Constitution* say about us. Just today they say that we create a nuisance, and we ask for something that we don't deserve. They ain't talked to a single one of us. They talk to the missuses we work for, who complain about us and speak against us."

Miss Birnbaum said, "I know. I saw that in the *Constitution*. They're wrong. What they did was wrong."

"How do I know you don't misrepresent us, just like the *Constitution*?"

"I can give you a copy of our paper to read. You'll see the point of view we take," said Miss Birnbaum.

"I can't read."

Eliza had never heard Mrs. Gardiner sound so combative. She said, "Mrs. Gardiner, I'd be glad to read the *Beacon* to you."

Mrs. Gardiner asked, "Young miss, what was your name again?"

Miss Birnbaum wasn't ruffled. Did Yankees not hear what a Southerner, especially a Black Southerner, could hear so plainly: the veiled rudeness of "young miss"?

Eliza broke in, "You heard it when she introduced herself. Miss Birnbaum. Nina Birnbaum."

"Well, Miss Nina, what can you tell me now to convince me you intend to tell the truth about us?"

Miss Birnbaum paused as she searched for the right way to put it. The church setting seemed to sober her. What kind of vow would she make? As an unbelieving Jew, neither God nor Jesus. She said slowly, "I swear it on my mother's soul."

Mrs. Gardiner didn't avert her gaze as understanding came to her. "You a motherless child?"

A shadow of sadness passed over Nina's face. "Yes, I am."

"All right," Mrs. Gardiner said. "I talk to you. Come see me tomorrow."

The next day, Nina appeared at Eliza's door. Eliza said, "You'll need to be careful with Mrs. Gardiner."

"She doesn't trust me. I know that."

Eliza didn't think before she spoke. She was getting to be like Ophelia herself. "I'll go with you. She doesn't trust anyone who's white."

"I'll keep that well in mind."

Nina started gently with Mrs. Gardiner, asking about her early life, her move to Atlanta, her family, her work with the church. She listened closely and left her note-book untouched. Mrs. Gardiner was clearly taken aback, since she expected harsher treatment. But these subjects were easy ones. Mrs. Gardiner relaxed in her chair, and her voice lost its careful, public cadence. Then she looked

129

right at Nina and said, "You softening me up to ask me about the strike, ain't you?"

"Mrs. Gardiner, you've found me out."

"Pity only take you so far."

"I'm aware of that." She didn't reach for the notebook. "Mrs. Gardiner, I won't press you. You tell me whatever suits you. If there's anything you don't want in the newspaper, you tell me. I'll respect that."

Mrs. Gardiner said, "Thought you would write down everything I say in that little book of yours. How you keep it straight?"

"I have a good memory, Mrs. Gardiner. Like you do."

Mrs. Gardiner, brought up in slavery, a woman who knew when not to look a white woman in the face, met Nina Birnbaum's eyes. "All right. What do you want to know about the strike?"

She picked up her notebook. "Anything you'll tell me."

Mrs. Gardiner talked to Nina Birnbaum for over an hour, and she ended by saying, "Miss Nina, I'll allow you to go out to see how we canvass. Eliza, you willing to take her along with you?"

Eliza looked at Nina. "Tomorrow morning, if you're ready."

Early the next morning, Eliza answered the door to Nina, who wore dark blue again. Eliza itched to see her in that heavy twill and wondered if Miss Birnbaum owned a dress better suited to the Atlanta summer. "Have you had breakfast yet?"

"Yes, I'm quite all right. I live with the Endicotts on

Peachtree Street. Mr. Endicott owns the *Beacon*, and Mrs. Endicott feeds me royally. Why? Did you think I stayed at a threadbare boardinghouse and had to eat stale biscuits and drink watery coffee?"

Exactly what Eliza had thought. Nina's sardonic accuracy made her laugh. "I'm glad you're provided for. We'll go out to talk to people. We'll pester those who haven't joined us and keep up the spirits of those who have."

"And do you meet every night?"

"Yes, and not just at Pleasant Grove. We fill up the pews at every Black church in Atlanta. I can take you to Bethel A. M. E. on Wheat Street and Friendship Baptist over in Jenningstown. I rotate, and I go to each church every week. All the smaller churches have meetings, too, if you want to attend those."

"I'll go anywhere, if people will talk to me."

"They should. The word will go around."

"The human telegraph."

"Eliza!" It was Ophelia, who had met Nina briefly at the meeting at Pleasant Grove. "She come along with us?"

Eliza said, "Miss Birnbaum will accompany us so that she can write about the strike for her newspaper."

"Yes, I hear Mrs. Gardiner give the say-so."

"What's bothering you?"

Ophelia spoke as though Nina wasn't there. "You think that anyone talk to us with a stranger hanging over their shoulder?"

Eliza heard the words Ophelia wouldn't say. *A white woman.*

Nina said, "Mrs. Taylor?"

Ophelia looked surprised that a white woman would address her as "Mrs."

"I'm sorry. I'm so eager to tell your story that I didn't think that I might be in your way. May I talk to you privately, whenever I can? Would that be all right?"

Grudgingly, Ophelia said, "Yes, I reckon so."

"I'm sorry we troubled you for nothing this morning, Miss Birnbaum," Eliza said.

Nina grinned. "This is a success. Mrs. Taylor will talk to me later."

After Nina left, Eliza asked, "Why were you so rude to Miss Birnbaum?"

"I don't care what Miss Amanda say. I don't trust her. She ain't in this for us. She in it for herself."

"I can tell she's ambitious. But I think she cares about telling the truth, too."

"I see the two of you at that meeting the other day. Don't be fooled because she like you and make you laugh. You watch yourself." Ophelia put a warning hand on Eliza's arm. "Come on. We got work to do."

They walked down the alley behind Fraser Street. At the first house they came to, the yard was empty. No washtub, and no washerwoman. Pleased, Ophelia said, "She on strike."

Next door, there was no washtub in the yard, either. A group of women sat on the back steps. One of them waved to Ophelia. "We all on strike, Miss Ophelia! We get in union!"

Ophelia waved back, beaming. "You stay in union! You need anything?"

"Miss Mary still washing," the woman said.

Ophelia said, "Miss Eliza and I go pay her a visit."

The woman turned to look at the three friends who were still seated. "Let's all go call on Miss Mary," she said.

They found Miss Mary bent over her washtub, and they surrounded her. Ophelia put her hands on her hips. "You should be ashamed, Miss Mary. Ashamed of yourself! Ashamed for washing!" The rest of the women clustered around her, pressuring her with their presence.

Miss Mary stopped stirring the clothes in the washtub. "Ashamed of making a living?"

Ophelia stepped forward. "Yes, when we all stop work and go on strike. Ashamed of not standing with us!"

Miss Mary looked up. "You shame me? What you do to me?"

"We come back and yell at you, day after day."

Miss Mary snorted. "I have a thicker hide than that."

Eliza joined Ophelia. "Don't you want a dollar a dozen?"

Miss Mary gave Eliza a disdainful look. "I might want a lot of things. Might want to be the queen of heaven and sit on a golden throne and wear a starry crown. Do I get that? No. Got to make a living. Got to keep working."

"What if we could help you?" Eliza asked. She threw a glance at Miss Mary's daughter, who listened intently, her eyes wide.

"Help me how? Stop yelling at me?"

"Feed you and your children. We have a meeting at Pleasant Grove every night, and we serve dinner. You'd be welcome."

Miss Mary said, "Still have to pay my rent. Who help me with that?"

"Who do you rent from?"

"Mrs. Toussaint."

Ophelia said, "She my landlady too, and she agree to

give up the rent for a month. Maybe two month, if this drag on. Would that help?"

Miss Mary didn't reply. In the silence, her daughter, carrying the baby, had joined the crowd of washerwomen.

Miss Mary said, "This is how you act, after I try to raise you right? Get in trouble?"

The girl edged close to Ophelia. Ophelia put her hand on the girl's shoulder. "Miss Mary, what do you say? You with us? You stand with us?"

The girl said, "Mama, stand with them."

Miss Mary stared at her daughter. Then she buried her face in her hands. When she took them away, they all saw the tears on her face. She wiped her hands on her wet apron. She asked, "You feed my children? You help us with the rent? You mean that?"

Ophelia rested a hand on her shoulder. "Yes. The Washing Society help you."

Miss Mary sighed deeply.

"Mama," her daughter repeated.

Miss Mary said, "Maybe I live to regret this."

"Maybe you don't." Ophelia pointed to the washtub. "Don't you finish that. Leave it sopping wet and full of soap. Bundle it up and dump it on your missus' front steps."

"I can't do such a thing!" Miss Mary said.

"Yes, you can. We all been doing it. It make them madder. Make them see that we mean business."

Miss Mary said tartly, "How I carry a wet load of wash through the street? Weigh even more wet."

"My husband have a wagon. He take it for you if you go with him and dump it yourself."

Miss Mary's daughter gave her a mother a long,

searching look. Miss Mary glared at Ophelia. "You crazy, you know that? And you get me in the worst kind of trouble."

Ophelia laughed. "Sometimes it's good to make trouble, Miss Mary."

~

A FEW DAYS LATER, AS ELIZA HURRIED THROUGH HER breakfast, her mother asked, "Will we see you at supper tonight?"

Eliza had never been so busy, not even at the height of her career as a student at Atlanta University. She spent her mornings with Ophelia, persuading and cajoling the washerwomen of Summerhill and Shermantown to stay in union. She spent her afternoons with Nina, introducing her to anyone who was skeptical that a reporter would be fair to the Washing Society. She spent her evenings in churches all over Atlanta, doing whatever Amanda Gardiner needed her help in getting done. She was in a permanent state of agitation, and despite her frenzy of activity, she found it hard to sleep.

She gulped her coffee. "I'll try," she said, setting down the cup with a rattle.

"I hear you spend all your time with the reporter from the *Beacon*. Miss Birnbaum. Introduce us. I'd like to meet her."

Eliza nodded, folded her napkin, and, as she rose, asked to be excused. She sighed. "Yes."

That afternoon, when she met Nina outside Bethel A. M. E. on Wheat Street, she said, "My mother wants to meet you."

"When?"

"Now. Let's go." She began to walk eastward.

"Where are we going? Your house is in Summerhill."

"Her office is on Wheat Street."

"Office? What does she do?"

"She runs a contracting business."

Nina was fascinated. "Really? A woman of color! May I interview her?"

"You'll have to ask her that yourself."

As they walked down the street, they drew stares from white ladies on the street. One of them sniffed and said to Nina, "You shouldn't let your servant act so familiar with you."

Nina bristled.

"Hush," Eliza whispered, putting her hand on Nina's arm. "Save your indignation for something that really matters."

Nina muttered, "Getting insulted every time you walk down the street, doesn't that matter?"

The composition of the crowd on the street began to change from white to Black. Eliza breathed easier. Now Nina drew the attention of strangers. She didn't flinch. She held her head up and slipped her hand into her pocket, touching her notebook like a talisman.

When they passed Kaltenbach's Dry Goods, Nina asked, "Is this your father's shop?"

Eliza stopped dead on the street. "How do you know that?"

"Matt told me."

Eliza fumed. "It isn't his to tell."

"It's as much his story as yours," Miss Birnbaum said.

"Do you say anything that comes into your head? That will get you in plenty of trouble in the South."

"I'm a Yankee. And a reporter."

Eliza thought of Ophelia's warning words. They were just as true for Nina Birnbaum. *You watch yourself.* "Let's go," Eliza said, tugging on Nina's arm. The shop door opened, and two well-dressed Black women emerged.

"Eliza!" the younger one said. It was Lavinia Oliver, the Atlanta University classmate who had proudly proclaimed her engagement and her upcoming wedding just after she graduated. "I haven't seen you for weeks! What are you doing?" She glanced at Miss Birnbaum but didn't acknowledge her.

Eliza laid a warning hand on Miss Birnbaum's arm, hoping that she would take the hint. She felt the full weight of her friend's scrutiny, and worse yet, that of her friend's mother. Mrs. Oliver, widowed and well-off by the standards of Black Atlanta, conducted herself like a Southern lady. She had been the one to summon Dr. Chesney, Eliza recalled. "I'm helping the Washing Society. The washerwomen. They're on strike."

"Yes, I know," Lavinia said. "We've had to do our own wash for two weeks." She wrinkled her nose. "I never thought I'd touch a cake of lye soap!"

"They have reason to stop work. They want better pay."

Mrs. Oliver said, "Don't tell me that you're out in the street with them, Eliza. What does your mother say to that?"

"She's all for the Washing Society as long as I stay far away from it."

Mrs. Oliver sniffed. "As well you should."

"Sometimes it's good to stir up some trouble," Eliza said, quoting Ophelia.

"Young lady, don't say such a thing. This could be real trouble. Do you know what I mean?"

Eliza thought of Cass County and everything that had gone wrong there. "I'm still Black, Mrs. Oliver, as are you. I know just what you mean."

Lavinia rushed in. "We were just in your father's shop. We bought a length of white satin for my wedding dress. And some lovely lace, too."

Eliza nodded.

Still trying to heal the breach, Lavinia said, "How is Mr. Mannheim? Have you seen him lately?"

"I haven't. He doesn't like the Washing Society, either."

Mrs. Oliver pulled on Lavinia's arm as Nina pulled on Eliza's. They turned away at the same time.

Miss Birnbaum asked, "Who were they?"

"Neighbors in Summerhill."

"I gather that they don't trust white people, either."

"You're right. They don't."

"May I pry a bit?"

Eliza sighed. "As though I could stop you."

"Who is Mr. Mannheim?"

"Ben Mannheim. We were at Atlanta University together. Before I joined the Washing Society, he was thinking of proposing marriage to me."

"What does he think now?"

"That's enough," Eliza said, and fell silent for the two blocks to her mother's office, where she pushed the door open. "Eliza!" her mother said, rising from her chair. "Is this Miss Birnbaum?"

"Yes."

Her mother said, "I've never met a reporter before."

"I've never met a woman of color who owns a construction company."

"We can be two oddities together," her mother said pleasantly, and Nina laughed. "I hear that Eliza has taken you all over Atlanta to talk to the strikers."

"I'm very grateful to her for it."

"Miss Birnbaum, please be careful. And that goes for my daughter, too."

"Is there danger?" Miss Birnbaum asked, in a pleasant tone.

"You must not know the South very well."

"You'd be surprised, Mrs. Coldbrook."

"Mama, don't badger her. And don't pester me, either. I talk to our neighbors in Summerhill in broad daylight. I go to the church down the street. I'm hardly in danger."

"A Black woman is always in danger." Her mother's voice was sharp.

She was right, and Eliza's fear made her testy in return. "We're in Atlanta now, not in Cass County!"

"I know. But I haven't forgotten a thing about Cass County, and you shouldn't, either."

Eliza felt the chill that always accompanied her nightmares. "We have to go," she said, tugging on Nina's arm again.

Surprised, Nina said, "So soon?"

Through gritted teeth, Eliza said, "Yes."

Still puzzled, Nina said, "Excuse us, Mrs. Coldbrook. It's been a pleasure to meet you." Outside, she said, "What was your mother talking about?"

Eliza dragged Nina to the backyard, a treeless strip of

dirt behind the building. Despite the full sun, despite the humid heat, Eliza felt cold.

Nina said, "Stop yanking on my arm. What's this about danger?"

Eliza suddenly found that she couldn't reply.

"What happened in Cass County?"

Eliza shook her head and turned away. She pressed her arm to her face and was flooded with a Cass County memory, of her aunt Adelaide telling her mother not to wipe her face with her sleeve because a free woman used a handkerchief.

Nina's voice was gentle. "What's the matter, Eliza?"

When she could talk again, Eliza said, "I don't understand her. She supports the Washing Society. She gave them a thousand dollars for the strike fund. But she hates that I've gotten involved with the strikers."

"She worries about you. Whether there's danger or not. Any mother would."

Eliza was so upset again that she didn't watch her tongue. "What would your mother think of your being a reporter, running around Atlanta, putting yourself in danger?"

Nina drew in her breath. "I wish she were here to tell me."

She didn't have to look at Nina's face to feel ashamed of herself. "I'm so sorry, Nina. For what I said. For your loss."

"Just four months ago. I still think of her all the time." Now Nina, the motherless child, was the one to rub her face with her sleeve.

Eliza asked, "Do you need a handkerchief?"

"I never have one when I need one." Nina wiped her face.

Eliza asked, "Now, may I pry?"

"Fair turnabout." Her voice was throaty.

"What was she like?"

Nina hesitated, and Eliza was about to apologize again. "No, it's good to talk about her. No one else lets me, not even Mrs. Endicott, who was her friend."

"She wants to spare you."

"She doesn't. It was just the two of us. I never knew my father. So we were doubly precious to each other."

"Oh, Nina."

Nina wiped her eyes again. "She was fierce in every way. She was fearless, too. She used to lecture on abolition before the war. She went all over the South. A planter in Charleston told her that if she wasn't a woman, he'd tar and feather her and run her out of town."

"So you do know about the danger."

"Of course I do."

"Was she afraid?"

"If she was, she never showed it. I'm in awe when I think of how brave she was. She was born in a little Jewish town in Poland. Her father was a rabbi, very religious. He wanted to marry her off when she was sixteen. She ran away."

"All by herself?"

"I don't know how she managed it. She got to Germany and then to England. She met some interesting people in London. She knew Karl and Jenny Marx." At Eliza's puzzled expression, she said, "I forget that not everyone knows. They were radicals. Famous in radical circles. It would be like knowing Frederick Douglass if you were an abolitionist."

"How did she come to America?"

"Her friends in London helped her. They got her started as a writer and a speaker in America, too."

"A radical," Eliza murmured.

"Oh yes. Antislavery before the war, and women's suffrage after." Nina was still throaty. "And if that wasn't scandalous enough, she never married. She said that marriage was a kind of slavery." She looked up at Eliza, her eyelashes wet, her expression defiant. "Have I shocked you?"

Eliza said, "Don't take this the wrong way."

"I'm braced."

"Mother a runaway? Never married? Child without a daddy? Except for the big ideas, it's a life any washerwoman would recognize."

Nina was still a little choked up, but her laugh was genuine. "Now that's something that never occurred to me. But you're absolutely right."

"We'll get you a washday dress and a cake of lye soap, and you'll fit right in. Every Black woman in Atlanta will want to talk to you."

"Hah!"

"Did your mother wear a corset?"

Nina made a sound like a half laugh and half snuffle. "All her life. It was vanity, pure and simple. She liked having a small waist."

～

ELIZA INVITED NINA TO THE NEXT MEETING AT BETHEL A. M. E., and when Ophelia saw them together, she made a point of walking with Mrs. Gardiner.

Nina said, "I like Mrs. Taylor, but I can tell she doesn't like me much."

"Has she allowed you to interview her?" Eliza asked.

"Not yet. She's very busy."

Eliza thought of both of them, tugging on her arms. "She is."

When they turned onto Wheat Street, Eliza saw the policeman who had blocked their way a few weeks ago. He stopped Mrs. Gardiner, who headed the crowd. "Where are you going?" he asked.

She replied with the same soft tone as before. "We go to church, sir."

"You go to church every night, all of you?"

Mrs. Gardiner placated him. "Oh, sir, we all very pious."

Nina whispered to Eliza, "I didn't think a policeman would bother women."

"They prefer to bother men," Eliza whispered back. "But they like bothering anyone who's Black."

The policeman, not content with harassing anyone who passed him, walked down the sidewalk, through the crowd, tapping his club into the palm of his hand. When he saw Nina, he stopped. "What are you doing here?" he asked her.

"Is there something wrong, sir?" Nina asked sweetly.

He drew the club across his palm as though he liked the feel of it. "You're with these people?"

"Is that a problem, sir?"

"Don't you backtalk me."

Alarmed, Eliza tugged on Nina's sleeve. She said, "Sir, we're just moving along. Going now, sir."

He laid his club on Nina's shoulder, and Eliza was suddenly mute with fear. The women around her stopped, watching, waiting.

He said, "A white woman. You ought to be ashamed of yourself." He let the club rest on Nina's shoulder as though he were getting ready to use it. "You cast in your lot with niggers, we'll treat you like one."

Nina went pale. Eliza said, "Sir, let us pass. We go on. We don't bother anyone."

He said, "Walk in the street." He lifted the club from Nina's shoulder and gestured with it. "Where you belong, both of you."

Nina glanced into the gutter, which was filthy with mud and horse manure. Before she could open her mouth, Eliza tugged hard on her sleeve. "Yes, sir. We go now." She stepped into the gutter and pulled Nina after her.

The policeman watched as Nina followed Eliza, and he kept his eyes on them both as they walked away.

Eliza trembled as she kept a tight grip on Nina's sleeve. When they were far enough away to return to the sidewalk, Nina said, with some difficulty, "You can let go of my arm now."

Eliza nodded. "I thought he was going to beat you."

Nina was ashen. "So did I."

At Bethel A. M. E., two women caught up with them. One of them asked Nina, "Are you all right?"

"Not hurt, at least," Nina said.

Her companion said, "She the reporter I tell you about.

Her name Miss Nina. Miss Amanda say she write about us in her newspaper."

"Reporter?" the first woman asked. She looked at Nina. "You testify about us in your newspaper?"

Nina gave Eliza a quizzical look. Eliza wished that she could stop trembling. "They mean 'bear witness,'" she said, glancing at the church front. "Tell the truth because God is listening."

Nina's face got a shadowed look, as it did when she remembered her mother. "Yes," she said to the woman. "I'll testify."

Inside, neither of them wanted to call attention to themselves by sitting up front. They tucked themselves into a pew near the back. Nina straightened her skirt and pulled her notebook from her pocket. The crowd buzzed around them, but Eliza was still too shaken to pay much attention.

Mrs. Gardiner stood on the pulpit, next to Reverend Carter. When he greeted them, saying, "Sisters, sisters!" they quieted. He introduced Mrs. Gardiner, and she took the pulpit for herself.

She said, "I talk to you, more than a few of you, as I come in. I hear that you tired. I know that you tired. I know you tired of coming to meetings every night. I know you tired of neglecting your families to do this. I know you tired of not working and not getting paid."

"Amen!" someone said, and someone else said, "You hush!"

Mrs. Gardiner waited for them to quiet. "We ain't finished. We just get underway. And how well we start out! Three thousand of us now, and everyone stop work. Even the white washerwomen join us, the Irish women.

They poor and overworked, too. If any of you here tonight, you welcome, too!"

Eliza looked around, but the only white woman she saw was Nina.

"And now all of Atlanta have weeks of dirty laundry, in the worst heat of summertime. They all go around in dirty drawers and sweaty shirts because of us. They take notice, don't they!" She grinned, and laughter rippled through the crowd.

"We got Atlanta roiled up. We trouble the water, all right. Don't know if you hear about this yet, but the city of Atlanta so riled up about us that the city council poke its nose in. They want to pass a law to make us buy licenses to do the wash. I hear they talk about a license that cost twenty-five dollars a year." A gasp from the crowd. "I know what that sound like to you. I know some of you strain every sinew to make a hundred dollars in a year. I think they bluff us. We don't give up, and we don't stop. We keep our eyes on what we aim for."

A whistle pierced the air. Ophelia called out: "A dollar a dozen!" and the crowd took up her rallying cry. "A dollar a dozen!" they chanted, clapping their hands and stamping their feet. "A dollar a dozen!"

Mrs. Gardiner waited for them to clap and stamp themselves into silence. "I know it hard for some of you. If it's the kind of hard that money can help, don't be shy to ask. The Washing Society got a fund for just that reason. It ain't charity. It's just like the Mutual Aid Society. It's there for folks who need it. And anyone in need deserve it." Deep breath. "But there's another kind of hard. What we do, to stop work and go on strike, it's hard on the spirit, too. But I know all of you got the strength in you.

146

You got to keep the hope in you, too. Nothing move us from that."

She had suggested the song, and it rose spontaneously from the crowd, the testament of faith and strength. "We Shall Not Be Moved," they sang, and Eliza felt a chill run down her spine. It was the anthem of the election of 1867, when the Black voters of Cass County marched to the polls and stared down the Klan on the way.

CHAPTER 11

DR. CHESNEY

AFTER HER MOTHER'S gift to the strike fund, Eliza thought anew of Dr. Chesney, who was caught between his yearning to help the Black people of Atlanta and his need to make a living. The Washing Society might help with more than food and rent. Why not with medicine? Why not with doctor's visits?

She decided to call on him in his office. No one could say anything against it. She'd go there to see him if she were ill.

Dr. Chesney had rented an office on Wheat Street, between her father's shop and her mother's place of business. It smelled of carbolic, sweet and tarry, which competed with the odor of the mud and manure of the Atlanta street. The walls had been recently whitewashed, and the floor was scrupulously clean. He sat at an oak desk that had seen better days; evidently he had little money for furnishings. Behind him was a shelf that held his doctor's bag and several leather-bound books that she assumed were medical references. The office was too small for a waiting area. Two chairs had been arranged on the other side of the desk, and in one of them sat an elderly woman, her face nearly unlined despite her age. Her name was Mrs. Marable, and she was well-known in Atlanta for the medicinal plants she grew in her backyard.

Eliza said, "Have I intruded?"

Mrs. Marable smiled. "Miss Eliza! No, you ain't in the way. Didn't come because I was sick. Wanted to meet the doctor, that's all." She rose.

"Mrs. Marable, it was good to meet you," said Dr. Chesney.

After Mrs. Marable left, Eliza said, "You know she's a root doctor."

"Of course I do."

"I'm surprised you'd give a root doctor any credence."

He smiled. "My grandmother was a root doctor. An herbalist. I learned a great deal from her. Black people will visit root doctors, whether I'm here or not. I might as well meet them and try to get along with them."

"That's very open-minded of you."

"Miss Coldbrook, what brings you here to visit me? Are you ill?" His tone was both concerned and hopeful.

"No, I'm not. I'm healthy as can be." She sat. "I came because I have a business proposition for you." The words came easily, as though she used them every day. Perhaps she was like her mother, a woman of business, in a way she had never contemplated before.

He smiled. "A business proposition! I can't imagine."

"Then you'll be surprised." She leaned forward. "I assume you've heard about the washerwomen's strike."

"I have. I support the strike. But it makes it harder for me to practice medicine and charge anyone a fee for it."

"That's why I'm here."

"Have you come into a fortune, Miss Coldbrook?"

In a way, she thought, and she felt as pleased as though the money were truly her own. "No. But the Washing Society has come into some money."

"The Washing Society?"

"A mutual aid society for the washerwomen. A strike fund. To replace their lost wages. To help them with food and rent, if they need it."

"A good idea."

"Why not help them with medicine?"

He sat up straighter in his chair.

She said, "And doctor's fees, too?" He didn't reply. She added, "Anyone who's sick should be able to afford a doctor. And medicine as well."

"I can hardly disagree with you."

"It's still only an idea. I'd have to convince Mrs. Gardiner, who's organized the strike and raised the money for the fund, that it's a good idea."

"They've already raised the money?"

"Yes, a substantial sum." She dropped her voice. "I shouldn't tell you how much."

"I'll trust you. What shall we do?"

She liked to hear that the two of them were in union. "Would you mind coming with me to talk to Mrs. Gardiner?"

"Miss Coldbrook, to assure the success of this plan of yours, I'd go a lot farther than that. Tell me about Mrs. Gardiner. What will convince her?"

Eliza laughed. "Once she gets a good look at you, I don't think she'll need much convincing."

She walked away, aglow with a feeling of enterprise.

Was this how Ophelia felt after she discovered her talent for organizing her neighbors to strike? *This is my way of striking*, she thought.

Mrs. Gardiner offered Dr. Chesney the best chair in the parlor and fussed over bringing him coffee. Then she began to interview him with more rigor than Nina Birnbaum had shown in interviewing her. She said, "I already meet you at Pleasant Grove, but we ain't properly acquainted. Who are your people?"

"My family? They're all in Philadelphia, Mrs. Gardiner. My father is a barber, and he's very successful at it and well-respected among Black and white alike."

"Do he serve white people?"

"He counts them among his customers, yes."

"Philadelphia. So you born free."

"I was, and my parents before me, both of them."

"No slavery in your family?"

"My grandmother, my father's mother, was born into slavery in Virginia, early in this century."

"Her master free her?"

Dr. Chesney smiled. "She freed herself, Mrs. Gardiner. Lit out for Pennsylvania and followed the Drinking Gourd to Philadelphia. After that, she conducted herself like a free woman, and no one ever questioned her."

"She ever look over her shoulder?"

"We all did, even in Philadelphia, after the Fugitive Slave Act became law. It made my family more resolute than ever about fighting slavery. My parents ran a station on the Underground Railroad before the war."

Satisfied, Mrs. Gardiner nodded. "So how do a Black man become a doctor?"

"I was fortunate in having a good education as a boy at the Institute for Colored Youth in Philadelphia. I was always interested in medicine. As a barber, my father knew men who were surgeons, and my grandmother was an herbalist—what Southerners call a root doctor." He met Eliza's eyes, and they both smiled. "I couldn't imagine anything nobler than alleviating the suffering of sickness and pain."

"I hear you attend Howard University."

"I did, Mrs. Gardiner. I completed the program at the College of Medicine. It wasn't easy. The courses were held at night because all of us had to work to support ourselves and pay the college fees. I was a medical student by night but a porter by day. Whenever I felt discouraged, I reminded myself that I wouldn't be a porter forever. Only until I earned my medical degree."

Mrs. Gardiner looked as though she didn't know whether to feel regret or hope. "That's why we on strike. So we won't be washerwomen forever. Our daughters go to college, like Miss Eliza here."

"I hope so, Mrs. Gardiner."

"What bring you to Atlanta? If you go back to Philadelphia, you doctor all them Black people who been free for three generations. Must have some money for doctoring, too. Atlanta ain't like that."

He sat at ease, as though he'd been asked the same thing before and knew his answer by heart. "We talked a lot about that, we medical students. We all wanted to make a living, but Howard encouraged us to help Black people less fortunate than ourselves."

"Uplift the race," Eliza murmured. "Atlanta University, too."

"That isn't quite fair to people who suffer from poverty and prejudice, through no fault of their own," he said. "I thought about it for a long time. I concluded that I wouldn't be useful in a small place in the South or in the countryside. The need in Atlanta is great, but so is the opportunity."

"You a man of business as well as a doctor."

"A doctor has to be a man of business, Mrs. Gardiner. But if he's only a man of business, he won't be a good doctor." He glanced at Eliza, and his smile warmed her. "That's why Miss Coldbrook's idea was so appealing to me. Miss Coldbrook, will you explain it to Mrs. Gardiner?"

She appreciated his courtesy in acknowledging her initiative, and she could tell that Mrs. Gardiner did as well. Eliza outlined the idea of using the Washing Society fund to pay for doctor visits and medicine for the strikers, explaining that it was as much a need as food or rent.

Mrs. Gardiner said, "You right." Her gaze moved to Dr. Chesney, who met her look with composure. "We never use the mutual aid fund for medicine or doctors before," she said. "But we never strike before, either."

Dr. Chesney knew not to interject.

Mrs. Gardiner said, "Eliza, could you put your mind to it? Study it?"

"With Dr. Chesney's help," Eliza said.

"I'd be glad to help you," he said.

"You figure it out, the two of you. And then bring your plan back to me."

"Of course," Eliza said.

As they rose and readied to leave, Dr. Chesney said, "I'm very grateful to you, Mrs. Gardiner."

She took the hand he proffered, but instead of shaking it, she patted it, as a mother would. She laughed. "Save your gratitude. I ain't said yes yet."

Outside on the sidewalk, Eliza felt unreasonably glad. She told Dr. Chesney, "She was joking with you."

"I know."

"She likes you. Of course she'll say yes."

"A little skepticism is a good thing, Miss Coldbrook," he said, but he was smiling.

Eliza said, "If Amanda Gardiner had a daughter old enough, she'd marry her off to you."

He laughed. "Now that's a hazard I hadn't reckoned on."

BEFORE SHE CALLED ON DR. CHESNEY AGAIN, ELIZA ASKED Mrs. Gardiner how the Pleasant Grove Mutual Aid Society disbursed its funds.

Mrs. Gardiner said, "Ain't a mystery. When someone in the congregation die, we all know about it. The widow come to us, tell us about her circumstance, and Reverend Jones pay out the money. We keep the fund in the Atlanta National Bank, and the reverend and I can draw it out when we need it."

Eliza nodded. Now she had a place to start with Dr. Chesney.

As on her earlier visit, an older woman sat in the visitor's chair. Eliza waited politely until she rose and left. Eliza asked, "A patient?"

"No, a midwife who treats female complaints in addition to delivering babies. She tells me she's paid in eggs."

"I have nothing against eggs. Our neighbors keep chickens. But I think we can manage a better form of payment for you."

He smiled. "Please be seated, Miss Coldbrook. Now, how should we proceed?"

She explained the mutual aid society's method of reimbursement.

"I don't think it would work for a medical practice. There's a great deal I need to keep private, like why people consult me or what I prescribe for them. I'd prefer to keep my fees private, too."

"So it's not like a dry goods shop, where cottons are so much a yard and silks, another."

"I have to take into consideration what the patient is able to pay."

She said, "My mother runs a construction company, and when she bids for a project, she thinks the same way. She'll bid differently on a house for a comfortable family than for a house for, say, a laboring man and a washerwoman."

"Your mother is a builder and a contractor?"

"Yes, a successful one."

"Do you assist her in the business?"

"No, unless you count listening to her bemoan the fact that no one will accept her bid on a commercial building. She's kept me at arm's length from the business."

"But you've absorbed it."

"As I absorbed the dry goods business of my father."

He looked a little puzzled. "I didn't know there was a Black dry goods merchant in Atlanta."

"There isn't. It's Kaltenbach's Dry Goods, just down the street, and if you've gone inside, you know who runs it."

"I have. He sold me cotton for shirts. A very courteous man." Understanding dawned. "A delicate situation. Is it generally known?"

"In Summerhill, at Pleasant Grove Church, it's well-known, if not openly discussed."

He sighed. "Slavery and its ghosts are still with us."

"Yes, they are."

"I've led us far afield."

"There's no need to apologize, Dr. Chesney."

His gaze was full of sympathy, and his eyes, a darker brown than his face, were easy to look into. "Shall we return to business?"

She nodded. "You were going to tell me about your records and your accounts."

"In one way, I'm like any man of business. I write every patient a receipt for medical services and medicines. And I keep track of my fees and my expenses in a ledger." He turned to reach for a familiar-looking leather-bound volume. Unlike the ledgers her parents kept, it was so new that it smelled of leather, and the word stamped on the binding was still bright gold. The undisturbed spine creaked in protest when he opened it.

He hadn't done a lick of business since he'd come to Atlanta.

She said, "No, keep it private. Debits and credits, I assume, as in any business."

"Yes, exactly." He returned the ledger to its shelf. "I also keep a daybook with notes on patients: the reason they consult me, the symptoms I observe, any diagnoses, and prescriptions. If they return, I have a medical history to refer to."

"And all that is even more private. Between you and the patient and no one else."

He nodded.

"How many patients does a doctor see in a day?"

He wasn't embarrassed or taken aback. "In a new practice, several a day. In an established practice, a dozen or more."

"So the strike fund could have dozens of people applying for reimbursement every week, for reasons they'd rather not tell us about or let us know by reading their receipts."

"I see where you're going, Miss Coldbrook."

"I don't know yet. You're ahead of me. What are you thinking?" In college, she found mathematics dull, but this dry subject interested her.

Perhaps because Dr. Chesney interested her as well.

He said, "It would make more sense to leave the record-keeping to me. I could summarize the visits in a way that assured the patient's privacy and report them to the Washing Society that way."

"How would the patients get their money?"

"There would be no need for that. I would treat any member of the Washing Society free of charge."

"So we'd only have to reimburse you."

"It's too much to leave to trust, Miss Coldbrook. Hence the need for careful record-keeping and accounting. Whatever would satisfy the Washing Society."

She laughed. "Whatever would satisfy me, since I'd have to examine the records."

"It would also have to satisfy the people who disburse the funds. Would that be Mrs. Gardiner?"

"Yes. We should put our minds to this, as Mrs. Gardiner says, to understand what information would be necessary. I wouldn't want to burden you, Dr. Chesney. We want you to doctor, not to keep records."

"We're in agreement in that, Miss Coldbrook."

They smiled at each other at the same time. His manner put her at ease.

He said, "I understand you just graduated from Atlanta University."

"Yes, the heavens ring with the news in Summerhill."

"They're proud of you," he said. "My family never tires of boasting of my medical degree. What did you study there?"

"The general course. Arts and sciences. Now you're going to ask me what I planned to do with my degree, teach or missionarize."

"Did you want to do those things?"

"Evidently not. I was casting about for something useful to do with myself, and it turned out to be the Washing Society."

He leaned forward, and she caught a whiff of wintergreen. "You could hardly have anticipated the washerwomen's strike!"

"No, but it was the right thing. For me as well as the washerwomen."

"What drew you? A college graduate, not a washerwoman yourself?"

"A Black woman nonetheless, Dr. Chesney." She held out her hands, with their unmarred skin and buffed nails.

"That's not something you forget, if you look in the mirror every day."

"Or if you walk down the street in Atlanta every day."

He sighed. "Yes, as I well know."

She leaned forward. "You told Mrs. Gardiner that you wanted to help Black people less fortunate than yourself. So you can understand my feeling about that, too."

"What does your mother think about it?"

"She wants me to stay out of trouble. She grew up in slavery and had a run-in with the Klan after the war. She never tires of reminding me of the difficulty the world can make for a Black woman."

"My older sister is a fighter. She's passionate about equality for Black people and for women. So far she's only fought with her pen, writing for the *Christian Recorder* in Philadelphia. But my mother worries about her, too."

"Is she married?"

"No. She says that there are a few things she has to do first. If that means righting all the world's wrongs, I'm afraid she'll never get around to it." He shook his head. "My dear, difficult sister."

No wonder Dr. Franklin Chesney got along so well with strong women. He had grown up surrounded by them.

"Dr. Chesney, do you think I've been forward with you?"

Now he laughed, a real laugh, a guffaw that came from deep in his chest. "Miss Coldbrook, you've come with an idea that could give me a living doctoring Black people in Atlanta. I can hardly fault you for it."

She had never worked alongside a man to do something useful and important in the world. She hadn't realized that it could be such a pleasure.

~

On Wheat Street, Eliza ran into Ben, who looked wilted in his business suit. His shoulders were slumped. She stopped on the sidewalk to say, "We haven't seen you for a while."

"Walk with me."

"Still no luck in finding a position?"

"No, not a bit."

"You could visit us nonetheless," she said. "My mother would be glad to see you."

"I can't. I wouldn't feel right." He sighed. "I can't go back home. There's nothing for me there. And I don't know how I'll find something in Atlanta."

He meant something dignified. Worthy of an Atlanta University graduate. "Might the Post Office be hiring?"

With scorn, he said, "That's a patronage job, and you know it. Do I have the connections to get a position as a post office clerk?"

She shook her head.

"What about you?" he asked. "What brings you to Shermantown?"

She felt a twinge about Dr. Chesney. "I was visiting my mother."

"Are you still occupied with the Washing Society?"

"Yes," she said in irritation. "I do what I can to help."

"I don't like it."

She thought of Dr. Chesney, with his ready smile, his smell of wintergreen, and his sense of purpose. "You don't have to. I'm not doing it for you, and I'm not giving it up for you, either."

"Eliza," he said, reaching for her hand. "Let's not

bicker. I've never felt so low. Can't you give a fellow a little sugar?"

She let her hand rest in his. His fingers, like his face, were damp with the heat. She wondered if Dr. Chesney had a sweaty touch or a cool one. She felt a surge of guilt. She and Ben weren't formally engaged, but before they graduated, they had an understanding to have an understanding about getting married. She should be embarrassed for being so spiteful to him. "I'm sorry, Ben. Don't stay away. None of us cares if you have a position or not. Come to see us when we're at home on Sunday afternoon."

He patted her hand. "I might."

She knew that he was still ashamed, and he was unlikely to call. But he stood up a little straighter. Her slight encouragement boosted him. He let go of her hand, and they parted to go their separate ways, in opposite directions down Wheat Street.

THE NEXT MORNING, ELIZA SAT IN MRS. GARDINER'S parlor and explained the idea for reimbursement that she and Dr. Chesney had shared. Recalling it, she thought of his compassionate look and warm smile, and she felt a delight unsuited to a matter of business. Did men feel a similar exhilaration as they did business? She'd never given it a thought.

Mrs. Gardiner said, "So he make an account, and we look at it. Or you do, and tell me what it say."

It bothered her to think that this competent woman couldn't read. "Mrs. Gardiner, if you'd like to learn how to read, I'd be glad to teach you or find someone who can."

"Miss Eliza, I try to learn, more than once. Them letters swim before my eyes, and I can't make head or tail of them."

"Would spectacles help?"

"No, my eyes just fine. Can't see them letters, that's all."

Eliza sighed. "I'll be your amanuensis."

"Dear Lord, what is that?"

"Fancy word for clerk."

Mrs. Gardiner said, "Save them fancy words for Dr. Chesney." She looked thoughtful. "Even though the bank know me as the president of the Washing Society, Reverend Jones have to sign for money, since I can't write. But we can put you down as an officer of the Society so you can sign, too." She thought again. "Do the doctor have his own account with a bank?"

"I don't know, but I can ask him."

"Because if he do, the Washing Society can write him a check. Our bank to his. Don't have to tote any cash around."

Eliza said, "My mother has a bank account for her company. She writes checks all the time."

"There you go. We take you to the bank, let them know you can write checks on behalf of the Society. Then you all set."

Eliza felt warmth creep through her. "I've never written a check. Just watched my mother do it."

Mrs. Gardiner gave her an odd look. "Your mama know all about business. Don't she school you?"

"No. I don't think she wants me to follow in her footsteps."

Mrs. Gardiner drew in her breath. "Do your mama know that you been talking to Dr. Chesney?"

"She told me that she doesn't mind if I help the Washing Society as long as I stay out of trouble. What kind of trouble can I get into in Dr. Chesney's office, talking to him about his accounts?"

Mrs. Gardiner laughed. "Young gentleman and young lady? Can't imagine."

Eliza felt her cheeks grow hot. "We've been very businesslike. Is it wrong for me to see him on business?"

"I tease you. I know your mama want you to be a lady. But being ladylike don't help with the strike."

"I'm beginning to see that."

"Your mama want to hold you close because she cherish you. But you a grown woman. Old enough to act for yourself and to keep some things to yourself. I let you tell her, if you want to."

"I know how you feel about trouble, Mrs. Gardiner. I promise you there won't be any trouble," Eliza said, even though a striker's potential trouble with the police wasn't the same as a young lady's with a doctor.

Mrs. Gardiner looked thoughtful. "Since the strike, we all do things we never expect to do. You the treasurer of the Society now, and we tell the bank you have permission to draw against our deposit."

THE ATLANTA NATIONAL BANK WAS SMALLER AND LESS imposing that Eliza expected, a classical building of red brick and limestone with its name emblazoned on the façade, and for good measure, the word "Bank" was sculpted just over the door. A white man brushed by them, giving them a scornful look. Eliza hesitated, asking Mrs. Gardiner, "Should we go in?"

Mrs. Gardiner shook her head at the white man's rudeness. "Well, they won't be glad to see us, but the Washing Society have a thousand dollars in an account. I reckon our money is as good as anyone's."

Eliza swallowed hard and followed Mrs. Gardiner within.

The interior was no more imposing than the façade: a large room divided by stone pillars, and against the far wall, a counter where the cashiers sat. At this hour, the bank was empty. A young white man, starched inside his business suit, approached them to demand, "What are you doing here?"

Mrs. Gardiner drew herself up. "We have business here, sir."

"What business? We don't hire women as porters."

Eliza knew she shouldn't bother to feel anger. She couldn't help herself. In her best Atlanta University diction, she said, "Sir, we represent a charitable organization called the Washing Society. The Society has a substantial account here. I'm the treasurer, and I need the authority to write checks against the account."

The man said, "You're a might uppity nigger, aren't you?"

The cashiers, all three of them, watched this exchange with interest. Eliza thought, *Why is there always a crowd to witness a Black person's humiliation?*

Mrs. Gardiner tried a placating tone. "Sir, if we could see your head cashier, Mr. Batchelder. He know me. We talk when I set up the account."

"How do I know you're telling the truth?"

"Sir, please, ask him if he know Mrs. Gardiner. He remember me, I'm sure of it."

"I believe he's occupied."

"Sir, it only take a moment to ask."

One of the cashiers disappeared into a back room.

"I'm going to have to ask you to leave," the man said.

"Please, sir," Mrs. Gardiner said.

Pleading for the use of our own money! Eliza thought. If it were up to her, she would stuff the Washing Society's money under her bed and let the National Bank of Atlanta starve for lack of funds.

A portly man with old-fashioned muttonchop whiskers emerged from the back. He said, "I hear there's a disturbance."

Mrs. Gardiner said, "Mr. Batchelder, we meet when I open an account for the Pleasant Grove Church. I come with Reverend Jones. Do you recall, sir?"

Mr. Batchelder stared at Mrs. Gardiner. "Yes, now I recall."

"Mr. Batchelder, we come to add our treasurer's name to the account so she can sign our checks."

He shook his head. "What is this world coming to? Colored people doing business. Women writing checks."

Eliza trembled with anger. She modulated her voice against it. "Sir, I believe that Reverend Jones and Mrs. Gardiner made a substantial deposit with your bank on behalf of the church."

"As though that excuses it! All right, come in back."

Out of sight, Eliza thought. He led them into a cluttered room not much larger than a closet. He sat at the desk, not inviting them to sit, and for the fifteen minutes that it took to establish Eliza's identity and affix her signature, they transacted their business in discomfort.

He snatched the paper away and said, "Get on with you," as though they were slaves who loitered in the yard instead of women of business with a thousand dollars deposited in his bank.

Mrs. Gardiner said, "Good day to you, sir," returning his rudeness with politeness, a form of subtle insolence common to slaves before the war. When the two of them returned to the sidewalk, Eliza had never been gladder to breathe the stink of the Atlanta streets.

ELIZA CALLED ON DR. CHESNEY AGAIN. THIS TIME, HE HAD no visitors. She teased, "Have you run out of wise women to talk to?"

"I could talk to them for weeks, but now I need some patients to see instead."

"I have good news for you."

"Are you ill?"

She laughed. "No. Better news than that. Mrs. Gardiner likes our idea for reimbursement. I'll tell her what your accounts say, and she'll need to approve them. I don't foresee we'll have difficulty."

"That is good news."

"And I've been appointed the Society's treasurer, so I can write the checks myself."

"Checks? High finance." He was teasing her again.

"The Society has an account at the National Bank of Atlanta. Do you have an account with a bank here?"

"Yes, I do, also at the National Bank of Atlanta. I had

God's own trouble getting them to open an account for me."

"They don't think that Black people have money. Or should have money."

His eyes glittered. "Let's prove them wrong."

"Yes, let's."

"How will you inform the Washing Society members about the new arrangement?"

"We can start tonight at one of our meetings. You should attend! We'll introduce you."

"I'd be glad of that."

She laughed, and he asked, "What is it?"

"Or I could just tell my friend, Mrs. Ophelia Taylor. The news would be all over Atlanta in an hour."

"Is she a gossip?"

"Yes, and she's also our best organizer."

Dr. Chesney and the plan would be public property by tomorrow morning. She wanted to relish the privacy of their initial effort for just a little longer. She held out her hand. "To a successful partnership, Dr. Chesney."

He shook it. "With my appreciation, Miss Coldbrook." His hand was dry in the Atlanta heat, and pleasantly warm. A healer's touch, and for her, more than that.

THE WASHERWOMEN APPLAUDED WHEN DR. CHESNEY WAS introduced at the meeting at Pleasant Grove and cheered at the news of the doctoring plan. Many of them were impressed by more than his education and medical expertise. Eliza heard one washerwoman say to another, "I hear the doctor ain't married. Maybe he want to court my girl."

The other scoffed, "Your girl? She can't even read. If he marry, he want someone educated like Miss Eliza."

Eliza smothered a laugh.

Within a week, Dr. Chesney had sent her an accounting, and she was glad to read it to Mrs. Gardiner. "He seem to do well, now that the Washing Society pay for doctoring," she said.

"Wasn't that the idea?"

Checkbook in her pocket, she went to call on Dr. Chesney at his office. When she opened the door, the office was crowded with a half dozen women. "If you here to see Doctor Chesney," one of them said, "you have to wait."

"I'm not ill," she said. "It's a matter of business. I'll come back later."

She returned late in the afternoon, hoping to find him as he was about to close. He sat at his desk, which was littered with receipts, and said, "I haven't had time to enter them in the daybook or the ledger. Thank the Lord, I never have a free moment!" He laughed. "I had to buy a set of chairs for the waiting room because so many patients come that they have to sit and wait!"

"I'm so glad to hear it," she said, and they basked together in the pleasure of his success.

"Was Mrs. Gardiner satisfied with the accounting?"

She nodded. She pulled the checkbook from her pocket with a flourish. "I'm here to reimburse you." She leaned on the desk and opened the checkbook.

"Ah, the sweetest words I could possibly hear."

She looked up, laughing. "For a man of business. I would hate to think that those are the sweetest words you'll ever hear."

"They won't be." He was teasing her.

"Hand me the pen." She dipped it in the inkwell and held the pen over the check.

"Don't hesitate," he said. "You'll have a blot."

"This is the first check I've ever written."

"Now you're a woman of business."

"I am," she said, pleased at their common happiness, and she filled out the check and signed her name in a large, impressive signature completely unlike the ladylike way she signed her letters to friends. She handed him the check. "To your continued success, Dr. Chesney."

He took it. "To my continued gratitude to you, for assuring it."

CHAPTER 12

IT AIN'T YOUR FIGHT

THE DOOR of the *Beacon's* office opened with a crash, and Nina came in, waving a large brown envelope in the air like a flag at a Fourth of July parade.

"Your article about the strike?" Mr. Endicott asked.

She handed him the envelope. "I made as clean a copy as I could manage." She grinned at Matt.

"Let me see, my dear. The editor's eye, you know."

"Oh, no changes!" Matt joked.

Endicott scanned the copy. He picked up a pen and scratched out a word to substitute another. And another. And yet another. "Just a little trimming here and there."

Nina held out her hand. "You took out my favorite sentence!" she said, pretending to be offended.

"Your most judgmental sentence. You didn't need it."

"Editors!" she said, handing the edited copy to Matt. "They're like cats. They have to walk on it to prove they were there."

Matt smothered a laugh and picked up his pen as Nina left.

After he read the piece, he no longer felt like laughing. He asked Mr. Endicott, "Do you ever worry about Miss Birnbaum's safety?"

He had never seen Endicott look so grave. "All the time, young man. All the time."

"Have you told her to be careful?"

Endicott sighed. "Yes. She promises me that she will, and then she does exactly as she likes."

Nina returned at midday, after Mr. Endicott left for his dinner. "Shall we go to Mrs. Harper's?" she asked Matt.

He was still writing. "In a moment."

"You read my piece?" She perched on the corner of his desk, an odd intimacy. The smell of soap wafted from her. Not the scented soap that ladies used, but the plain, harsh soap used to launder.

He put down his pen and nodded. Despite the worry that gnawed at him, he took Endicott's words to heart. *Don't press her*, he thought. "Are you getting your laundry done?"

"Don't worry. I'm not breaking the strike. I rinse out my things in a basin at night. My mother and I always looked after ourselves like that."

"Maybe you could teach me. I can't tell you how much I want a clean shirt. When do you think the strike will be over?"

"How much do you want a clean shirt? Are you desperate?"

He laughed. "Very near."

"I'll tell the ladies at the Washing Society."

"I liked your piece. It did its work. It made me angry."

"Good!"

"And it made me worry, too. I see that the police have been bothering the strikers."

Nina shifted her weight on the desk. Her tone was blithe. "Oh, they've bothered me, too."

He sighed. "Nina, be careful."

"When my mother lectured on abolition in the South, she had threats on her life. So I have a lot to live up to."

"This is serious. It could be dangerous."

"Mrs. Gardiner, the head of the Washing Society, says the same thing."

"She knows what she's talking about. When she was a girl, the slave patrollers, the slave catchers, were the police."

"Matt! We live in the city of Atlanta, not in some godforsaken corner of Georgia!"

"I grew up there," he said. "I haven't forgotten it, not a bit."

His concern about Nina didn't upset him. It warmed him. It was an unaccustomed pleasure to care about someone in Atlanta. As they returned from their midday dinner, he asked her, "May I call on you at the Endicotts'?"

"Why would you want to call on me? You can talk to me whenever you like."

"I thought it would be pleasant to see each other when we aren't working."

She said, "I have a better idea. I'll wrangle you an invitation to Sunday dinner."

When his face fell, she said, "Mrs. Endicott will be delighted to see you."

"But I want to see you."

"You will. At the dinner table."

And the next day, Mr. Endicott issued the invitation. "My wife worries that you might feel lonely."

Matt spoke carefully. "Sir, may I presume?"

"You never presume, my dear boy."

The endearment warmed him. "Did Miss Birnbaum put you up to this?"

He got a sly look. "Did she? I've always told her that even freethinkers need a day of rest. Please, join us."

On Sunday, he pulled his best suit from the clothes press. He rummaged in his father's room, hoping for any kind of clean shirt. He had to resort to the shirt that was the least noxious.

If the Endicotts noticed or objected, he would remind them of the words on the masthead of the *Beacon* about the dignity of labor.

But if Laura Endicott could tell that his linen was unwashed, she was much too polite to say. She settled him in the parlor and sent for a cool drink, and when it arrived, she inquired after his happiness and his comfort. She glanced affectionately at her husband, who was on the floor, letting his littlest son ride him like a pony, and at Nina, who rubbed the dog's ears and said to him, in affection, "Teaser, you bad dog, you!" She wore a summer dress in lightweight striped cotton. Was that Laura Endicott's doing? Nina must have balked, even though the dress suited her. She didn't seem to care that the dog shed fur on it.

Mrs. Endicott said to Matt, "It's pandemonium here, as usual. Thomas, get up and say something cordial to young Mr. Kaltenbach."

Mr. Endicott looked up. He was red in the face. "We're very glad to see you, aren't we?" He panted a little as he tousled his youngest son's hair. The boy laughed and grabbed his father's leg.

Matt wondered if his own father had ever shown him that kind of affection. He said, "Likewise," glancing at Nina, and her cheeks were also pink, but not with exertion. She rubbed her cheek on the dog's head.

At the table, Mr. Endicott announced, "Nina's article about the strike will be published in next week's issue."

"After you rewrote it for her, I bet," his wife teased.

"Not at all. I was very pleased with it."

"And you wore yourself out to make a clean copy, didn't you?" she said to Matt.

"Mrs. Endicott, I never weary of my tasks at the *Beacon*," he said, with a sly sideways glance at his employer.

Laura Endicott laughed. "Thomas, do you hear that? Mr. Kaltenbach feels enough at ease to josh you."

"I would hope so, Laura. He's one of the family now."

Matt had to duck his head as affection washed through him.

Mrs. Endicott said, "The washerwomen have taken to Nina. One of the organizers has befriended her, and after that, all of them were willing to talk to her."

"Mrs. Gardiner?" Matt asked.

"No, a Miss Coldbrook. An educated young woman of color with lovely manners, too. If she weren't your source, Nina, I'd hope she would be your friend."

"Miss Eliza Coldbrook?" Matt asked.

"Yes. Do you know her?"

He hoped that Laura Endicott, unlike clever Nina Birnbaum, didn't know German. "I know the family."

She looked at him with a curious expression. "For someone who hasn't lived in Georgia since you were small, you seem to know many people in Atlanta."

He thought, *I know my own relatives, even if they won't speak to me*. Suddenly, he was careful to be polite. "Atlanta is a small place, as you know, Mrs. Endicott."

After they rose from the table, the parlor seemed stifling, even with the curtains drawn against the sun. Nina picked up the discarded newspaper from the settee and fanned herself with it. Mrs. Endicott smiled indulgently at her. "Nina, why don't you show Mr. Kaltenbach the garden? It's always shady under the arbor. Much cooler than indoors."

Nina blushed again. Matt hoped she wouldn't call Teaser to take him along. "Shall we?" she asked him, and he held out his arm as though they were going on a promenade.

The garden, like the house, showed the hand of someone with money who loved to display it. The beds had been planted with every deeply fragrant, showy shrub that could grow in Atlanta. Magnolias competed with roses in every hue from deepest red to purest white. Heavy clusters of wisteria, both purple and white, enveloped the arbor.

"It is cooler here," Nina said, as they sat on the bench in the arbor, lifting her hair from her neck.

"You look different today."

Nina blushed again. In the dappled shade, under the oaks that had grown tall and thick since the war ended, she looked girlish and pretty. "Mrs. Endicott shoehorned me into this dress."

"I like Mrs. Endicott, very much."

"They both like you, too. They mean it when they say you're like a member of the family."

"I don't mind," he said. "After the way my own family has behaved, it's good to be welcome somewhere."

"You're welcome at the *Beacon*. I hope you know that."

"More than welcome, I'd hope."

"Matt, don't flirt with me, I can't promise to be any good at it."

He teased, "Do you ever do things you aren't good at? To get better at them?"

"I'm not interested in beguiling." She hesitated. "Suitors."

That gave him hope. "But sources, that's a different story."

"That is different. I gain their trust."

"So you've become quite friendly with my—" He caught himself. "Eliza."

"I like her. She likes me, too."

"Don't deny it. You've beguiled her." He thought of a friendship between Nina and Eliza, and he tried to tease. He didn't manage it. "How did you do it? I wish I could."

"I'm not a Southerner. And I'm not related to her."

"I can't help that," he said. He shook his head. "Why is she so angry with me?"

"Matt, what happened in Cass County?"

Startled, he said, "Did she tell you?"

"She wouldn't tell me. All I know is that it bothers her. Upsets her. Probably frightens her."

In this lovely, scented yard, he recalled the smell of

smoke. He rested his hands on his knees. "It was a long time ago."

"So was the war. And no one's forgotten that, either."

He turned toward her. "Nina, today of all days, can we put that away? I came out here to tease you and flirt with you, even if you don't want me to. Can you give me that? What Southerners call a little sugar?"

"I'm sorry. I've overpowered you again. I shouldn't talk to a friend the way I interview a source. I know it isn't right." She reached out and tapped the back of his hand with her ink-stained finger. "Forgive me?"

Her touch brought him back to the present. The past faded away. "Only if you promise me something, Nina Ariadne Birnbaum."

"Am I in trouble? My mother used to call me that when I was in trouble."

"No, not if you promise me. Will you?" Now he was flirting shamelessly, but he had the upper hand. He had made her feel guilty.

"What are you asking?"

"To take a promenade with me. And to talk to me as a friend. Can you promise that?"

She let her finger rest on his hand. "Yes." She looked up. "Is that enough?"

He turned his hand over and closed his palm over her finger. "For now," he said, teasing her.

"What happens later?"

"We'll see," he said, feeling happier than he had in weeks.

～

THAT MONDAY, AS THEY WALKED BACK TO THE OFFICE FROM Mrs. Harper's, Matt asked Nina, "Do you attend meetings of the Washing Society every night?"

"Not every night. But often."

"Could I come to one of them?"

"Men do come to the meetings. Husbands or fathers of washerwomen. And a few white washerwomen attend, too."

"Would I stand out?"

"Yes." She rested her hand on his arm, and he wished that he could take her hand. "Is this about the Washing Society or about Eliza?"

"Both."

She sighed. "Why do you want to go where you know you aren't welcome?"

"Has that ever stopped you?"

"I'm not related to anyone in Atlanta. Black or white."

"Where is the meeting? What time is it?"

She met his gaze, and he was struck anew by how lovely her eyes were. She couldn't hide that the way she hid her shape. "There's a meeting tonight at Pleasant Grove Church in Summerhill. At seven. I believe Eliza will be there."

MATT HAD SEEN THE WOMEN WALKING TO CHURCH, BUT HE hadn't realized that they were washerwomen on strike. Tonight, a few minutes before seven, he shut the door behind him and walked into the still-hot, magnolia-scented air to mingle with the crowd. Some of the women gave him a wide berth. Even in Summerhill, where a Black person was loath to walk in the street, they deferred to prevent trouble. Others, who recognized him, didn't greet him. One of them murmured to the friend who accompanied her, "That's young Mr. Kaltenbach. He Mr. Henry's boy."

Matt had passed Pleasant Grove Baptist Church many times, but he had never been inside. An indifferent Jew, he felt a twinge of discomfort at setting foot in a church. The entryway was so crowded that he didn't want to use his prerogative as a white man to part the crowd. Ill at ease, he lingered near the door, taking in the smell of sweat and starch that emanated from this gathering and the smell of greens and bacon that wafted from somewhere else in the building.

To his relief, he saw Nina and waved to get her attention. She moved easily through this throng, smiling, chatting, touching an arm in amity, or stroking the hair of a child. He overheard someone call her "Miss Nina." *They like her*, he thought.

She said, "I'll find you a place to sit. The pews will be full. It's like this in every Black church, all over town. Packed every night."

"Do you feel strange being in a church? As a Jew?"

"I'm not here to pray."

She took his arm, which sent a shiver of pleasure through him until he realized that she was defusing his presence with her own. She led him into the church proper.

He glanced around the room, struck by how plain it was: unadorned white walls and a pulpit bare of decoration save a simple wooden cross. He was used to the Reform temple in San Francisco, which modeled itself on a German Lutheran church. Sherith Israel sported stained glass windows that dramatized scenes from the Old Testament.

A familiar figure tripped down the aisle in a white dress he recognized from the disastrous Sunday dinner: Eliza. Seeing him, her face fell. "What are you doing here?" she demanded.

"I wanted to support the strikers."

"Give some money to the Washing Society strike fund."

"I'd hope I can help more than that."

She raised her voice. "We don't need your help."

Nina said, "Eliza—"

Eliza put her hands on her hips, as his aunt Rachel did when she was angry. Now Eliza stared at Matt with eyes afire with dislike. She spoke loud enough for anyone in the front pews to hear. "This ain't your fight!"

She lost her educated diction in her ire, just as her mother did.

Someone seated in a nearby pew asked, "Miss Eliza, do this man bother you?" Her voice carried as well as Eliza's. Before Matt could reply, a well-dressed, dignified man hurried down the aisle. "Is there some problem here?" His voice was mellifluous, and it wasn't hard to guess who he was.

Nina said, "Reverend Carter, this is Matthew Kaltenbach, who works with me at the *Beacon*."

"There's a Mr. Henry Kaltenbach who is a good friend to Atlanta's people of color. Is there a connection?"

Nina put a restraining hand on Matt's arm. "Father and son. Reverend Carter, all of us at the *Beacon* are in sympathy with the strike. Mr. Kaltenbach hopes to support the strike and help the strikers."

Reverend Carter glanced at Eliza, then at Matt. "I see."

A Black woman he didn't know, who would be stately when she wasn't in such a hurry, propelled herself down the aisle. She scolded, "Eliza! What is this fracas you're making?"

The women who crowded the pews watched with interest. Matt heard smothered laughter.

"Mrs. Gardiner," Nina said, and introductions were made afresh.

She asked Nina, "Is this Mr. Henry Kaltenbach's—"

Nina interrupted her. "Yes."

Mrs. Gardiner repeated the reverend's quick glance, from Eliza to Matt himself. He saw sadness as well as understanding on her face. "Young sir, you're welcome to stay, but it's best if you set quietly in the back."

"No, I really should go."

He walked away quickly, his head down, and this time the crowd in the entryway parted for him as easily as the Red Sea parted for Moses. Once on the sidewalk, he didn't look back. He kept his gaze on the pavement.

He was furious with himself and just as angry at Eliza. He thought he was past being hurt by Eliza. He'd been wrong.

That night, even though he wished for a glass of whiskey, he denied it to himself. He fell into an uneasy sleep, and the nightmare came to him in full force. The burning schoolhouse. The shouts of the Klansmen and the screams from the crowd. The sound of shots and the frenzied cry. "They're killing us!" Himself and Eliza as children, their arms around each other, in too much terror to comfort each other.

THAT MORNING, NINA CAME TO THE *BEACON*'S OFFICE JUST after he and Mr. Endicott had settled down with the morning coffee. Mr. Endicott said, "Nina, my dear! A pleasure to see you. No strikers to talk to today?"

"There are always strikers to talk to. I came to see Matt. Can you spare him?"

He had never gotten back to sleep, and now his head ached. "I'm right here. You can talk to me," he said, not hiding his irritation.

She walked up to his desk and stood before him, her hands on her hips. "Mr. Kaltenbach, may I take you from your labors for a few minutes?"

Matt rose and Nina said, "Walk with me." She held out her arm, but he shook his head. Today he was angry with her, too.

She led him into the alley behind the *Beacon*'s office building, a strip of dirt bordered by a rutted path big enough for a wagon. Commercial buildings, two-story, three-story and taller, hemmed in the space on both sides and cast it into shadow. The alley, like the street, smelled of mud and manure. It was a spot that suited his misery this morning.

She said, "I am so sorry about what happened last night."

His head throbbed and he erupted in anger. "Stop apologizing for her! That ain't your fight, either!" He turned and strode away.

She ran after him and reached for his hand. Short of breath, she said, "It seems to be. Since I care about both of you."

He pulled his hand away. "All you care about is being a reporter. All you care about is getting a story. There's nothing else you care about."

"That's not true," she said, in the smallest voice he had ever heard from her.

"I don't see it." He turned toward the other end of the alley and began to walk.

She followed him. "Matt!"

The alley dead-ended. He was trapped here with her. With his back to her, he said, "Leave me alone." His voice was shaky.

"I won't. What's wrong? I've never felt less like a reporter. Tell me as a friend."

The dream and the memories returned, and he felt sick with both. Nina tapped him on the shoulder, and he turned around. "She acts as though she hates me. Can't she remember? I haven't forgotten. I'll never forget."

"Forget what?" Her voice was soft.

"Cass County. What happened in Cass County."

"What was it?"

Now that he'd stirred up the memories, he couldn't bear to talk about them. He shook his head.

She said, "Eliza won't talk about it, either."

He jerked his head up. "How do you know that?"

"It came up when Eliza and her mother were arguing. It upset her terribly, and she wouldn't tell me why."

The memories deluged him. He looked at Nina without seeing her.

She grasped his wrist. Her fingers were roughened, as

though she labored at something harder than writing. "Tell me."

"It's too awful to say."

"Tell me," she repeated, and nothing ever sounded less like a reporter's inquiry. Her voice was a croon. It was a caress.

He had never described the terror of that night to anyone, not even his mother and stepfather, who had soothed his nightmares long after they left Georgia. Now he let his hand rest in Nina's. He met her eyes, which were dark with compassion, and he told her.

CHAPTER 13

DISORDERLY CONDUCT

Eliza's outburst at Pleasant Grove hadn't gone unnoticed. The next morning, when she met Ophelia to go canvassing, Ophelia asked her, "Why you yell at young Mr. Kaltenbach last night?"

Eliza had spent a restless night waking up several times in a sweat of embarrassment. She snapped, "Don't you have anything better to do than gossip about people?"

"Kin or not, it ain't a good idea to raise your voice to a white man."

"I'm well aware of that."

"You don't act like it. And he is your kin. Even if you don't claim him and don't like him. That even more disrespectful."

Eliza glared at Ophelia. "Did you ever meet a Black woman who was forced by her master?"

"That don't even bear asking."

"If your massa forced your mother, would his son be your brother?"

Ophelia said, "We all know Mr. Henry, and that ain't

the truth here. Everyone understand that he love Miss Rachel, God help both of them. You can't be mad at your daddy for getting married first and having a white son. And you shouldn't be mad at that white boy for who his daddy is."

Guilt whipped through her like a tornado. Eliza raised her voice, even louder than last night. "You can go out by yourself today. I don't want to listen to you."

Ophelia shrugged and walked away.

THAT EVENING AT THE DINNER TABLE, HER MOTHER WAITED until Eliza filled her plate. In the hearing of her doting father, her inquisitive brother, and her clever little sister, her mother asked, "What's this I hear about you and Matthew Kaltenbach last night at Pleasant Grove Baptist? Did you really shame him away from the Washing Society meeting? At the top of your lungs, and in public?"

"Where did you hear that?" Eliza asked, even though anyone in Summerhill or Shermantown could have told her.

"Mrs. Gardiner came to see me. She doesn't care whether you act like a lady. But she wants you to act sensible, and that means decorum in public. You can say whatever you like about Matt in private, even though I wish you wouldn't. But you don't air our family's dirty laundry"— she paused, relishing the bad pun—"before half of Atlanta."

Eliza sulked. "You don't like my being involved with the Washing Society."

"I've lost that battle. I just want you to be prudent. And

careful. Henry, you tell her. She'll listen to you. Remind her that a Black woman can still get hurt, even in Atlanta in 1881."

Cass County again. "You don't have to remind me."

"Don't I? You seem to have forgotten."

She hadn't forgotten. The smell of magnolia that drifted through the windows reminded her. That night, in Cass County, magnolia blossom had fought with the fug of smoke and cordite. The memory made her feel too queasy to eat. "May I be excused?"

Her mother said sharply, "Stay and eat your dinner. I know the Washing Society doesn't meet until seven."

THAT NIGHT, ELIZA WOKE FROM THE ALL-TOO-FAMILIAR nightmare. She sat up in bed, sweating and shivering at once. Her mother stood in the doorway in her nightdress, her hair bound in a scarf, her eyes puffy with sleep. "Eliza? Are you all right?"

"Did I wake you?"

"You were crying in your sleep."

A small figure in a white nightdress appeared beside her mother. "Mama? Why are you awake?"

Her mother hugged Ada. "It's all right, sugar. Eliza had a bad dream."

Ada cast a worried look at her sister. "Was it about those bad men? The men in the Klan?"

How did she know? Did all Black children lose their innocence about violence and danger, just as white children lost their faith in the Easter Bunny? Eliza sat up straight, even though she felt dizzy. "There are no bad men here. We're perfectly safe here in Atlanta."

When she was younger, her mother had come into her room to comfort her, enfold her into an embrace, and stroke her hair until she was soothed enough to fall asleep again. Now, neither her mother nor her sister moved or replied. They all listened to the familiar nighttime sound of the crickets.

Her mother glanced at Eliza, who thought, *Leave me alone so I can stop pretending I'm all right.* Her mother sighed. "Let's all go back to sleep."

THE NEXT DAY, WHEN NINA APPEARED ON THE FRONT STEPS of the Coldbrook house, her first words to Eliza were, "You don't look well."

"Just tired." She'd awakened with a headache that wouldn't go away.

"I'm going to talk to Mrs. Gardiner this afternoon. Will you come with me?"

Eliza leaned against the doorframe. The headache sapped her strength. "Why? So she can chastise me, too?"

"For what? You're doing fine by the Washing Society, as far as I can tell."

"For losing my temper at the meeting the other night."

Nina laughed. "That? That's nothing. People lose their tempers all the time."

Her head hurt so much that she spoke without censoring. "I made a fool of myself."

"Did you?"

"If there was anyone who didn't know that Matthew Kaltenbach was my brother, they know now."

Nina said, "I thought he was your kin but not your brother, as you explained it to me once."

"Don't twist my words. I can't argue with you. My head aches too much."

"Eliza, he cares about the connection. It matters to him. He still remembers your childhood together."

Eliza shook her head.

Nina said, "He remembers Cass County." When Eliza didn't reply, Nina said, "He has nightmares, remembering it."

Tears started in her eyes, and Eliza turned her head away. In a low, hoarse voice, she said, "Go see Mrs. Gardiner without me. I don't feel well. I'm going to lie down."

THE POLICEMAN WHO STOPPED THEM ON WHEAT STREET was now on duty during the day, and he and a partner began to follow the canvassers. Mrs. Gardiner reminded them that anything might start trouble. Every canvasser became adept at pretending she was on a social call or in a discussion about church business.

Mrs. Gardiner had said to Eliza, "You keep your temper low and your mouth shut."

"Yes, ma'am," Eliza said, too tired to explain that she understood the prejudices of the police just fine. She reserved her ire for her relations.

Mrs. Gardiner was equally sharp with Nina. "The same goes for you. Don't try anything like that business last time, when you sass the police. You act like that, you start trouble. The police just itching for trouble with us."

"I know."

"Then you behave yourself."

"I don't like it," Nina said.

"You think we do? As long as you with us, you stay low. Because if any trouble start, being white don't spare you. You in as much danger as any Black woman."

In the wet heat of an Atlanta summer, Eliza felt so cold that she wrapped her arms around herself. Unbidden, she remembered the night that haunted her dreams. Matt had held her like that, in a tight grip born of fear.

THAT AFTERNOON, ELIZA AND OPHELIA STOOD ON WHEAT Street with Mrs. Gardiner and Mrs. Bell from Jenningstown. They found themselves a spot where they weren't obstructing anyone on the sidewalk. They spoke in quiet tones as they planned on how they would visit the courtyard behind Houston Street, where the washer-women in Shermantown gathered to work before the strike and where they now congregated to bolster each other to keep the strike going.

The Wheat Street policeman ambled up to them, staring at all four of them, his hand on the club he wore at his hip like a gun. "What are you doing? You're blocking the sidewalk."

Mrs. Gardiner moved into the street, and the three of them followed her.

"You're causing trouble, aren't you?"

Mrs. Gardiner said meekly, "No, sir. We just talking among ourselves. We on church business."

"What business?"

"We collecting money for charity, sir. Our church run a charity for widows and orphans."

"In the middle of the day? Why ain't you working?"

Mrs. Gardiner gave him a dazzling, obsequious smile. "Sir, we all very lucky," she said. "Married to men who make a good living. They take care of us. We don't have to go out to work. We can do good works for our church."

Slowly, he drew out his club. "I don't believe you."

"Sir, I swear, it the truth."

"If you're loitering, I can arrest you."

"No, sir. We ain't loitering. Just about to move along. Going to the church down the street." She smiled again and took a step in the direction of Bethel A. M. E.

He blocked her path. "Did I say you could walk away?"

"Sir, we glad to move on."

He laid his club across her chest. "Stay put."

Mrs. Gardiner didn't move. Her smile faded away. Eliza began to feel deeply uneasy.

The street teemed with passersby, Black and white, but no one stopped. No one challenged the policeman. No one white cared, and no one Black wanted to get entangled in a police matter.

As they waited, five more policemen began to push through the crowd on the sidewalk. One of them shoved an old Black man into the gutter, saying, "Out of my way, nigger."

The man stared after the policemen and shook his head.

The policeman who had challenged Mrs. Gardiner said, "I'm going to take you in for disorderly conduct."

Eliza began to tremble, but Mrs. Gardiner spoke in a voice she hadn't used since the days of slavery. "We ain't being disorderly, sir."

"Are you being uppity with me?"

Mrs. Gardiner shook her head and dropped her eyes. She stood perfectly still.

The policeman said, "Uppity and disorderly." He raised the club. Eliza's breath caught in her throat. The policemen hit Mrs. Gardiner in the eye. Her hands flew to her face, and she began to moan.

Suddenly all four of them were surrounded by policemen. One of them grabbed Ophelia's arms to pull them behind her back. "I ain't done a thing!" she shouted, trying to twist free. "I ain't been disorderly!" Another policeman hit her in the face, splitting her lip. As blood gushed from her lip and dripped onto her dress, as she struggled and screamed, the second policeman hit her again.

Mrs. Bell, who had never raised her voice to anyone— she did her persuading softly, too—yelled at the top of her lungs, "How dare you! Hit a woman who ain't done a thing! What kind of a brute are you!" The exertion made her wheeze. The policeman who had hit Ophelia went after her, and before he could grab her arms, she kicked him in the shins as hard as she could. He yelped in pain and pressed his club across her neck. She wheezed so badly that Eliza was afraid she would stop breathing. In terror, Eliza screamed, "She has asthma! She can't breathe!"

Then Eliza felt the club come down on her shoulder blades. On her back. Someone was beating her, over and over, and she couldn't catch her breath to defend anyone. She bent over, too stunned to feel the pain, and someone forced her upright and grabbed her hands to pull them behind her back. She heard the handcuffs snap shut, and metal bit into her wrists.

"That's it," said the first policeman. "Handcuff them all. We'll take them to the station."

Eliza looked up. One of the policemen said, "Eyes on the ground, you nigger bitch." Before her eyes flooded with tears, before she cast them to stare at her feet, she saw the pale, horrified face of Nina Birnbaum in the crowd.

THE HANDCUFFS STAYED ON AS THEY WERE TRANSPORTED TO the station in an open wagon that exposed the shame of their arrest to everyone on the street. They stayed on as the four of them were booked, shamed again by the accusation of disorderly conduct. They stayed on as the arresting policemen rifled their pockets. Eliza carried a tiny reticule in her pocket to hold any contributions to the Washing Society. She had ten dollars in that reticule.

The handcuffs stayed on as the policeman behind the desk said to the policeman who arrested them, "I hope you don't arrest any more nigger women today. We're full up."

The policeman who arrested them said, "That ain't my problem. I arrest them, you find a place to put them."

The policeman behind the desk said, "We'll put them in with the whores. It'll be tight."

The arresting policeman laughed in derision. "They ain't here for their *comfort.*"

The handcuffs chafed Eliza's wrists, and the position of her arms made her back hurt more. She couldn't bear to look at Mrs. Gardiner, whose eye was beginning to blacken, or at Ophelia, whose dress was now soaked with blood from the cut on her lip. Her eyes filled with tears again as she thought, *My mother would die to see me like this.*

They were handed over to the jail warden, a short, bald man with an unseemly air of cheer. He led them down a dark corridor that smelled of sweat, dirt, and fear. He stopped before a barred cell, unlocked the door, and herded them inside, leaving their handcuffs on. The cell was about eight feet square, the size of a slave cabin before the war, with two narrow wooden benches on the walls facing the locked door. A bucket stood in the corner; the smell of urine from it was strong. On the bench opposite sat four beautiful women, all in fashionable silk dresses. One was older, her skin the palest brown, and the other three, a generation younger, were ivory in complexion. The younger women folded their uncuffed hands in their laps. They smelled of perfume, which failed to overpower the stink from the bucket.

The older woman asked the warden, "Are they murderers?"

"Of course not."

"Take their handcuffs off, for God's sake."

He laughed. "What will I get for it, Miss Florette?"

"Come see us after I get out."

Miraculously, the handcuffs came off, and all four of them crowded onto the empty bench. Mrs. Bell wheezed.

Eliza put her arm around her, trying to soothe her, and winced at the pain from her back.

Miss Florette gave them an appraising look. "What in God's name happened to you?"

Mrs. Gardiner put her hand to her eye. "We all washerwomen. We belong to the Washing Society. We on strike."

"Oh, so you're the ones responsible. No washing! It's been terrible for our business. No clean sheets, unless we wash them ourselves."

Speaking with difficulty, Ophelia said, "They call you whores at the desk."

"That's cruel of them. It's not true. I run a parlor house. You can see what my girls look like." She gestured toward the three lovely young women beside her. Was there a family resemblance? Were they her daughters? Eliza felt sick at the thought. Miss Florette asked, "What did they arrest you for?"

"Disorderly conduct," Mrs. Gardiner said. "And that a lie, too. We stand on the sidewalk, quiet and orderly as can be."

"Of course," Miss Florette said, as though she heard people lie all the time.

Mrs. Gardiner said, "We all good churchgoing women."

"And you see where that gets you."

Ophelia asked, "Why you in here?"

The younger women didn't speak. They looked disgusted. Miss Florette sighed. "I've never seen men as greedy as the Atlanta police. Last year we paid them plenty to leave us alone. They asked for more not three months ago. When they asked for even more a few days ago, I said, 'How do I know you won't come back in a few weeks to ask for even more?' So they arrested me and my girls. And now I'll have to pay them to let us out."

Eliza asked, "If we paid them, would they let us out?"

"That's bail, not a bribe. They didn't offer you bail?"

Eliza shook her head.

"They must have it in for you. They never lock up the disorderly conduct arrests and refuse them bail. If they did, the jails would be overflowing."

Eliza buried her face in her hands. She felt ill, and the smell of the open bucket made her feel worse.

Miss Florette said, "You won't stay here long. You'll go to court in a few days. Recorder's Court, right here in the station. Arraignment, trial, and judgment, all in an hour."

"How do you know so much about it, Miss Parlor House?" Ophelia said.

"I wasn't always in a parlor house," she said. "I started my career on the street, and believe me, I saw the inside of Recorder's Court more often than I want to remember." She cast a fond eye at the sullen, silent beauties beside her. "I've taken better care of my girls than that."

The girl sitting next to her snarled, "We're here now, ain't we?"

Within the hour, a dapper man, his complexion a no-man's-land between Black and white, came to see them, and they left, Miss Florette on his arm, the other three trailing behind.

Mrs. Gardiner said to Mrs. Bell, "You want to lie down on that bench? Would you feel any better?"

Mrs. Bell was breathing easier, but she was still wheezing. She slumped back against the wall. "Nothing make me feel better. When I get out of here, I die with the shame."

Ophelia said, "Why? You don't do anything wrong. They maul us and beat us and make up a reason to arrest us. We don't belong here. You ain't got a thing to be ashamed of." After her speech, she put her hand to her lip. In a much softer voice, she said, "It hurt when I talk." She looked down at her dress. "All over blood," she said, trying not to strain her injury.

"Eliza?" Mrs. Gardiner asked. "Eliza, sugar? How you doing?"

Eliza didn't reply. Her back and shoulders ached and burned. It was the spot where she would have been beaten, back in slavery days. The thought hurt as much as the bruises.

CHAPTER 14

THE ALLY

NINA BURST into the office with such force that she slammed the door shut. She was red and panting and her hair had flown from its pins. She cried, "Eliza's been arrested!"

Both Matt and Mr. Endicott jumped to their feet. Matt said, "Why? What happened?"

Nina stumbled into the office and leaned against Matt's desk for support. She gasped out the words. "Along with Mrs. Gardiner, Mrs. Bell, and Mrs. Taylor. Standing on the street, as innocent as can be, and all of them were beaten up and arrested for disorderly conduct!"

Mr. Endicott asked, "Are they at the police station?"

"Yes." There were sobs mingled with the gasps. "I came right here. I ran here! I didn't know what else to do."

Mr. Endicott hurried to put his arm around her shoulders. "You did absolutely right, my dear." He looked at Matt. "I know a lawyer who's represented people of color unjustly accused. Let me send word to him. He'll want to help."

Matt asked, "Does Mrs. Coldbrook know?"

Nina took a deep breath. Matt handed her a handkerchief, but she didn't wipe her face. She balled it up in her fist. "It was on Wheat Street. Plenty of people saw it. I'm sure someone told her."

"First we summon the lawyer. Depending on what he says, we—that is, the two of you, who know Mrs. Coldbrook—take him to see her."

Matt envied Mr. Endicott his ease in touching Nina to quiet her. "Let me talk to the lawyer. Nina, can you go back to Mrs. Coldbrook's office? I'll take the lawyer there."

"If she knows, she may have gone to the police station," Mr. Endicott said.

"Where is the police station?" Matt asked.

"On Pryor Street."

Matt pulled on his jacket and reached for his hat. "Mr. Endicott, how do you know so much about this?"

"I've spent more time defending the dignity of Black people than I care to mention," he said. "The lawyer's name is Sefton. John Archibald Sefton. He's on Whitehall Street." He scrawled the address on a scrap of paper.

Matt stuffed the paper into his pocket and ran out the door.

As he hurried down Whitehall Street, Matt thought of the last time he'd visited a lawyer here in a fruitless effort to find a position. Mr. Sefton's office was in the next building over, a modest three-story structure, with no one to guard the door. Matt ran up the stairs, his hand

SABRA WALDFOGEL

sliding over the worn wooden railing, his shoes echoing on the treads.

He opened the door to a modest room, the desk piled with papers, the walls lined with bookshelves. The man who sat at the desk looked up. "You were in a hurry on the stairs," he said. He was young, with dark curly hair and blue-gray eyes. He had an accent that Matt couldn't place, not quite a Southerner's and not quite a Yankee's. "Is someone in trouble?"

Matt had to wait a moment to catch his breath. He nodded.

"Sit down," Mr. Sefton said, gesturing to the chair he kept for guests.

"It's not me," Matt gasped.

"It can wait ten minutes while you tell me. Please, tell me."

"You hear this all the time," Matt said.

"Sadly, yes. Who is in trouble? What happened?"

"Do you know about the Washing Society?"

"The strike? I do." He sighed. "I read the *Beacon*."

"Some of the strikers have been arrested. Four of the strike organizers."

"And what is your interest, sir?"

"I work for the *Beacon*," he said. "For Mr. Endicott."

"Justice, then."

Matt found himself short of breath again. "Why would you take this on? Is it hopeless?"

"I'll take it on regardless."

He was more than a friend to Mr. Endicott. He was a friend of anyone oppressed by the law of the post–Civil War South. He reminded Matt of his stepfather, the Ohio abolitionist who had joined the Union army to fight against slavery. Sefton was too young to have been a soldier. He must have absorbed his antislavery sentiment from his family in his youth. He was both brave and foolish to have taken it south.

Sefton asked, "Do you know one of the strikers?"

"It's more than that."

Sefton gave him a quizzical look.

"She's my half sister."

Mr. Sefton rose. "Let's go. Wherever we're going, whoever we need to see, you can tell me on the way."

By the time they reached Mrs. Coldbrook's office on Wheat Street, Mr. Sefton knew the story. Matt opened the door. Nina sat in the guest chair, and behind the desk sat Mrs. Coldbrook, silent, her face a terrible grayish color.

The lawyer held out his hand. "Mrs. Coldbrook?"

She nodded.

Nina said, "I told her about the lawyer."

In a dull voice, Mrs. Coldbrook said, "I have a lawyer. He drafts my contracts. He's never handled anything like this."

Mr. Sefton said, "I have. I'll do everything I can." He didn't sit. Gently, he addressed both women. "Do either of you know where they were taken?"

"To the police station," Nina said. "I was there. I saw it happen. All of it."

"I'll want to talk to you later. We should go to the police station first. Mrs. Coldbrook, you don't have to be there."

She raised her head. She raised her voice. "Of course I should be there! My daughter is in jail!"

"It will be very upsetting for you."

"I'm already upset! Will it be any worse?"

Matt brushed past Nina to lean over the desk. "Aunt Rachel."

She stared at him, but she didn't object.

He reached out to rest his hand gently on her arm. He had a sudden painful memory of Eliza saying, "This ain't your fight." Softly, he said, "Aunt Rachel, let us help you."

She didn't shake him off. She rose and Matt lifted his hand away. She addressed the lawyer in a forced tone that told Matt she was struggling to retain her educated diction. "Let's go. I've never been to the police station. Where is it?"

MATT THOUGHT THAT A POLICE STATION WOULD LOOK sordid, reflecting what went on inside, but the building on Pryor Street resembled any number of commercial buildings downtown. Three stories tall, clad in red brick, with plate glass windows gleaming in the sun, it wasn't much different in appearance from Mr. Sefton's office.

Mr. Sefton led them inside with the practice born of experience. They joined a line that mixed those arrested—some handcuffed, some in the literal clutch of a police officer—with the supplicants like themselves. Those who had been arrested were varied, many more men than women and many more Black people than whites. One of the white men, unsteady and smelling of whiskey, was telling the officer who had handcuffed him, "I ain't guilty of a thing. It ain't a crime to have a drink in the middle of the day. You can't lock me up for that."

Mr. Sefton shook his head as they waited for their turn.

A policeman stood behind the counter, like a clerk in his father's shop. Matt ran his hand over the wood. The policeman said to him, "Hands off." He was middle-aged and running to fat under his uniform.

"Excuse me," Matt said, pulling his hand away as though he'd been burned.

Mr. Sefton said, "We're making an inquiry about four women who were arrested earlier today."

"Names?"

His aunt Rachel gave them.

"Who are you?"

"One of them is my daughter."

"Oh," he said. "The nigger women from Wheat Street." He looked at Mr. Sefton. "What do you want to know?"

"We want to pay their bail."

The policeman rummaged through some papers on the counter. "No bail."

"What was the charge?" Mr. Sefton asked.

"Disorderly conduct."

"You're going to hold them without bail for disorderly conduct?"

"And assaulting a policeman," he added.

"Was she armed?"

"Says here that she kicked him. That's assault. Who are you?"

"I'm their lawyer. I'd like to talk to them."

The policeman snorted. "Lawyer! For niggers in Recorder's Court!"

"Let me talk to them," Mr. Sefton said, escalating his tone.

"All right. We'll take you back later."

Rachel pushed forward and pressed her hands on the counter.

"Hands off!" the policeman said.

She removed her hands. She didn't bother to sound servile. "May I see my daughter?"

"No. No visitors."

Rachel leaned against the counter. She looked so gray that Matt worried for her. "Can I bring her anything? Some food or clean clothes?"

The policeman shrugged. "This ain't a hotel."

"When is the trial?" Mr. Sefton asked.

"They'll get to it whenever they can."

"Will it be a day? Two days?"

The policeman shrugged again. Mr. Sefton pulled a ten-dollar bill from his pocket and laid it on the counter. "Will this help?"

The policeman put his hand over it. "I'll see what I can do. Come back first thing tomorrow."

MR. SEFTON LED THEM OUTSIDE AGAIN. IT SEEMED WRONG that the sun was shining and that the Georgia sun beat down with its usual summer ferocity.

Nina said weakly, "They take bribes?"

The lawyer sighed, a delicate sound of agreement.

Nina, who had been red in the face earlier, was now very pale. Rachel was still gray. Neither of them were inclined to faint, but Matt was worried for them both.

"Can we stand in a shady spot?"

"I'm sorry," Mr. Sefton said, and they moved into the shadow of the station's roof. "This will only take a moment, and then I have to hurry." He turned to Rachel. "I'll need the names of witnesses."

"Why?" Rachel asked. "Miss Birnbaum was there. She can tell you what happened."

"Character witnesses. This isn't about what happened. It's about moral character."

"I was there!" Nina spluttered.

"Yes, whatever you can tell me will be useful. But believe me, I've argued in Recorder's Court before. That's how it works."

Rachel said, "Our minister. And several other ministers who've been involved in organizing the strike." She gave the names.

"Anyone else?"

Rachel rubbed her forehead with her hand as though her head ached. "My daughter just graduated from Atlanta University. Is that evidence of good character?"

"If there are teachers who can speak well of her, it would help."

"Miss Emma Ware. Her English teacher."

Nina asked, "Will you want the witnesses to testify? Will I testify?"

"No. Recorder's Court doesn't work that way. I'll talk to them and testify on their behalf when I defend the accused. And as a reporter, you shouldn't testify at all."

"My character?"

"Your bias."

"Will it be successful?" Nina asked.

"We'll have to do our damnedest with it."

After Mr. Sefton left, Matt asked Rachel, "Are you all right? Should we see you home?"

"I'll walk. It will clear my head." Before he could object or insist, she walked away, her shoulders slumped, like a woman dragging a cotton sack.

Matt looked at Nina. She was still pale, but she seemed a little less inclined to faint. "Let me see you home."

"I can't believe that lawyer bribed the police. In broad daylight! Like paying for a bar of soap at the druggist!" Outrage brought some color to her face.

"I can find us a hansom."

"I think I'd like to walk, too."

He held out his arm. She took it, and he felt how shaky she was. "You're sure?"

"Matt, I don't ask for something by denying I want it. I'll be all right."

She was arguing with him and teasing him at the same time. She must be feeling better. Nonetheless, she walked slowly, much to the disgust of the crowd around them, most of them men of business in an Atlanta hurry. He didn't mind. It was like the Sunday promenade that he had asked for. She had yet to take a stroll with him.

He said, "I hope you aren't planning on going back to Wheat Street. Or to a Washing Society meeting tonight."

"I should."

"It will keep, you know. They won't forget overnight. They'll still be mad tomorrow."

She nodded. She slowed down even more. In a low voice, she said, "Matt, I never told you because I knew how upset you'd be."

"About what?" he answered, his heart starting to race.

"The policeman who arrested Eliza threatened me. He told me I'd get the same treatment the strikers did."

He'd suspected that. "Mr. Endicott told me that he'd warned you away from danger. And that you didn't pay him any attention."

She stopped and collided with a man who said, "Excuse me," in the same tone of distaste that ladies used when they said, "Bless your heart."

"I'm putting you into a hansom," he said. "And seeing you home in it. Don't argue with me. Even women with strong spines can feel faint. Did you see how awful my aunt Rachel looked?"

In the hansom, which smelled powerfully of tobacco and sweat, she slumped against the cushions and closed her eyes. He watched her with a tenderness so profound that it was painful. He thought, *She tries too hard to live up to her mother's memory. She's haunted by the past, just like I am.*

She fell asleep and didn't wake until the hansom stopped. She was too groggy to object that he paid the driver or that he handed her out. He gave her his arm again. "Please, lean on me," he said, feeling the tenderness again.

Outside the door, in the shade of the portico over the door, her arm still twined in his, she turned to him. She looked troubled.

"Were you dreaming?" he asked her.

She tightened her hold on his arm. "No, remembering."

"Tell me." He let the words reverberate between them.

She took a deep breath. "Matt, I saw it. All of it. They

were blameless. Standing on the street, talking quietly. I saw the policemen club them, one after another. Hurt them. They could have been badly hurt. If it had happened at night, with no one to watch, they might have been beaten to death."

He nodded.

"It's one thing to talk about being brave. It's another thing to see what it's like for people who don't have any choice." Tears filled her eyes. She wiped them away with her hand. "And it's just as bad to stand on the sidelines and watch because anything you do to help will make it worse for them. Matt, if I'm an ally and a friend, I'm a failure at it. I should be ashamed of myself."

He said, "That's your fight. To do whatever you can and to feel guilty about it. Because it's never enough."

Her laugh was shaky. She nodded.

He gently extricated his arm from hers and reached to touch her cheek. Her skin felt soft under his fingertips. He wished he had the courage to kiss her cheekbone. He laughed too, a low chuckle. "Do you need a handkerchief?"

"Always," she said.

MATT MADE HIS WAY DOWN PEACHTREE STREET TO RETURN to Summerhill. In the heat of late afternoon, his head was completely clear. He felt a purity of purpose that he had never felt before in Atlanta. And he knew exactly what he wanted to do with it.

At the Coldbrook house, he didn't hesitate. He rapped on the door and waited, feeling no qualms.

Rachel opened the door. She was still tired and strained, but the awful gray tone in her face was gone.

"Aunt Rachel," he said, letting her hear the bond that had never gone away.

She said only, "Matt."

"I came to see if there's anything I can do for you."

Cass County was long gone, but something else shimmered in the air between them. She stepped back to invite him in. "We're sitting down to dinner, even though no one is very hungry. Please, join us."

CHAPTER 15

JUSTICE IN ATLANTA

AFTER MISS FLORETTE and her entourage left, the corridor was quiet. The air in the cell was unbearably hot, and the bucket smelled worse than ever.

Throughout, Mrs. Gardiner remained silent. Now she stared at the bucket. "In slavery days, they put out a bucket of water at the end of the cotton row. It sit there all morning. Get warm, get bugs in it. But you drink it anyway because you got to drink water. That's what that bucket make me think of."

Eliza had never heard her sound so bitter. No one tried to cheer her.

In a little voice, Ophelia said, "How long we wait like this?"

Eliza said, "They don't seem likely to tell us."

"Do you think anyone come to see us?"

Eliza hated to hear Ophelia sound so small. "I wish I knew."

"Can we get water, Amanda?" Mrs. Bell asked. "I'm thirsty."

Eliza licked her lips and realized how parched she was. She splayed her hands on her knees and tried not to think about water.

"When do you think we go into that courtroom?" Ophelia asked.

They waited for Mrs. Gardiner to say something, but she didn't reply.

Eliza rested her head in her hands. Her back hurt. She sat up. "Ophelia, can you tell me if I have blood on the back of my dress?"

"Turn so I can see."

Eliza obliged.

"No, whatever they do to you, it don't draw blood. You mighty dusty, though."

Footsteps sounded in the corridor and keys rattled. It was the cheerful warden, with two policemen in tow.

Ophelia asked, "You letting us out?"

He said, "There's a man to see you." The policemen stood sentinel behind him.

Mrs. Gardiner asked, "Who is it?"

The warden shrugged. "Don't know."

The warden opened the cell, and the policemen stepped inside. One of them grabbed Ophelia's arm and Eliza's, and the other took hold of Mrs. Gardiner and Mrs. Bell. "Stand up!" the policeman commanded Mrs. Bell.

Mrs. Gardiner said quietly, "She do her best. She don't feel well."

"This ain't a hospital," the policeman said. He pulled on Mrs. Bell's arm again. "All of you, come with us."

Eliza didn't resist the tug on her arm. *It will only hurt worse*, she thought. They made uneven progress down the corridor, and the policemen pulled them into a window-less room furnished with a battered wooden table and equally abused chairs. At the table sat a white stranger whose dark hair curled over the collar of his sober suit jacket.

He rose as they entered and remained standing as the policemen forced them to sit. "You'll leave us?" he said politely.

One of the policemen snickered. "You're not going anywhere, any of you. We'll be right outside." He let the door slam shut.

The suited man sat. "I'm John Sefton, and I'm a lawyer. Mr. Endicott of the *Beacon* asked me to talk to you."

"The *Beacon*?" Ophelia asked. "You know Miss Nina?"

He looked puzzled.

Eliza said, "Miss Birnbaum, who works as a reporter at the *Beacon*."

"Yes," he said, his eyes moving from one of them to the other.

We look a sight, Eliza thought.

"I've spoken to her. She's very worried about you, and she wants to do whatever she can to help. I've also spoken to Mrs. Coldbrook. I understand that her daughter, Miss Coldbrook, is among your number."

Eliza felt sick. Her mother knew. She forced herself to look at Mr. Sefton. "I'm Eliza Coldbrook."

He nodded. "Please introduce yourselves, the rest of you." He wrote their names down as they told him. "I want to talk to you about what happened. It will help me put together your defense."

Mrs. Bell, who was forcing herself to breathe slowly to

minimize her wheezing, asked him, "Sir, do you think we could get a cup of water first?"

His eyebrows rose. "They haven't given you water?"

Amanda Gardiner raised her head. "No, sir, they have not."

He opened the door, and they could hear him asking for a pitcher of water. They heard him say, with anger in his voice, "Yes, I know this isn't a hotel. It's a jail. And even in a jail, it's only decent to give people water."

The warden returned with a pitcher of water and a tin cup. He banged them on the table, not caring that some of the water slopped onto the wood. Mrs. Gardiner stared at the cup. "A bucket and a dipper," she said, in the same bitter, distant tone she had used in the cell. "Like in slavery days."

Ophelia reached for the pitcher. She poured a cup of water, and with great courtesy, she handed it to Mrs. Gardiner. "Miss Amanda, may I offer you a cup of water?"

Mrs. Gardiner said, "Ophelia, we in jail. We accused of something we don't do. We go to court for it. How do playacting make us feel any better?"

"They can try to treat us like we back in slavery. We don't have to act like it."

In a grudging tone, Mrs. Gardiner said, "You don't have to remind me."

Ophelia proffered the cup again. "Yes, I do."

Mrs. Gardiner wasn't smiling, but her face lost some if its bitterness. "If you want to act polite, give it to Susan first. She thirstier than I am."

Ophelia's right, Eliza thought. *It helps to remember what it's like to have your dignity.* Mrs. Bell drank slowly, as though the water were medicine.

Ophelia asked, "Miss Eliza?"

"Yes, thank you." Her back hurt. *Beaten like a slave.* She remembered all the afternoons she had spent drinking tea with her classmates at Atlanta University. She sipped daintily from the tin cup and handed it back to Ophelia. After Mrs. Gardiner took a drink, Ophelia poured some for herself. "I ain't as refined as the rest of you," she said, and she drank her cup in one draught.

Mr. Sefton watched them with interest. "Are all of you friends?"

"Yes," they all said at once. Ophelia added, "We all washerwomen, except for Eliza, who just graduate from Atlanta University. We all work on the strike together."

Mr. Sefton asked, "Have the police been harassing the strikers?"

"How do you know about the strike?" Mrs. Gardiner asked.

"I read the *Beacon*. And I have friends who talk about it."

Eliza wondered who he knew besides Mr. Endicott.

He said, "Please, tell me what happened. Mrs. Gardiner, would you start? Then I want to hear from the rest of you."

He listened, nodded, and made notes. He sighed as he put down his pen.

Ophelia asked, "What happen now?"

"I'll talk to more witnesses. I'll need to hurry. The case may come to trial as early as tomorrow morning."

Mrs. Gardiner asked, "What happen at the trial?"

Eliza remembered Miss Florette's sarcasm: *All in an hour.* But she wanted to hear a lawyer tell them.

"We'll go to Recorder's Court. It's for lesser offenses.

The docket is full, so there's not much time for each case. The first order of business is an arraignment, when the judge reads the charges against you. Then the judge calls witnesses for the prosecution—that is, the evidence gathered against you. Then I present your defense. After that, the judge decides whether you're guilty or not, and if the verdict is for guilt, he pronounces your sentence."

Mrs. Bell cried out, "We go to prison?"

"I've never seen a case in Recorder's Court end up in a prison sentence, Mrs. Bell."

"Sir, when we go into court, everyone see us?" Ophelia asked.

"The judge and all the officers of the court, yes. And the court is open to the public. There are reporters and spectators, too."

She gestured to her dress. "Hate to be seen like this," she said. "Wish I could get a clean dress."

His eyes were dark with sympathy. "I'm sorry, Mrs. Taylor. If this were a jury trial, I'd have you dress to the nines. But it's evidence. I want the judge to see that you were injured, and your dress is eloquent on that score."

Eliza asked, "What will you say in our defense?"

"The prosecution—the judge—will want to make this about the strike. But we won't."

"How do we do that?" Mrs. Gardiner asked.

His mouth twitched a little. If he was used to shading the truth, he didn't like it. "That you're innocent because you're good Christian women who would never cause a public disturbance."

Mrs. Gardiner said, "How you show that we good Christian women if we go into court all dirty and bloody?"

"Good Christian women who have been badly wronged." He rose. "You'll have to excuse me. I have three ministers to talk to yet today."

~

THE NEXT MORNING, THE WARDEN APPEARED, AGAIN accompanied by two policemen behind him. Eliza couldn't tell if they were the same men as yesterday. They all looked alike, and it wasn't just their uniforms. They shared the same expression, unyielding and contemptuous. The warden said, "You're going to court!"

As though it were a jolly jaunt.

The four of them weren't handcuffed, but they were roughly escorted, a policeman's grip tight on the arm. The policemen frog-marched them down a corridor, up a flight of stairs, and into the courtroom. At the door, Eliza quailed. The courtroom was as crowded as a Washing Society meeting, although not with the same people. Most were white, and they had the amused, expectant look of an audience.

Eliza glanced around the room. Her eyes found her mother, who was dressed in black, suitable for business or mourning. *Wasn't this both?* Eliza had never seen her mother look so tired and upset. Beside her sat Nina, and next to Nina was Matt.

She thought, *Lord, help me. All of them here to see my humiliation.*

Her father was absent. She understood why, but it hurt nonetheless.

The policemen hustled them down the aisle, and Eliza thought with a pang of every meeting she had attended in the past weeks at Pleasant Grove Church, where she walked between the pews.

Mr. Sefton was already seated at the table before the judge's bench. The policemen released their arms and told them to sit. Eliza rubbed her arm where the policeman had yanked on it.

The judge's face was a blur, and all Eliza saw was the black of his robe. His voice was too sonorous for the charges he read against them. For Mrs. Gardiner, Ophelia, and herself, disorderly conduct. For Susan Bell, disorderly conduct and assault. That kick in the policeman's shins had cost her dearly.

Their accusers' witnesses were next, Eliza recalled.

There was only one witness, whom they all recognized. He had harassed them, threatened them, and brought a gang of his fellows to arrest them. He explained that the four of them had been arguing among themselves, haranguing passersby, and blocking traffic on the sidewalk. When they were asked to quiet down and leave, he said, they refused and began to use vile language. And after they were put under arrest, they resisted, assaulting one of his fellow officers in the process. He added that they were washerwomen on strike, known to disrupt the peace, and he had often seen them haranguing others to join them.

The lies were so brazen that Eliza drew in her breath. She cast a despairing look at Mr. Sefton. His jaw tightened as he whispered, "It's not done yet."

The recorder asked about the assault, and the policeman who had been kicked appeared as well and pulled up his pants leg to show the judge his bruise. When the judge bent to look, the spectators in the audience tittered as though they were in a vaudeville hall.

Eliza thought, *We're figures of fun, like the poor souls reviled in the* Constitution.

The judge asked, Mr. Sefton, "You're representing these people?"

Mr. Sefton rose. "Yes, I'll be speaking in their defense."

The judge said, "Best be quick about it."

Mr. Sefton asked Mrs. Gardiner to stand. He drew out the facts of the matter, that they stood talking quietly on the street, bothering no one. He then asked her about her efforts for Pleasant Grove Church and made it plain that she was engaged in collecting money for the church's charity to help widows, orphans, and laundresses who were without work. He emphasized her minister's praise for her efforts.

He called Ophelia next, in her bloodied dress, and Eliza knew that her friend was red with shame under her dark complexion. He asked her about her involvement with the church, and once he had established her penchant for good works, he asked about the blood on her dress. Ophelia froze. Mr. Sefton had to coax the truth out of her.

At least the audience didn't laugh.

Then, to her surprise, Mr. Sefton asked Eliza to stand. It was sweltering in the courtroom but she was even hotter with embarrassment. She tried to still the misery that welled through her. *Answer what he asks*, she thought, *and hope that the truth comes out.*

What he asked—what he wanted the judge and the room to know—was that she had attended Atlanta University, where her teachers had thought highly of her intelligence and her morals and from which she had recently graduated with honors. *My sterling reputation*, she thought. Soiled, like the white dress she had worn since she was arrested. When she got home, she would burn it.

After she sat down, the judge didn't hesitate. He said, "Despite your nimble defense, Mr. Sefton, it's clear that there is ample proof that these women are guilty as charged." He picked up a piece of paper and read from it. "Amanda Gardiner, disorderly conduct. A fine of five dollars." He didn't look up. "Ophelia Taylor, disorderly conduct, a fine of five dollars. Susan Bell, disorderly conduct and assaulting a policeman, a fine of twenty dollars."

Mrs. Bell began to labor for breath. In a choked, frightened voice, she said, "Twenty dollar! I don't have twenty dollar! How do I pay a fine like that?" She put her hand to her mouth as though it would control the wheezing.

"If you can't pay the fine, you'll be put on the chain gang list for forty days."

Mrs. Bell gasped for breath. Eliza jumped to her feet. "You can't send this woman to the chain gang! She's ill! You'll kill her!"

The judge looked up. "Eliza Coldbrook, is it? Eliza Coldbrook, disorderly conduct and contempt of court, a fine of twenty dollars." He went back to the papers before him. "Case dismissed. See the clerk about your fines."

Outside the courtroom, her mother waited. Eliza turned her face away, but her mother enfolded her, held her close, and stroked her hair, as she always had when Eliza woke from a nightmare. The embrace hurt her bruised back, but she buried her face in her mother's shoulder to hide how she bit her lip against the pain. She whispered, "I'm so ashamed."

Her mother whispered back, "You got nothing to be ashamed about."

Mr. Sefton touched her sleeve. "I'm so sorry, Miss Coldbrook. Mrs. Coldbrook."

In a bitter voice, like Mrs. Gardiner's in the cell, her mother said, "So we got justice. What pass for justice in Atlanta."

"Let's pay the fines," Mr. Sefton said.

Mrs. Bell asked, "Will they send me to the chain gang?"

"No," Mrs. Gardiner said. "Because we pay your fine." She raised her voice, not caring who overheard. "The Washing Society pay it."

Her mother opened her reticule. "Reimburse me later, Miss Amanda. I have money. Mr. Sefton forewarned me."

At the desk, the clerk took the money and stamped "paid" on a piece of paper. *Like a receipt at my father's shop*, Eliza thought. He asked, "Who's Eliza Coldbrook?"

"I am."

He pulled a small, lumpy object from the shelf behind him and tossed it on the counter.

It was her reticule, dirtied and torn as though someone had stomped on it. It was ruined now. When she looked inside, it was empty. "I had ten dollars in here. Where is it?"

The clerk shrugged. "I don't know."

"I thought you made a record of everything when you emptied our pockets."

"There's no record of it."

"That money wasn't mine. It belonged to the Washing Society." Her voice rose. "And you stole it from me!"

"You shut up," the clerk said. "Or you can go right back into that cell."

"Stole my money!"

Mr. Sefton laid his hand on her arm. "Please, Miss Coldbrook." Gently, he led her away.

THAT EVENING, MRS. GARDINER INSISTED THAT ALL OF them attend a Washing Society meeting. "Not at Bethel A. M. E.," she said. "We stay away from Wheat Street for a while. We go to Pleasant Grove." Ophelia's husband drove them the few blocks in his cart.

As the four of them filed into the church, wounded and bruised, Eliza stared down the aisle and thought of the courtroom, where a similar walk had filled her with shame. Now she held up her head as row after row of eyes followed the four of them. Face after face registered shock and outrage. For once, Pleasant Grove Church was silent.

A woman with a sweet, resonant voice began to sing. The melody was familiar. It was "Gospel Plow," with its refrain about keeping your hand on the plow. But these words were new. They retold the story of Paul and Silas, who were punished by the Romans for spreading the faith. As she repeated the verse, other voices joined in her improvisation, singing in outrage about being sent to jail and denied bail. The singer invented a new verse about how the prisoners were freed from their chains by an earthquake sent by God. Only the refrain was familiar, and it was from the traditional song that had already inspired the strike: the admonition to hold on. They all learned it and joined in it, and the church filled with voices in unison. In union.

On the pulpit, Mrs. Gardiner took Ophelia's hand, and Ophelia took Eliza's, and Eliza bolstered Mrs. Bell by clasping hers. Mrs. Gardiner pulled Ophelia's hand into the air, and the rest of them followed, hands linked, a gesture of benediction and triumph at the same time.

When the song ended, Mrs. Gardiner let go of Ophelia's hand and stepped forward. She grinned and then winced. She said, "I'm all right. We all are, even though we feel a little puny." She gestured toward her eye.

They applauded and whistled their relief.

She said, "You all say it better than I can. Hold on. Hold on. Hold on."

CHAPTER 16

OPHELIA TAYLOR

AFTER THE TRIAL, I don't feel right. I remember standing in the courtroom with my dress all bloody, and I have to look down to be sure that the dress I wear today is clean. I wash and wash, but I still feel dirty.

Eliza find the article in the *Constitution* and read it to the rest of us. The paper call us "the ebony quartette" like we players in a vaudeville show. Make us figures of fun. Publish our names, too, so that every white person in Atlanta know what to call us when they laugh at us.

My lip slow to heal, and it bother me all the time. It hurt when I eat. It hurt when I try to kiss my children, no matter how easy I take it. It hurt too much to kiss my husband, and believe me, we both miss that kind of loving. Worst of all, it hurt when I talk.

A few of the churchwomen think that I get what I deserve, but they always been high-rumped, and I never like them much. Washerwomen, members of the Washing Society, they tell me they furious at the police and the judge and they proud of me. I hear it a lot, and not just in Summerhill but all over Atlanta. It don't help me none. I still feel low.

Eliza understand. I ask her how she feel, and she tell me the bruises ain't the worst of it. She upset in her heart. She say that they beat her like she was a slave, and she brood over it. She won't be over that for a while.

Oh, I understand all too well.

I start to wonder if God judge me, and that feeling an awful one. It hurt me so much that I go to see Reverend Jones at Pleasant Grove Church to see what he say. His wife a washerwoman, and she a member of the Society. If anyone understand, he do.

I tell him about the dirt and the guilt, and the burden I carry because of it.

He say, "Mrs. Taylor, you were wrongfully arrested. Wrongfully beaten. Wrongfully imprisoned. Wrongfully tried. And wrongfully convicted. All the blame lies with the police and the Recorder's Court. You are blameless! All the world knows it."

I gesture toward my lip. I say, "All my life people tell me I talk too much and too free. I feel like this wound a judgment from God, too. This is how God punish me."

He look kind and sad at the same time. He say, "Mrs. Taylor, I believe being injured like that was a coincidence." He lean forward. "I know that God isn't cruel like that. God gave you a strong voice—"

"A big mouth," I interrupt him.

He smile. "As a gift, to use in praising Him and speaking out against the things that are wrong. To inspire and persuade and lead the strikers. To win the strike."

"You really think so?"

"I believe it from the bottom of my soul."

My eyes fill up with tears. And I say, "Don't make me smile, Reverend. It hurt to smile, too."

CHAPTER 17

WE MEAN BUSINESS

WHEN ELIZA RETURNED HOME, her brother and sister waited in the foyer, their faces drawn. Ada asked in a small voice, "Did the bad men hurt you?"

"No, sugar. A policeman hit me, but I'm all right." She knelt and gathered her little sister into her arms.

Ada sniffled as she said, "You smell bad."

"I do. I need a bath."

Charles hung back as he said, "I wanted to come to the courthouse, but Mama wouldn't let me."

Eliza rose. "She was right. It was nothing for you to see."

Her mother said, "Ada, Charlie, let your sister go upstairs. Eliza, I'll see to a bath." She put her hand on Eliza's back, and Eliza winced. On the stairs, her mother said, "You're hurt."

"It's nothing. Don't bother to draw a bath. I can't wait that long. Just send up some hot water."

After the maid came upstairs with a pitcher of hot water, Eliza peeled off her dress, chemise, and petticoat.

She threw the dirtied, hated dress on the floor. She would never wear it again. She told herself, *After this I'll burn all of it.*

She washed herself until the water went cold. It was an exquisite pleasure to have clean skin and to smell of lavender soap. She had just pulled on her dressing gown when her mother called her name and knocked gently on her door.

"What is it?"

Her mother opened the door. "I know you're hurt. Let me help."

Eliza drew the dressing gown tighter around her body. "Just bruises, Mama. It's nothing."

"I can get the arnica for you. Let me see."

"No, Mama, I'm all right."

Her mother's voice hardened. She took that tone when Ada refused to obey her. "Let me see."

All right, Eliza thought, suddenly furious. *I'll show you.* She turned and let down the dressing gown to reveal her back.

Her mother gasped. She cried out, "Dear God, I ain't seen anything like that since slavery days!" All diction of freedom was gone.

Eliza covered herself and turned around. She wanted to say, "Are you satisfied?" But the look on her mother's face stopped her cold. She looked worse than she had in the courtroom.

Tears started in her eyes, and she felt as small and frightened as Ada. Her mother enfolded her into an embrace, as she had when Eliza woke from her nightmare as a child. Eliza wept, and her mother wept with her.

~

Now, as Eliza shifted on the settee, the shame as bad as the hurt, there was a hard, urgent knock on the door. Her mother said, "Don't get up."

At the door stood a sweating, disheveled Dr. Chesney. Trying to catch his breath, he said, "I heard that Miss Coldbrook was injured. How is she?" Without waiting for an invitation, he rushed in.

"Who told you I was hurt?" Eliza asked.

He stood before her, looming over her. "Mrs. Taylor came to see me. She told me all about it."

"Goodness," Eliza said, not responding to the alarm in his voice. "What did she say?"

"That the police beat you across the back with a club."

She tried to mollify him, as with her mother. "That's true. But I'm only bruised, Dr. Chesney. Otherwise I'm all right."

His voice rose. "Can you walk? Do you feel numbness or weakness in your limbs?"

"Dr. Chesney, I can walk just fine. Nothing is weak or numb." She rose, as if to show him, and winced.

"You're suffering. I can see it." His emotion was much more than a doctor's. "Please let me examine you. I beg you."

Even through her hurt and upset, she knew it wasn't a doctor's urgency. But she had no desire to be a patient to this distraught doctor. "Dr. Chesney, I didn't summon you. I don't need a doctor's attention."

He dropped his doctor's bag on the floor. He usually coddled that bag and its contents like a newborn baby. "Let me be the judge of that."

Eliza put her hands on her hips. She raised her voice. "Franklin Chesney, I *do not need a doctor*. Go back to your office and treat some people who are truly ill. They need a doctor. I don't."

He reached for her hands. "Eliza, please. I would never forgive myself if I neglected any serious injury."

"And I'd feel like a fool being examined for a bruise."

"On my authority as a physician—"

"You don't have any in my parlor!"

Her mother looked puzzled. "Excuse me, but I wasn't aware that the two of you were acquainted."

"Mama, of course we are. Dr. Chesney attends our church."

"This ain't from meeting on Sunday at church. Well acquainted, from the sound of it. How did this happen?"

Now Dr. Chesney looked puzzled, too. "Mrs. Coldbrook, I thought that Eliza had told you."

"Told me what?" Her mother's voice rose in alarm. Eliza's imagination supplied the worry: *That you're in the kind of trouble no young lady should be in.*

"About her responsibility for the Washing Society."

"The organizing? And what it leads to? I'm well aware of that."

"She hasn't told you about her duty as the Society's treasurer? About the plan to provide medical treatment to the members of the Washing Society?"

Her mother's eyebrows rose. "No, not a word."

"She and I meet in my office on the business of the Society. The strikers consult me free of charge, and the Society reimburses me for their visits. Your daughter goes over the accounts and disburses the funds."

"You meet to do accounts?" her mother asked.

"Mrs. Coldbrook, I swear on my honor as a physician, that's all that's passed between us."

"Eliza?" her mother asked.

"It's the truth, Mama."

"But you didn't tell me."

"I should have."

"Is there anything else you haven't told me?"

"I can't swear to it like Dr. Chesney can. But there isn't, Mama."

Her mother sat back in her chair. She looked worn out. "It ain't the first time two people flirted over an account book."

Eliza said, "Mama, don't. It isn't like that." But her cheeks were hot because it was true.

Dr. Chesney, much calmer now, said to her mother, "Mrs. Coldbrook, I like your daughter very much. It's been a pleasure doing business with her. But she's behaved with perfect decorum, and so have I."

Her mother said, "I didn't say it was a terrible thing to flirt over an account book."

"Mrs. Coldbrook, I never intended to ask it under these circumstances, but I've been thinking of asking whether I can call on Eliza at home. I thought I'd wait until the strike was over and do it properly. Since it's now in the open, I'll ask. May I call on your daughter?"

"I believe that's up to her."

"As long as you don't insist on a medical examination," Eliza said.

Now she saw the familiar smile. "Not in the parlor."

Eliza said, "We're at home on Sunday afternoons."

"Eliza, we can do better than that." Her mother

addressed Dr. Chesney. "We have dinner together after church. Join us, and you can meet the whole family."

A DAY LATER, WHEN THE *CONSTITUTION* PUBLISHED THE article about the trial, Mrs. Gardiner was furious. The article in the *Beacon*, which told the truth, didn't mollify her. She called Mrs. Bell, Ophelia, and Eliza together for a meeting. They sat in her neat, crowded parlor as Mrs. Gardiner said, "I been thinking about this business with the licenses."

In the heat of the arrest and the trial, Eliza had forgotten about the licenses. She had to force herself to remember that the city council debated an ordinance to charge every washerwoman twenty-five dollars to ply her trade.

Ophelia said, "Licenses! And after we get arrested and convicted. We should be in the streets, yelling and crowding and carrying on."

"No," Mrs. Gardiner said. "Not unless you want a lot more washerwomen to get beat up and arrested. No, we say something about them licenses. We write to the mayor and the city council."

"Don't see how writing to the mayor about the licenses help the strike."

Mrs. Gardiner's eyes gleamed, or at least her uninjured eye did, since the other was still puffy. "I think they try to scare us by threatening us with them licenses. But we ain't afraid. We stand up to them and see how serious they are." She cast her impaired gaze on each of them. If Mrs. Bell felt any dread, she didn't dare say so. Mrs. Gardiner said, "We tell them we mean business, and we see if they do. That's how we fight back. Miss Eliza, will you write it down proper for us?"

Eliza always carried a little notebook and a pencil in her pocket to keep track of any donations to the Washing Society. She drew them out and brandished her pencil.

Mrs. Gardiner said, "We address it to the mayor."

"Mr. James English," Eliza said.

"No. Call him Mr. Jim. Give him a nickname, like a dog's name. Like they call us."

"Ain't that an insult?" Mrs. Bell asked.

"Write it down," Mrs. Gardiner insisted. "Mr. Jim English, mayor of Atlanta."

Eliza wrote it down.

Mrs. Gardiner said, "Tell him that the Washing Society stand by what we ask for: a dollar a dozen. We willing to pay that twenty-five dollars, or even fifty for a license, so we get the price we insist on. We in charge of the washing, and we in charge of prices for doing the wash in Atlanta."

Mrs. Bell asked, "How do we pay so much for licenses?"

"If this go right, we don't pay a thing. The city council get shamed into saying that the licenses a bad idea. They vote against them. Eliza, sugar, you getting this?"

Eliza had to smother a smile. "Yes, ma'am."

"Tell them we want to hear their answer tomorrow."

Ophelia said, "Ain't that rushing it?"

"It tell them we ain't in a mood to wait. We mean business! They do this, or no washing!" Since the trial, she had been downcast. Now she glowed with purpose. "Eliza, what have you got? Would you read it back to us?"

THE DAY PASSED IN A FRENZY OF ACTIVITY AS MRS. Gardiner hurried to get the agreement of the Washing Society members in Shermantown and Jenningstown. Eliza wrote the final version of the letter in a rush and put it into the best envelope in her mother's desk. "Shall we find a messenger?" she asked Mrs. Gardiner.

"You take it down to City Hall."

Eliza laughed. The thought of this gesture of defiance cheered her. "We mean business!" she said, sealing the envelope.

At City Hall, Eliza talked her way past the Black man who sat at the desk in the foyer. She ignored the stares of the white clerks and aldermen who thronged the hallway. She marched into the office of the mayor and held out the envelope. "I'd like to leave this for the mayor," she said to the surprised clerk.

He recovered enough to sneer. "What is it? Who are you?"

She dropped the envelope on his desk. "It's from the Washing Society." She didn't wait for his reply. Before she turned away, she said, "We mean business!" She laughed as she flew down the hallway and out the door, oblivious to anyone who might yell, "Hey, you!"

THE NEXT DAY, IN THE DROWSY HOUR AFTER MIDDAY dinner, Eliza and her mother sat in the parlor. "I have to go back to the office," her mother said. "Are you meeting Mrs. Gardiner today? Or Miss Birnbaum?"

"We're catching our breath after running around to get that letter to the mayor."

Her mother said, "You seem better."

"I think so."

"Have you seen Dr. Chesney?"

"Not yet. But I do need to talk to him about some accounting."

Her mother laughed. "Did I ever tell you that your father and I fell in love over a ledger?"

"You did not!"

"Go see Dr. Chesney," her mother said.

His office was closed to consultations over the noon hour, but when he saw her at the door, he let her in, greeting her with a smile. "You must be feeling better."

"I am. Arnica has worked wonders."

"As my worry did not. I'm sorry for bursting in on you like that. I was so angry for you, and worried for you, that I forgot myself."

"Don't give it another thought."

"How are your spirits?"

"Is there medicine for that?"

"I wish there were. The bruises go away, but the damage to heart and mind often linger."

She thought of that night in Cass County still causing pain years after the fact, and tears rose to her eyes. He saw the distress and held out a handkerchief. That made her laugh, and she recovered. "Is that part of practicing medicine, Dr. Chesney? Handkerchiefs?"

"Sometimes," he said, and his smile warmed her, too.

"Don't wait to call on us. Are you free this Sunday?"

"I am, and I'll be there, if your mother agrees."

"Don't worry. She does. Now, is there a ledger we can look at?"

A DAY LATER, STILL RECOVERING, SHE OPENED THE DOOR TO Ben Mannheim. He looked dapper. "Is that a new suit?" she asked.

"Yes, it is."

"And you're getting your laundry done."

"My landlady settled with her washerwoman. It wasn't hard, since she's her sister. May I come in?"

She let him in, and they settled in the parlor. "Your mother isn't home? We can talk in private?"

"She's at the office." Her heart began to beat faster. Unless a young man had bad intentions—and Ben had never had such an intention—there was only one reason that he would want to talk to a young woman in private.

She wished that she wanted to say yes to talking with him in private.

He said, "I know I've been remiss about seeing you. I've been so busy trying to find a position. But now I have one."

She knew, as every woman knew, that a man waited until he was fixed to propose marriage. "What will you be doing?"

"I'll be employed by Mr. Hightower."

"The undertaker? You're hoping to be an undertaker?"

Ben's eyes gleamed. "No. He wants to start selling burial insurance. He's put me in charge of it."

"Isn't that what the Mutual Aid Society does? Won't you be in competition with them?"

"We'll see who does best," he said.

She began to wonder if she'd been right about his reason to come here. "Congratulations."

"Eliza, there's something that I've been meaning to say to you for a while."

Ah, here it was. "What, Ben?"

"It's time for me to get established. Time for me to make a decision."

Get to the point, she thought.

"Eliza, I never liked that you worked for the Washing Society."

Now he'll ask me to give it up.

"That was bad enough. But when you got arrested, when you went to jail, when you went to court, when you were convicted, that was more than I could bear."

Eliza searched his face. But there was no sympathy in his face or voice.

"I have a future before me. I need a wife with a sterling reputation to help me. Eliza, I can't be connected with a woman with a reputation like yours. I can't marry you."

"You're breaking it off," she said.

"How can I break it off? We were never engaged."

The words were like a slap. "An understanding to have an understanding," she said.

"I don't want to mislead you."

Just to hurt me.

He softened. "I'm sorry, Eliza."

For a moment she saw the Ben she had always known, the Ben who had been her childhood friend, beneath the adult he had become. Then he vanished.

"You knew I was arrested. Did you know the police

beat me up? You didn't ask me how I am. Is that how little you care about me?"

He shifted uncomfortably in his chair. "I don't know why you're so angry. We were never engaged."

"We've known each other since we were children, and we've been friends for years. Doesn't that count for something?"

He began to get angry too. "I didn't think you wanted to marry me. At least that's what the gossips are saying."

Even though she had been free in saying so, she lost her temper. "And why should I? Marry an Atlanta University snob who'd rather blame a Black woman for getting arrested than blame the police?"

With some heat, he said, "That's just the attitude that bothers me. Shouting on street corners! Associating with washerwomen! Hardly a credit to your family or to your race."

The room was summer-hot, but anger made her hotter. "What is being a credit to your race? Wearing white gloves and drinking tea and pretending that poor Black people deserve every misery that comes to them?"

She'd gotten to him. Poor Black people would be the customers who gave the burial insurance agent their hard-earned dimes every week for a proper funeral. If he despised them, he'd have a hard time making a living. "Of course we should sympathize with them. Help them. But that doesn't mean we should socialize with them or emulate them."

She rose. She wanted to tower over him. "How Black are you, Ben Mannheim?"

He glowered. "I look in the mirror every morning, Eliza. I know what color I am."

"Then act like it."

He stood, too. "I think we're done."

"Yes, we are."

Before he turned to leave, he said, "What's this I hear about you and Dr. Chesney?"

Her anger flared afresh. "That I do business with him? That's nothing to hear."

"That you go to his office every week, by yourself, and spend an hour there with him."

She heard the insinuation of people like Mrs. Oliver and her daughter. Her anger extended to them, too. "It's business and nothing else," she said, her temper very high. "As though it's any business of yours!"

"It's not. Not anymore." Before he turned to go, he said, "Eliza, I'm sorry to end it like this."

"No, you're not."

After the door closed, she sat down heavily, twisting her hands in her lap. She found herself pressing on the ring finger that had never held a ring.

She hadn't wanted to marry Ben Mannheim. He was right about that. She had declared it, over and over. She had no reason to feel so injured or so angry.

THAT SUNDAY, DR. CHESNEY WALKED HOME WITH THEM from the service at Pleasant Grove Church to join them at dinner. Seeing him at the table, Eliza felt affection bloom in her chest like a rose in her mother's garden.

He charmed her father. He had studied German to read the latest medical works, and he nodded in comprehension when her father spoke in his native tongue. Dr. Chesney said ruefully, "I'm afraid I don't have much conversation in German, unless you want to talk about lesions."

Her father beamed. "We'll have you reading Heine's poetry in no time."

Blunt and ambitious as usual, Charlie said, "I didn't know Black men could be doctors."

Eliza said, "Goodness, Charlie, that's not polite."

Dr. Chesney said, "I don't mind. I have plenty of nieces and nephews, and believe me, I've heard a lot worse." He turned to Charlie. "Of course Black men can be doctors. They can study at Howard College of Medicine or Meharry College in Nashville. Are you interested in being a doctor?"

Ada interrupted, "When I grow up I want to be a doctor, too."

"You can't. You're a girl," Charlie said.

Dr. Chesney said, "There was a young woman at Howard who graduated a few years before I did. A Miss Eunice Shadd, from Canada. She married a fellow doctor and now they both practice medicine in Ohio."

Her mother didn't remind Ada of her manners. She listened to this exchange with interest.

After Sunday dinner, Eliza asked, "Mama, may I walk with Dr. Chesney in the garden?"

"Please do." Her mother smiled. "Perhaps you'd like an account book to take along?"

Ledgers! Eliza wanted to stick out her tongue at her mother. "I'll let you know if we need one."

In the yard, they walked slowly, side by side. Her mother's roses were in full bloom and intensely fragrant.

Eliza led them to a shady spot, and Dr. Chesney said, "It seems that your mother has forgiven me, too."

"Yes, she has. She likes you. And she's a much tougher case than Mrs. Gardiner."

"Mrs. Gardiner had only to decide if she could trust me with her money. Your mother wants to know if she can trust me with your happiness." He smiled at her, and she thought she would drown in the dark pools of his eyes.

This kind of talk from Ben annoyed her. Why did hearing it from Franklin Chesney make her so glad? "She can. I'll put in a good word for you, too."

"Then I'm welcome back?"

"Are you sure that you want to associate with a jail-bird?" she teased.

"Who thinks that of you?"

She should let him know the field was clear. "I had an understanding with someone else. He's just ended it. He told me that a rising young man can't be saddled with a wife who's been arrested and tried and found guilty."

"He didn't see the injustice?"

"Of course he saw it. He didn't want to admit to it. It was easier to blame me for the trouble."

"He was dead wrong, you know. You did the brave thing. The noble thing. The right thing." He reached for her hand, and they laced their fingers together in an easy union.

"Like my friend Ophelia says, good trouble."

"Absolutely." He let go of her hand to rest both of his hands lightly on her shoulders. "Does that hurt you?"

"No. Why do you ask?"

He gently pulled her close and kissed her. His mouth

was soft on hers. Warmth suffused through her, a slow and pleasant fire in her chest and belly. She kissed him back, letting the fire grow, and cradled his head in her hands. He kissed her with greater passion. She thought, *You swear to a life together because of love. You seal it with desire.*

When they broke apart, he said, "Will you trust me with your happiness? Consider sharing a life of walking side by side? Doing good, and making good trouble?"

"There's nothing I'd like better," she said.

A FEW DAYS LATER, OPHELIA ASKED ELIZA TO WALK AROUND the neighborhood to talk to anyone who might be flagging. Atlanta was sick of the strike, and everyone knew it. The city council hadn't voted to throw out the license ordinance yet, but a Summerhill neighbor, who worked as a messenger at City Hall, heard rumors that they would. Mrs. Gardiner had said to her committee, "Did I tell you?"

Eliza said to Ophelia, "You look better."

"Feel better." Ophelia gestured toward her lip. "Healing up. It don't hurt so much to talk."

"As though that ever stopped you," Eliza teased.

Ophelia grinned and winced. "It still hurt to grin. What's this I hear that you and Ben Mannheim are done with each other? And that Dr. Chesney pay attention to you?"

Eliza laughed. "You'll never learn to mind your own business, will you? It's all true. You can go tell it on the mountaintop, if you like."

"Dr. Chesney a fine man."

"That he is." Eliza leaned close to whisper in Ophelia's ear. "Like you say about your husband, he light a fire in me."

Ophelia chuckled. "You keep it burning."

They ambled down the alley, waving to the women who gathered in the yards. "Still in union!" they called to Ophelia.

They'd never had occasion to stop at Amy Alexander's house before. Amy was her nickname. Eliza recalled that her given name was "America." She attended the very first meeting at Pleasant Grove and remained stalwart throughout the strike. She was married to a mason, and his income helped her feed her less-fortunate sisters night after night.

Now they found her at the washtub. Ophelia said, "Miss Amy! What you do?"

Amy straightened up. "No, I ain't breaking the strike." She grinned, a look of pure happiness. "I settle with someone." She wiped her hands on her apron. "For a dollar a dozen, and I have a receipt to prove it." She pulled it from her pocket. "Got it from young Mr. Kaltenbach. Mr. Henry's boy from California. Big eyes. Soft voice. Earnest. Guilty conscience. He pay me in advance, he feel so guilty."

Eliza wanted to laugh. That was Matt, all right. "May I see the receipt, Miss Amy?" She had never seen Matt's handwriting before.

"What do it say?" Ophelia asked, breathless with excitement.

Eliza read it aloud.

At that, Ophelia shrieked, "Miss Amy! Your strike over!" She flung her arms around Amy, who smiled and allowed the embrace. She said, "Ophelia, quiet. You loud enough for all of Summerhill to hear."

"Shout it from the mountaintop!" Ophelia said, smiling at Eliza.

"If they on strike up there, they hear you," Amy said.

Eliza asked, "Miss Amy, may I take this? Mrs. Gardiner will want to see it. She'll be able to make use of it."

"Mrs. Bailey think so, too. Say that every washer-woman should know to get a receipt."

Eliza cradled the receipt in her palm. She gazed at the signature. *Matthew Kaltenbach. Paid in full.* Their ally. And for her, perhaps, more than that.

CHAPTER 18

SAFE HARBOR

MATT WAS ALONE in the *Beacon* office, making a fair copy of the articles for next week's edition. Mr. Endicott was out, trying to woo an advertiser, and Nina was following the washerwomen in search of another story. Matt had learned to pace himself. He rarely had a cramp in his hand these days. He had also learned how to keep a cup of coffee on his desk without spilling it.

He had just laid down his pen to sip some coffee when the door opened. He expected one of his colleagues, but it was Rachel Coldbrook, dressed for business in sober black with a white collar and white cuffs.

He rose. "Mrs. Coldbrook."

"Only in the office. I hope we won't stand on ceremony elsewhere."

"Please, sit. Can I get you coffee? It's still warm."

"I'd like some." She flashed a smile.

When she was settled, she said, "I do have some business to transact with you. With the *Beacon*, at any rate."

Puzzled, he said, "We'll do our best to oblige you."

"I want to advertise in your newspaper."

He laughed. "Mr. Endicott will be delighted if you do."

"I'm pleased for him. But I'm doing it on my own behalf. Coldbrook Construction is well-known among people of color. It's time to reach beyond that." She leaned forward, and under the lavender soap she now used was her natural scent, familiar from his childhood, a spicy odor like sassafras.

"We'll do our best to help you."

"Tell me about your readership and your advertising rates."

He felt a surge of joy entirely unsuited to a business proposition as he fumbled for the rate sheet.

As he tried to explain, she laughed. "Oh, Matt. You've never sold anyone advertising, have you?"

"Everyone has to start somewhere."

"True enough."

"Be patient with me."

She reached out her hand. The capable, work-roughened fingers he remembered were now smooth, like his own. He thought she wanted to shake on it, but she clasped his hand instead. "I will."

They pored over the advertising rates together, and when she had decided what she wanted, and better still, had written the *Beacon* a check, she said, "Mrs. Alexander told me that you met her terms, and she settled the strike with you."

"I did."

"That receipt you wrote for her has been a model for the washerwomen. They've all studied it, as they say, and when they settle, they ask for one just like it."

"So the strike is ending."

"House by house and missus by missus."

"I'm glad to hear that."

"And the washerwomen have all learned to ask for their money in advance."

He laughed. "Even better."

She rose. She was smiling. "Give my best to Mr. Endicott."

"I will." He also rose. "Aunt Rachel?"

She inclined her head, accepting the endearment.

He said, "Give my best to Eliza."

THAT SUNDAY AT THE ENDICOTT TABLE, NINA WORE HER pretty dress, but she looked tired and strained, and she was unusually quiet. After midday dinner, Matt asked if she'd like to walk in the garden, and she accompanied him with a subdued step. The air was hot, fragrant, and still. Even the birds and crickets were hushed in the heat.

Matt held out his arm to her, and she took it without enthusiasm. They ambled to the pergola, where the sweet smell of wisteria hovered in the air. They sat. He asked, "What's the matter, Nina?"

She brooded. "I thought I would feel happy after I'd found a good story," she said.

"But you don't."

She turned to face him. Her sad eyes were still beautiful. "Shouldn't I have gone to jail with them?"

He reached for her hand, and she let him take it. Her fingers were inert and damp with the heat. "How could you write about them if you were in jail?"

She turned away. "Oh, Matt. My mother risked her life

246

every time she set foot in the South. Compared to her, I'm a coward."

He gently pressed her hand. "Was your mother happy, do you think?"

"She was happy when she was railing against something she thought was wrong. She never tired of that."

"That was her work, which she chose. I mean in her life."

"Her most private life."

"Yes."

Nina looked down at their intertwined hands and reflected. Then she looked up, and her expression was sadder than he had ever seen. "When I was a little girl, I never thought about it," she said. "I thought everyone lived like we did. When I got older, I began to wonder. I asked her where my father was, and she told me that he was dead. I asked her why she wasn't married, and she snapped at me. 'Marriage is slavery,' she said, and believe me, she knew about slavery."

"Do you think that's true?"

"Marriage can swallow a woman up. If my mother married, I don't think she would have been able to write and lecture anymore. She would have lost that."

"What about love? Do you think she missed that?"

"Matt. She and I loved each other. We both knew it."

"Was that enough for her?"

"Why are you asking me?"

In the quiet, a large, lazy bee bumbled into the wisteria behind Nina's head. He said, "I think I'm in a position to understand about love withheld. And lost." He stroked her hand with his thumb. "And found."

Nina looked into her lap.

He asked, "Is it a bad memory?"

She looked up. "Bittersweet. If I tell you, I'll probably cry."

"Tell me," he said, as she had once said to him.

"It was about six months before she died. Now I know that she knew how sick she was, and she knew that it would kill her. She had trouble sleeping but she refused to take laudanum because it would dull her mind. One night, I found her in the parlor, in her dressing gown, with only a candle for light. There was a glass on the lamp table, and I could smell the brandy. She was sobbing." Nina took a deep breath. "She said, 'Why are you out of bed?' as though I was a child of five. 'Go back to sleep.' I took her hands and asked her what was wrong. She said, '*Loz mir aleyn.*'" Nina looked at Matt. "It's Yiddish."

"The German is close enough. She wanted you to leave her alone."

"Something was wrong. She only spoke Yiddish when she was very upset. I said, '*Zag mir.*'"

"Tell me."

"She said, 'I'm dying, Nineleh. I won't live to see you grown. I won't live to see you established in life. I'll never know if you'll be happy, or how.' And I said, 'Mameleh, no one knows if life will bring happiness, or not.' She said, 'I haven't done right by you. And I haven't done right by myself. There's so much I haven't been able to give you. So much I've denied myself by doing so.'"

Matt nodded.

"I asked her, 'What do you regret most?' She had to fortify herself. She drank some brandy before she answered. Her eyes were wet. Her cheeks were wet. 'Your father,' she said. 'That you loved him? That he didn't marry you?' And she said, 'All of it.'" She looked away. "I told you I would cry."

"It's all right."

She said, "I asked her the one thing I wanted most to know, the one thing she would never tell me. 'What was my father's name, Mameleh?' And she smiled at me through her tears. It was her beguiling smile. 'I'll carry that secret to my grave, Nineleh,' she said." The tears came in full force. "And she did."

He couldn't bear to let her cry. He didn't care that it might be forward or presumptuous or wrong for a man to embrace a woman he wasn't engaged to. He put his arms around her and drew her so close that her tears wet his shirt. He stroked her hair and murmured, "Nina. *Liebchen.*"

She rested for a while in his embrace. Then she lifted her head so that she could look him in the face. "I don't want a life like that. It was like being on a stormy sea, all alone, all the time."

He touched a wayward curl and smoothed it. "Oh, Nina. Does the metaphor help? Does it lessen the pain?"

"Words have power. You know that as well as I do." She met his eyes, and her gaze was full of pain. "I want to voyage, Matt. But I want a safe harbor to come home to."

"You have it." He didn't move to kiss her; it seemed wrong. He pressed her close again and whispered, "You have it, in me."

All his life, he had thought that kindness was a form of weakness. He had seen his kind-hearted father make a mess of his own life and the lives of everyone he cared about. Matt had never realized that kindness could be a form of strength. His heart swelled with tenderness. He whispered, "We'll voyage together. And harbor one another."

She drew back. "I'm so afraid of getting swallowed up."

"I would hate that, too."

The tears in her eyes gleamed. He didn't have to ask. He leaned forward and gently kissed her on the lips. She wrapped her arms around his neck and kissed him in return, with a surprising passion for someone who felt so conflicted.

When they broke apart, he said, "I love you, and I want to spend my life by your side. However we do it."

She nodded.

"We never did promenade together," he said, teasing. He held out his arm. "Will you walk with me?"

She laughed. "Now, that I can promise. Yes, I will."

MATT DIDN'T BOTHER TO GO ROUNDABOUT. A FEW DAYS later, at the office, he told Nina that he planned to call on Eliza. "I'd be glad if you'd go with me. But you don't have to."

"Of course I will."

As he stood before the door of the house on Fraser Street, Nina slipped her hand into his. "Are you sure about this?"

"Yes."

Today the maid answered the door, and Eliza called from the parlor, "Who is it?"

"Miss Nina. She's brought Mr. Matthew."

Eliza rose from her spot on the settee. She wore a clean white dress that smelled of starch. They must have settled with their washerwoman, too. She asked, "Have you come on business again?"

Matt stepped forward. "Not this time."

"Sit down, both of you."

When they were all seated, the silence was thick and awkward between them. Nina didn't interrupt to make it easier. Matt had asked her not to. He said, "Eliza, things haven't been easy between us."

Her smile was rueful. "I haven't made it easy for you."

"I don't have any illusions that we'll fall on each other's necks to weep and reconcile," he said.

"That's good of you."

"I understand full well that we can't acknowledge each other publicly as brother and sister. I understand why."

"It has to be that way."

"I'm sorry for it, and I always will be."

She didn't reply. If she was sorry for it, she wasn't going to say.

"But we're connected. We're kin. And even if the world can't admit to it, except behind our backs, we can."

She sat very still. "What do you want from me?"

"To acknowledge the connection. I know it will have to stay at arm's length. Coldbrook and Kaltenbach."

She glanced at Nina. "Did you have any part in this?"

"Only in that I care about both of you."

She hesitated, then looked at Matt. "My mother told me how you helped the strikers. The receipt."

"I don't expect thanks. It was the right thing to do."

She struggled to reply. Matt thought, *She knows she owes me an apology, and she's damned if she'll say so.* The legacy of slavery weighed on them both. She couldn't forgive him for that. He understood why, but he still yearned for her to do it.

She said, "I can do my best to be civil to you. I can promise that much."

"I want to be a friend. But I'll do it quietly. At arm's length. That's my choice, and it's for me. Gratitude doesn't enter into it."

"Fair enough." Her voice was cool at the mere mention of gratitude. She clearly hated the thought.

He rose. "Please excuse me. I need to go."

Eliza asked, "Nina, will you stay?"

"Not right now. You'll have to excuse me, too."

He was relieved that Nina refused to linger and let Eliza express her true feelings in his absence. Nina would have to maneuver this new alliance, too.

Outside on the sidewalk, he thought of his stepfather's stories of the war, about the flag of truce raised at moments when the two warring armies had common cause for temporary peace: when they exchanged prisoners and, more prosaically, when they handed over mail. He and Eliza weren't finished with their conflict. But they could raise the flag of truce. For now, it would have to be enough.

CHAPTER 19

AMANDA GARDINER

MISSUS KERSHAW, the one who cause me a lot of trouble before the strike, send word that she want to see me. I know why. But I don't know how it will go.

I wait in her kitchen, and she swish in to see me. She got on a nice dress, but she smell bad. No wonder. Wearing a dirty chemise and a dirty pair of drawers and sleeping on dirty sheets. I remember sitting in jail in a dirty dress, and my thought ain't kind. *Now you know what it feel like.*

I don't smile or say how do. I wait.

She peevish, like always. More reason to be peevish now. She say, "I want you to come back to work."

"Well, ma'am, that depend on something," I tell her.

"Are you being insolent with me?"

I feel like the whole Washing Society in the room with me, holding me up. "No, ma'am," I say, because it's the truth.

"What does it depend on?"

As though it don't go all the way through Atlanta,

ringing through the streets, published in the *Constitution*, and now that her friends start to settle, flying from one white lady to another. I say, "A dollar for a dozen pounds of wash."

"That's highway robbery!" she say, standing there in her dirty, smelly clothes.

I say, "Then no washing," and I start to turn away.

"No! Wait!"

"A dollar a dozen," I repeat.

She get a sly look on her face. "I'll find someone else."

I think, *Don't you learn a thing these past two months?* "Ma'am, there ain't anyone else. All the washerwomen in Atlanta agree that we don't do the wash unless we get a dollar a dozen pounds. Otherwise, no washing." And I start to turn away again.

"Don't you turn your back on me!"

I face her. "It ain't a matter of respect or disrespect. It's how we do business. If you want your washing done, that's how we do it."

Her face get red. She look like she have a headache start. That's too bad. But I ain't here to doctor her. I'm here to settle with her, if she want to. If she don't, I go on my way.

I have the upper hand now, and I admit, I gloat a little with it. Like they used to say when the war end, people who used to be slaves taunting the masters and missuses brought low, "Bottom rail on top now!"

I don't say a thing. I don't smile. I wait.

And she say, "I don't like it, you hear me? Not one bit."

All right, she ain't quite done yet. So I keep waiting.

Then she start to look pitiful. A sad, mean woman who

stink as bad as any field hand. Headache because she so upset that I don't act the lickspittle.

Like the song say, *I shall not be moved.*

She say, "A dollar a dozen?"

I never tire of repeating them words, Ophelia's words, our battle cry. "A dollar a dozen."

"I have a lot of dirty laundry. I don't know what it weighs."

I cast my eyes around the kitchen. "Ma'am, if you have a kitchen scale, we weigh it," I say.

She open the kitchen door and yell into the house, "Lottie! Bring the dirty laundry! All of it!"

And Miss Lottie stagger into the room with a huge bundle wrapped up in a sheet and dump it on the kitchen table. Missus Kershaw lose her temper. "Not on the table! Put it on the floor!"

I'm about to rescue poor Miss Lottie, who's just a slip of a girl. But she say to Missus Kershaw, calm as can be, "It easier to weigh, ma'am, because we put the scale on the table."

Missus Kershaw give her an angry look. "Insolent! Not you, too!"

I have to smother a smile. The maids and the waiters thinking about striking now that we show them the way. I'll have to say a word to Miss Lottie. Now she get the kitchen scale and set it on the table next to that big bundle.

I open the bundle. Phew! Dirty laundry never smell like roses, but they been wearing everything over and over for weeks at the height of summer in Atlanta. I let it fill the kitchen and let Missus Kershaw smell the stink she made.

I can't read, but I know that a kitchen scale measure up to two dozen pounds. I know when the arrow point to the twenty-four-pound mark. So I take a piece from the pile, a man's drawers, and I put it on the scale. I look at the arrow. I put another piece on the scale.

Missus Kershaw say, "We'll be here all day at this rate."

"It go easier once we used to it." I keep putting laundry on the scale and watching the arrow. When I have two dozen pounds, I put it aside in a pile. "That's two dozen," I say, making sure everyone in the room know it.

It go easier the second time because I get a good idea of how many pieces in two dozen pounds. And even easier the third time. Missus Kershaw act I like her waste her time on purpose, tapping her foot and glaring at me, but I take it slow. If she say anything nasty, I free to remind her, "No washing," and walk out.

Free to say no to a white woman! My heart glad of that.

We end up with ten dozen pounds of wash. I say, "Can't carry all that. Have to bring a wagon for it."

"If you don't want to take it—" Missus Kershaw snarl.

"Didn't say that, ma'am. Just said I can't take all of it right now. Carry part of it and arrange for a wagon for the rest."

"When can you get the rest?"

"Before the day over."

"How much?" she say, through gritted teeth, even though she know.

"Ten dollars, ma'am."

"I don't have that much," she say.

I look at the bundles of dirty laundry that cover the table. I start to turn away. "No washing," I say.

"No! Wait! I have five dollars."

"Well, ma'am, either I take five dozen pounds now, or I come back when you have ten dollars."

She say, "I'll pay you next week."

"No, ma'am. You pay me in advance, and you write me a receipt, so we both have a record of how much wash and how much money."

"Receipt! What do you need with a receipt! You can't read."

Miss Lottie sneak me a smile. *I can*, that smile say. I say, "That's how we do business now, we washerwomen. Need a receipt."

She send Lottie for paper and pen and ink.

I say, "For five dollars, I take five dozen pounds now. That's what the receipt should say."

"I can't believe the gall!"

"Five dollars. A receipt. Or no washing."

She write it, all scrawl and blots, and she throw it on the table. Then she rummage in her pocket like it hurt her to do it, and she take out some bills all wrinkled up and toss them on the table next to the receipt. I smooth them out to count them. "Ma'am, this only four dollars."

She glare at me again and pull another bill from her pocket.

I smooth it, too, and then I fan the bills out. Five dollars. "Thank you, ma'am," I say, and I put the bills and the receipt in my pocket.

She watch me while I bundle up the five dozen pounds, like I just hoping and praying to cheat her. I say, "I can take this much with me. Won't have to wait for a wagon."

I rest my hand on the bundle for a moment. Missus Kershaw still watching me.

And then it come to me, and my soul fill with it.

We win. We ask for what we deserve, and we stand firm and hold on until we get it. Black women, washer-women, we get in union and stay in union, and we stand up to all of Atlanta. And we win.

I smile at Miss Lottie.

I hoist the bundle of laundry onto my head, and it feel as light as an angel's feather.

The End

THANK YOU FOR READING *THE NEW SOUTH*!

IF YOU WANT TO KNOW WHERE THE STORY BEGAN, DIVE INTO the captivating, enthralling, sweeping Georgia series, starting with the award-winning *Sister of Mine*. Rachel is a slave. Her half-sister Adelaide owns her. Slavery them made kin. Will the Civil War make them sisters?

IF YOU LIKE TALES OF LOVE AND COURAGE AT THE TIME OF the Civil War, you'll enjoy *Charleston's Daughter*, first in the Low Country Series. Emily is a tormented Southern belle. Caro is a rebellious slave. In South Carolina in 1858, no friendship could be more dangerous…

. . .

Want another stirring tale of love and freedom at a time of war? You'll adore *The Fall of Natchez*. Rosa was a Southern belle—until she met a Union officer...

Sign up for my newsletter, *The Latest on the Past*, for exclusive giveaways and sneak peeks of new books. I greatly appreciate your help in spreading the word about this book, including telling a friend. Reviews help readers find books. Please leave a review on your favorite book site.

HISTORICAL NOTE

The Atlanta Washerwomen's Strike of 1881 is little known, and that's a shame because it was historic. It was one of the earliest successful strikes in the United States.

This novel closely follows the historical facts of the 1881 Atlanta Washerwomen's Strike, which are as follows:

- In late July of 1881, twenty washerwomen met at a church in the Summerhill neighborhood of Atlanta to establish the Washing Society.
- Shortly after, the washerwomen of Atlanta went on strike for better pay and better working conditions; within two weeks of the Society's founding, they had three thousand members.
- As the Society's membership grew and the strike spread, the Atlanta City Council, in an effort to discourage the strikers, proposed an ordinance that would require every

washerwoman in Atlanta to pay twenty-five dollars for a license.

- Around July 29, six women were arrested, ostensibly for disorderly conduct but in reality because they were organizing for the Washing Society. Their names were Matilda Crawford, Ophelia Turner, Sarah Collier, Sallie Bell, Carrie Jones, and Cora Jones. They were tried in Recorder's Court, found guilty, and five of them were fined five dollars. Sarah Collier was fined twenty dollars; she was unable to pay her fine, and her name was put on the chain gang list for forty days.

- On August 1, the Washing Society wrote to the mayor of Atlanta, letting him know that they were unfazed by the prospect of licenses and that they, not their employers, would set the price for washing. The letter concluded: "We mean business."

- By August 16, the Atlanta City Council had tabled discussion of the ordinance, and many employers had acceded to the washerwomen's demands. The strike was over. The washerwomen had won.

While the strike was swiftly organized and swiftly won, it was a long time coming. Washing was heavy labor, but washerwomen were not servants; they were self-employed. They worked in their own homes, not on the employer's premises. They set their own work pace and provided their own work tools—washtubs, irons, and soap. Black women found that washing let them arrange their work around their domestic and childcare responsibilities. It also allowed neighbors and friends to work together. In 1881, *Harper's* illustrated washerwomen in the Shermantown neighborhood working as a group beneath a canopy as shelter against the sun. The 1880 census enumerated 1,445 women in Atlanta with any job title related to laundry work (including *washerwoman, washing, washing and ironing,* and *laundress*). Of those 1,445, only twenty-four, 1.6 percent, were white. All the rest were Black. They represented a cross-section of Black working-class Atlanta. Some were single and self-supporting, many were widows, and a surprising number were married to men whose occupations ranged from the comfortable (drayman or mason) to the precarious (day labor). It was clear that their households needed their pay, which before the strike was set at a dollar for a load of wash.

From the beginning of the strike, the washerwomen were admirably organized. They set up branches of the Washing Society in every Black church in Atlanta. They articulated a clear and easily understood goal: a dollar for a dozen pounds of wash. They combed their neighborhoods for fellow washerwomen, encouraging those who had struck and shaming those who had not. They held nightly meetings to bolster the strikers. They weren't new to running a movement. They were experienced at it.

For fifteen years, the Black women of Atlanta had been the stalwarts of Black churches, not only as congregants but as the founders of mutual aid societies to help people pay for funeral expenses. Women weren't often presidents of these societies, but they served as vice presidents, treasurers, and secretaries. Running a mutual aid society provided a generation of Atlanta's Black women with an education in organizing and fundraising. The women who had been the organizational bedrock of the church's mutual aid societies applied those skills to leading and organizing the strike.

The strikers were intentional about the timing of the strike. Atlanta was due to host the International Cotton Exposition in October 1881, showing the world the vibrant economy of the New South that was bolstered by a docile Black labor force. The strike was a glaring contradiction to the story that white Atlanta wanted to tell, and the washerwomen were well aware of it. They were also canny in striking at the height of Atlanta's hot, humid summer. There was no better moment to subject white Atlanta to the intimate hell of dirty clothes.

Many other aspects of the novel are based on fact. The behavior of the Atlanta police was taken straight from the historical record. The *Weekly Defender*, Atlanta's Black newspaper in the 1880s, remarked—with considerable bitterness—on the brutality of the police in arresting Black men. The complaints are sadly familiar.

Atlanta did have two Black dentists in the 1880s: the Badgers, father and son.

The presence of Dr. Chesney—and the scheme for health insurance—was a figment of my imagination, as was the presence of Coldbrook Construction. The *Beacon*, a newspaper focused on racial justice and women's rights, did not exist in nineteenth-century Atlanta, although I wish it had.

I finished this book just as Georgia made history by

electing two Democrats to the US Senate in the tight and contested races of 2020. That one was Black and the other was a Jew had special resonance for me. It was good to write about a successful struggle for freedom and dignity in Georgia while witnessing another.

ABOUT THE AUTHOR

Sabra Waldfogel grew up far from the South in Minneapolis, Minnesota. She studied history at Harvard University and got a PhD in American history from the University of Minnesota. Since then, she has been fascinated by the drama of slavery and freedom in the decades before and after the Civil War.

Her first novel, *Sister of Mine*, published by Lake Union, was named the winner of the 2017 Audio Publishers Association Audie Award for fiction. The sequel, *Let Me Fly*, was published in 2018.

Made in the USA
Las Vegas, NV
27 August 2022

54158221R00163